In The End

Dyslexia-friendly Edition

**In The End series
By G J Stevens**

In The End
Before The End
After The End
Beginning Of The End

In The End

Dyslexia-friendly Edition

G J Stevens

Scorpius Books

Copyright © GJ Stevens 2018

The right of GJ Stevens to be identified as the Author of the Work has been asserted by him in accordance with the Copyright, Designs and Patents Act 1988.

First Published in Great Britain in 2018 by GJ Stevens

This edition published in Great Britain 2022 by
Scorpius Books

This is a work of fiction. Names, characters, businesses, places, events, locales, and incidents are either the products of the author's imagination or used in a fictitious manner. Any resemblance to actual persons, living or dead, or actual events is purely coincidental.

A catalogue record of this book is available from the British Library.

ISBN 978 1 8383660 7 0

All rights reserved.
No part of this publication may be reproduced, stored in a retrieval system, or transmitted, in any form or by any means, without the prior permission in writing of the publisher, nor be otherwise circulated in any form of binding or cover other than that in which it is published and without a similar condition including this condition being imposed on the subsequent purchaser.

Scorpius Books have made a commitment to reducing their environmental footprint and being good stewards of the planet.

Scorpius Books
www.scorpiusbooks.com

DEDICATION

To the women in my life.

For Jayne, for giving me the space to create, for being the other side of my coin, my constant.

For Sarah, for giving me inspiration, for our late-night conversations, for my confidence and being my Annie Wilkes.

For my mum who I hope would have read with pride.

ACKNOWLEDGMENTS

To Adrian, who reads anything I give him and keeps me grounded whenever I stray from my station.

To Ismena, who believes in me and is constructive in her criticism.

To Scott, who long ago sparked my imagination and who understands a good story if he ever saw it.

To James, for his wonderful talents touching every area where I am weak and his boundless enthusiasm for anything artistic.

To Al, for his contribution. Less words, more inspiration.

To my first readers, Sarah and Janna. Nothing spurs me on more than a late-night text message screaming excitement across the ether.

For my sister, knowing one day she might actually read this.

Thanks to all those who helped me along the way, be it big or small, I am grateful.

1

LOGAN

The first sign was the internet going down and the music streaming into the floor speakers going quiet without warning. A sudden loss of connection; Wi-Fi box rebooted twice and still nothing. The dimming of the lights came next. Not total power failure, with the solar panels on the roofs to thank.

Still we drank, draining the supply down to a bottle of port bought from the local supermarket on a hangover-fuelled run.

It was New Year's Eve 2017. We'd rented a holiday cottage on the edge of Cornwall, almost Land's End. The cottage was one of nine in a gated development, each built the new way but made to look old. The doors were a funny size; building regulations, I'm told.

Each cottage was built out of the way of the rest in a wide circle, a thick copse of trees between each one. In the centre stood a manager's house, a small shop and a bar. Where a tenth cottage could have sat was the wide road leading out and in.

There were ten of us, the cottage full. Twin and double rooms were shared, despite all but four of us not being coupled. We'd been there four days already, the recycling bin emptied with the ring of bottles each morning. A maid cleaned out the jacuzzi we'd used all night until the Atlantic air got too much and we headed back to dry around the wood-burning stove.

We lasted an hour before myself and Andrew dressed and walked the couple of hundred steps to the centre of the circle.

We weren't the only ones there. A huddle had formed at the open door of the manager's house, a half-drunk crowd shouting over each other.

I remember the concern on Andrew's face. Our worst fear; the little shop had run out of its overpriced alcohol. The mob were about to lynch

IN THE END

the grey-haired manager unless he'd drive a rescue party to the nearest twenty-four-hour supermarket. The door closed in our faces.

People turned to each other. Some were strangers. Some were not. All were confused by his actions.

The door re-opened and out came the guy with a radio in his hand, distorted words and static rattling from the paint-flecked speakers.

The crowd hushed as more joined at our backs. We were now in the middle of a group, listening to a voice settle. A handful of words came clean from the speaker. A power station had been attacked by terrorists; the nuclear reactor in Somerset.

Panic rippled through the group, the adrenaline working to cancel the effect of the alcohol. Two of the group pushed outwards and I turned to see them running back to one of the nine houses.

We continued to listen, my heart pounding in the near silence.

The sudden drop in power to the grid had damaged the network;

emergency breakers had surrendered the Southwest to save the rest of the nation from total darkness.

The radio broke up as the word radiation became isolated from the rest of the sentence by static.

Andrew and I stared, soon turning to other. Then came the assurance that the damage was not to the reactor but to the distribution system. There was no direct danger of radiation leaking. The core was stable.

Torn between the silence from the radio and sharing the news with the others, we peeled away back to the cottage. Thoughts of alcohol were long gone, but we found the house quiet, bedroom doors closed up tight.

It could wait for the morning. The voice from the radio had made it clear there was no instant danger.

The second sign was the hammering at the door in the early hours. With the power still dimmed, rationed between the buildings, I was the first to answer.

I was the one to see the silver-haired guy rush to tell me to get the

IN THE END

hell out of here. I was the first to hear him mumble the word evacuation as he moved away, running towards the centre of the circle before I had a chance to question him.

2

After five minutes, I'd only managed to repeat the explanation twice. Toby and Amy, the couple in the closest room to the door, watched through a hangover haze as we fought through their disbelief that it was just some elaborate trick.

Then to Leo and Daniel. Daniel hid under the covers and I was sure I could hear him snore as I recounted the guy's strange words, trying my best to get across the urgent look in the guy's eyes.

It was Toby who came up with the offer to trudge with me to the centre of the circle and find out what the hell was going on. I could see in his eyes he had a mind to give the owner a stern talking to.

The cottage fell silent as we headed out in tracksuit bottoms and dressing gowns and trekked through the fresh morning dew. My own questions about the situation were in full bloom until we found the manager's house locked up, a paper notice written in heavy bold ink pinned to the door:

Evacuate. Head north.

A freephone number was scribbled below.

I turned to stare at Toby as he gaped in my direction. Both of us turned on our heels as we searched out the circle for any sign of someone about to jump from behind a tree with a phone pointed in our direction to capture our faces as the words sank in.

We must have stood for over a minute before I fumbled in my pocket, reading the number aloud as I tapped the digits into my phone.

No Service was the message that came back. We ran the gravel path back to the house.

Breaking the quiet of the cottage, we flung doors wide to the protests of the others, shouting for everyone to get their arses into gear.

"The nuclear power station. Radiation," I shouted over and over.

Toby followed my lead. Neither of us stopped to answer questions. Instead, I headed to my room, pulling off Andrew's covers as I frantically dressed then stuffed what I could grab of my things into a small suitcase.

Within another ten minutes the cottage was alive with action. Even the most sceptical, Zoe and Naomi, who thought it some elaborate scheme to scare them witless, were making moves to get their things together.

It was still half an hour before we were ready to leave. Half the group were not convinced, insisting on stuffing all of their things away and packing them into the three cars before they would let us start the engines.

Still my inner distrust forced me to lock the place up, checking twice before pocketing the key instead of pushing it back through the manager's letter box like it said in the welcome pack.

Driving one of the three cars with Zoe and Naomi in the back, Andrew sat at my side, tuning the digital radio to each of the stations, flicking to the next as the No Signal message replied on the display.

"Where are we going?" Zoe said.

IN THE END

"The way we came," I replied, looking to Andrew for approval. His nod gave confidence to my words. The journey to the cottage had been made four days earlier, five hours from London via two motorways and a dual carriageway through Cornwall.

The same people were in the car now. Zoe I'd known for twenty years since graduating. We were close; about as close as you can get without being in a relationship. I took up tenancy in the friend zone a long time ago.

Naomi was Zoe's best friend, a new fixture since she'd moved from their childhood town to London last year. Naomi was attractive, if you like the blonde knockout sort, but she made it very clear to us all that her interests lay elsewhere. Still, she'd blended with the group easily, even putting Andrew in his place early.

Zoe's voice broke into my drifting thoughts.

"Have you seen any other cars?" she said.

"Since when?" Naomi replied.

I didn't need to look to know everyone was gazing around the road. We'd driven through two villages on the route to the A30, but she was right; I couldn't remember seeing any other cars on the road.

At first I put it down to my sleep-deprived state and the effects of alcohol leaving my body.

I think we all did. Now, paying attention properly, there wasn't a car to be seen.

"It's New Year's Day," I heard Andrew say.

"But..." Zoe started, her words tailing off until I twisted in the seat, watching as she paused.

Her head moved from side to side. "I haven't seen any cars. Not even parked."

"Shit, look out," came the urgent words from Andrew.

I turned back around to the sight of a figure standing in the road.

I had no time to react before his head hit the windscreen to an eruption of screams.

3

I won't ever forget the dull thump or the loud snap as a dark head cracked the glass. The body rolled up the car and slipped down again, hitting the road as I slammed hard on the brakes.

With no time for what I'd seen to sink in, Toby's car slammed into our rear. The jolt went unfelt, my body numb, my gaze fixed on my foot stuck on the middle pedal.

I sat frozen. Andrew was already out of the car.

Lifting my head, I watched as he turned back, his eyes wide at the car behind.

His head slowly turned, his gaze catching mine as he followed down the bonnet to what I should have been the first to see. The shock should be mine. The pain in the centre of my chest was for me to bear alone. I caused the disaster; I was the one to affect our lives forever.

Detached from my body, limbs cold

and numb, I pulled open the door.

Toby joined me. I brushed away his concern and his offered hand to help me out. The journey around to the bonnet took an age, but was over too soon.

I watched on, detached from my flesh while Andrew knelt over a pair of corded trousers, the only visible sign of who I'd hit.

Shouts repeated as Andrew reached under the car, the shouts growing in volume as he pulled his head high to look past me.

I turned, not hearing the words and Toby was gone. I twisted around to see him back in his car as he let it roll backwards.

Climbing to his feet, Andrew pushed me with gentle force to the side of the road before he climbed in my car.

I turned, alcohol-laced bile rising, projecting to the tarmac. I twisted back, hopeful what I'd seen had been a vision.

It wasn't, because there lay an old man with grey hair and wrinkled skin. His eyes were closed and sunken. His bloodied face held no expression, his head folded at ninety degrees.

No one checked for a pulse. It was a sight I knew I would hold until my days came to an end.

Andrew turned me away by the shoulders, gripping my upper arms as he spoke.

"He was flagging us down, tripped and fell into the road."

I had no idea of the truth in his words. Was he saying this for me? Was he telling me to get my story straight?

I didn't know how he'd come to be in the road.

I hadn't seen a thing.

I knew what had to be done and I pulled my phone out. Tapping the three digits, I barely heard the flashing pips in my ear.

No service.

With my mouth open wide, I turned to the others and watched my friends hugging, tears falling as they looked in my direction with sorrow in their eyes.

I hated the pity flowing towards me. All I could do was shake my head as I held out the phone. Hands grasped for their own mobiles, but all soon came back shaking their heads the same.

I threw up for a second time as Andrew patted my back.

Looking around, I took in our surroundings as if for the first time. My gaze followed the dusty back road to a short wooden bridge a few paces from where the car had stopped. The view spread out to fields either side, the horizon dotted by a column of grey smoke rising in the direction we'd been heading, the sight only adding to the guilt squeezing my throat. Had I really been paying such little attention as I drove?

Swallowing down the new bile, I watched the rising smoke blow high in the sky. The sound of hushed voices caused me to turn, to look over at the group of two stone houses just off the road. The right one had its bright-red door wide open.

Much to Andrew's protests, I walked in its direction.

"Let me," he said, stepping past.

I shook my head. Still he walked at

IN THE END

my side, his knuckles arriving first at the door, his high greeting echoing inside.

Andrew turned and waved Toby to its neighbour as he took a timid step over the threshold.

Inside, the air hung still, the silence clinging to my throat. It was Andrew who spoke again, repeating the greeting. Only silence replied; a thick, heavy quiet.

We both spotted the phone at the same moment, Andrew's hand reaching first. He paused to listen before replacing the receiver.

We heard Toby's knock, his call next door and his footsteps as he joined us.

"No answer."

The TV didn't work as I clicked its buttons and I remembered the power was out, trying the light switch with my finger.

Toby coughed, the noise violent in the silence.

"We can't stay here," Andrew said, pulling a blanket from the armchair.

My eyes widened as I understood its purpose.

"I can't, I can't."

Andrew held up his hand. "It's okay," he replied. I watched as Toby, red-faced, followed Andrew, rounding up two of the others.

I turned away and headed into the kitchen.

Andrew drove, peering around the mess of a circle in the centre of the windscreen.

I sat in the back, silently grateful for Zoe's arm around my shoulder. Time drifted in fits and starts. One moment it dragged, the world going by so slow, the next minute the scenery had changed, the sky darker, the sun covered by the smoke, thicker than before.

The car slowed, but I couldn't make out the reason; the blocked view through the windscreen only forcing the blanket of guilt down further.

Stopping the car, Andrew opened the door and was half out, peering between the gap. He turned back as he pulled himself all the way out, his face flat and colour drained.

I didn't want to move from the

IN THE END

seat, didn't want to leave the comfort, but I had to see why we'd stopped. I had to see what had caused the fear in Andrew's expression.

Zoe made the choice for me, pulling away and grabbing the door handle. The others were already at the side of the car, their stares forward and mouths hanging open.

Toby turned and caught my eye, his head shaking, pupils wide.

A chill ran down my spine.

4

A long parade of cars wheeled out, silent to the extent of my vision as I climbed from the car. My face fixed as my friends held their mouths wide, locked with bewildered stares.

Engines lay at rest. The traffic filled the two thin lanes bordered by dry stone walls. Each empty, with few of their owners having the presence of mind to close their doors.

"What the fuck?" were the words I barely heard from Toby's mouth; words I knew weren't meant for anyone.

"Why the fuck?" My words came without command, my feet the same. One in front of the other, slowly at first, building and building until I was flat out.

My gaze jerked this way and that, searching for new information. Searching for the end of the line as I swerved left and right around cars which became three across as each one tried and failed, despite the brush of metal on metal, to squeeze past. Shoes and bags, luggage and holdalls littered the gaps, slowing me to more of a hurdle as I raced to the head of whatever this could be.

I swerved right at the bumper of a van that had smashed the wall before bogging down on the grass. Its doors were wide, a glance of a hand imprinted red to the white paint of the bonnet.

I turned away, my progress doubling as I ran along the grass. Slowly, the number of cars seemed to increase, leaving no air either side, but it had done them no good. Each car had wedged with their windows smashed.

A vision flashed of people pulling themselves out, biceps tight, clawing to climb from the crush of metal.

I turned back ahead, knowing my day-mare was still only a patch on reality. My breath caught as I saw the queue suddenly stop, the road blocked with three cubes of concrete stacked at the junction. I stopped just as quickly.

Shaking my head with my hand reaching for my chest, the drum of my heart reassured me I was awake. As my breath slowed I took a hesitant step, renewed guilt washing over me when I realised I hadn't thought of the shadow hitting the windscreen as I ran.

With a deep breath I climbed the wall, stones crumbing to the ground as I leapt to the roof of a sports car, easing my way forward to the next. Ahead I could see the concrete blocks were like those used to put across deserted carparks, like those used to protect the unwanted occupation by families armed only with their homes towed behind them.

Beyond the concrete there was nothing. Nothing at least when I took my first look. No traffic, cars, vans, the spray of glass. But as I blinked, I realised there was plenty else to see. Bags, clothes and suitcases littered the junction cutting left to right, its third way blocked by the concrete. But it was the blood, more than anything else, which forced my hand to cover my mouth.

Glancing back at the sound of panting breath, I saw Toby and Andrew

IN THE END

hurrying forward on the grass. Their eyes were not as wide as mine, looking only to the abandoned cars. Soon they would be as wide as they could be on seeing the despicable scene spread out in front.

The moment was clear when they fell on the three piles of clothes, each looking out of place. Both climbed on the car as I stood without words. Both took steps with me, jumping over windscreens, landing to the clear tarmac.

Soundless, we headed on. Our gazes fell to the blood, our feet stepping sideways. Our glances met for the first time as my foot knocked something we all recognised, the spent cartridge like a tiny bell as it rattled across the floor.

Soon the sound came again, this time in chorus like a tiny orchestra. Our feet swept the path left and right, clearing the way to avoid the slip and fall while together we took our unspoken journey to the closest of the dark bundles. Definition grew, its shades of greens, browns and black recognisable.

We arrived and I reached out. Pulling at the shoulder, I stood back, the body of a young woman, an officer according to her lapels, rolled under her own weight.

My stomach reacted first, gripping like a vice, but it was already empty. My gasp of air was enough to control my alarm at the crushed side of her face, a muddy footprint to the other. The same could not be said for my friends.

As the body came to rest on her back, I spotted the handgun underneath. I turned left and right to the pair standing bent over with their hands to their mouths in unison, their gazes fixed on what I'd seen.

Toby nodded. Andrew gave no reply.

The gun was still warm, but it nearly fell from my fingers as an almighty rumble ran deep in my chest, ripping through the silence and lighting the horizon.

5

Diving for air, I turned toward the cloud. My breath rasped as I watched the smoke build, waiting, desperate for its form to become clear.

Panting, I read its shape in vain. Could it be a mushroom? There was no bright flash. No wind battering across me, knocking me off my feet.

My breath slowed and I turned to Andrew and Toby, shaking my head. Solemn nods came back in reply as Toby seemed to get energy from somewhere. He bounded around to the other two bodies, staring for a moment at each but never closing in.

Without words we turned back along the row of cars. Our pace was steady as we started the return journey. Their faces were grey and I imagined mine was the same.

"What do we say?" I heard Andrew's words as we walked along the endless string of cars.

"Tell them everything," Toby said,

his voice quick and stiff.

"No," I said, shaking my head, my gaze fixed on my feet. "They'll panic."

"I'm panicking," Toby replied.

I looked up and slowed the breath I hadn't realise had been racing. I took a moment to feel the energy building in my chest.

"We tell them what they need to know. Tell them we found a roadblock…" The words caught in my throat and I took a deep swallow. "We tell them we found chaos the other end. We tell them everyone has gone, evacuated."

"Not everyone," Andrew said.

I waited a moment to answer, knowing the full extent of what our words could do to our friends.

"We tell them about the panic. We tell them people didn't make it," I said, picking up my pace with the gun heavy in my jacket pocket.

Their reply was silent. I hoped if I turned I would see them nodding. To say anything else wouldn't make sense.

"Then what?" Toby said finally.

"We find another way out." My gaze

fell on the parade of cars stretching to the horizon. "All this in just a few hours?" I said, not asking anyone in particular.

No one replied, but Andrew slowed.

I turned, watching as he cut across to the wall, his hands testing the stone before climbing. I joined him high at his side as he took in the view.

All around us were fields rolling gently up and down, with only the rare wind-battered tree pointing skyward to dot the horizon. The packed road at our front was the only sign of anyone having ever set foot on the earth.

Our gaze carried to the left; we were about a third of the way back to the cars and our friends. Breath stole from my lungs, my stomach a cavern as I thought of Zoe and the others back at the car. I thought of their fear for us, their fear for the unknown. They would have heard the explosion but weren't in the same head space as us and had yet to see what we had.

"What the hell is going on?" came Toby's voice at our backs.

I climbed down and offered my hand, helping him up as we jumped down the other side. I was about to open my mouth, about to speak, about to tell him I had no idea, when we looked skyward, trying to spot what was making the low rumble sound.

Breath came fast, my look swapping between my two friends. Their eyes were as wide as mine.

We moved quickly, soon building to a run, winding our way through the metal and jumping the messy belongings clogging the road.

The roar grew, rising too quick to a climax as a grey fighter jet ripped through the air high above.

"Invasion," I shouted, my instant reaction. "It's World War Three..." The words tailed off as I ran faster than I dared.

6

Breathless, I spotted the missing car at the back of our own short convoy before I saw Zoe stood next to Toby's young wife.

Lily waved her arms high above her head in unison with Zoe, their faces lit with relief.

Lily ran towards us as we grew closer, rushing past me to clutch her husband. I turned away when no one came running in my direction.

Slowing my pace and with Andrew at my side, we watched Naomi climb from our car, followed soon by Matt and Chloe pulling out of Toby's silver Mercedes.

"What is it?" Zoe asked, her hands at her mouth, dread covering her face. "The explosion," she said, turning towards Naomi who eyed me with interest.

"It's a roadblock," I said, not ready to give the details. "Where's Leo and the others?"

Zoe and Naomi exchanged looks. Matt stepped forward, glancing to Chloe before he spoke.

"They didn't want to sit around waiting. They were pissed off you upped and legged it."

"I was coming back," I said, my voice high and defensive. "Of course, I was always going to come back."

Matt shrugged, looking to the distance.

"So where did they go?" I said, catching the gaze of each of the five.

Matt spoke again. "They're going to find another way around."

Zoe shook her head, a look of distaste on her face.

"Leo said some scary shit," Matt continued. "Dan thinks we're being invaded. World War Three or something."

Zoe looked at me the entire time, not hiding her interest in my reaction. "Max reckons they blew up the rest of the power station to stop a build-up of heat, but that must be bullshit," she added, her eyes wide for an answer.

"Well, what is it?" she said, her

voice rising.

"I didn't reply straight away, the pressure of the question weighing heavy.

"I don't know," I replied, shaking my head, speaking my true feelings. "It's not an invasion," I said, adding more words than I needed to. "I don't think. I did before, but it makes little sense now."

I watched Zoe's eyes widen and Naomi's contract.

"If the Russians or the Chinese have invaded then why the evacuation? The skies would be teaming with fighters," I said, shaking my head.

"But the explosion?" Zoe replied, noticing the rest had gathered around us, watching.

"I don't know."

The only reply was silence. Each of my friends looked on, waiting for me to come up with some idea, some plan, some theory they could latch on to. I read the disappointment on their faces when my lips didn't move.

I couldn't remain silent for long. "All I know is there was supposed to be an evacuation. Everyone should be gone, but we missed the bus. Quite literally," I said, turning to Andrew for support that I'd said the right thing.

He gave a shallow nod and silence followed, but I knew what came next.

It was Zoe who spoke first. "Evacuated from what?" As her words came out, a tear rolled down her cheek.

"I don't know," I replied, stepping forward with open arms. I dropped them to my side as she instead turned and sunk into Naomi's embrace.

Drawing a deep breath and pushing down the rising emotion, I broke from the group to circle my car and closed the passenger doors. Taking the driver's seat, I pushed down the locks as the engine started.

With emotional faces staring back, I turned the car, rolling it to the side of the road. I killed the engine and walked to the last empty car in the long queue, a Freelander.

Leaning through the open driver's door, I turned the key one notch and watched the fuel indicator spring to the right.

They soon got the idea as I pulled open the boot and lugged suitcases to the side of the road. Each lent a hand, pulling our bags from my car with the smashed screen.

Without words we started the convoy once more, pleased for every mile I put between us and the reminder of the worst day of my life, although the heaviness in my chest wouldn't let me completely forget.

We drove for hours, following the map on Andrew's lap, Toby's car never leaving my mirrors. Taking turn after turn, each time we found a line of abandoned traffic, sometimes longer, sometimes shorter than the one we'd left.

At the first few we checked the head of the line, gaining hope when there had been no repeat of the conflict; no cold bodies left behind.

Until we came to a short queue of upwards of fifty cars.

Zoe was the first to see the bodies lying in pools of blood. We checked no more road blocks after, instead turning the car away each time we came across the beginning of the snaking line.

The skies had darkened, the air chilling. It must have been the tenth or so road north we'd found blocked. This latest line was right back to the trunk road, but to its right we found the dry-stone wall smashed through.

The first car to knock the barrier down had been abandoned to the side, the windscreen smashed, the bumper tossed at the gap. Great welts dug into the earth told us many more had followed.

I looked towards Andrew and he gave the nod as I turned the wheel through the gap.

The going was chaotic and the Freelander loved the terrain. At first I thought it was a farmer's field, but instead it turned out to be wasteland potted with rocks hidden below the waist-high wild grass swinging in the winter breeze.

The same could not be said for the Mercedes in the rear-view mirror. With

IN THE END

no surprise, smoke soon billowed from under the bonnet.

Circling around, we watched our friends pile out.

7

With the blue sky only a memory and our luggage tossed to the long grass, Chloe squeezed up against Zoe, sliding Naomi to the door. Without complaint, Toby, Lily and Matt were left to fold themselves into the rear. Holdalls bursting with our precious things rested in every other space.

No one was keen to hang around in the dark, knowing death was close by. The spooky, distant orange lights helped to urge us on. Towering black smoke told of its source burning on the horizon.

Despite the cramped conditions, I felt the relief in the car as we moved away with a slow pace, knowing each bump rushing through the axles amplified tenfold for those tight together in the back.

With the main beam lights dancing across the road, another ten minutes past before I saw the remains of a stone wall smashed through in too many places to count, many cars discarded at its foot.

IN THE END

Swinging the four by four in an arch, the headlights swept across the barrier and I spotted the largest of the gaps near to the head of the silent line of traffic.

We rolled forward, the movement slow.

I glanced to Andrew in the passenger seat, watching his shallow nod.

The going was easy, the gap more than ample. Relief rushed through my body, excited that we were through the roadblocks. At my back, excited whispers joined my thoughts.

Through the gap and lit by our main beam, we saw the pickup truck which I guessed had cleared the way as we passed through. Its mass was pointed high, tilted to the horizon, the front wheels resting on a stone wall on the opposite side. Its doors were wide open.

Turning the wheel, the headlights revealed a view we'd seen so many times before. Bags, holdalls and luggage scattered around, but this time we weren't so foolish to the sight of the larger shapes surrounded in dark shadows.

A difference caught my eye the others too, if the sharp intakes of breath were anything to go by. We'd seen the face of a man, his body encased in an oversized orange hazmat suit. His eyes reflected through the wide clear window punctured by bullet holes.

Still turning, trying to find a way around the biggest of the rubble, I pushed hard on the brakes and we all looked forward as I saw something I knew to be a trick of light. Or so I thought, until Andrew jumped forward in his seat.

Leaning against the windscreen, he stretched his neck to get a better look. He, too, had seen the body in the headlights move in the beam.

I looked left, expecting to see Andrew's hand pulling the handle, but he was still staring forward, his mouth open.

It was Chloe's form that dived into the light before I felt the chill of air coming from her open door, the chorus of voices calling her back.

I joined in with the frantic calls, her nursing instinct hard-wired.

Drawing a deep breath, I followed her into the night. The darkness brought fog to my breath.

I watched Chloe kneel at the body's side. With her head low, she listened to the gentle moan of death.

I forced myself to breathe through my mouth, the powerful stench of blood and ripe, overflowing toilets sticking in my throat. I couldn't look at the scene for very long as I drew closer, instead assessing the wider view, despite knowing I should avoid it for the sake of my dreams.

This was by far the worst we'd come across with the highest body count. Double figures ticked off, despite my need to avoid the detail. This roadblock was also unique because on this side of the concrete blocks were cars. Some hadn't got away. Bullet holes peppered their sides, shell casings glinting in the powerful light.

I was grateful to arrive at Chloe's

side, despite the growing stench giving me an excuse to look away.

With a stolen glance I watched the last moments of a woman Chloe's age; mid-twenties, blonde hair streaked with scarlet. Half her face was blown off, her lips missing from one side of her mouth. The one intact eye remained closed.

She was moving, cradled in Chloe's arms.

Chloe made no effort to stop her death. Even I could tell there was nothing to be done, other than to give the final gift of not letting her be alone when the last moment came.

The moment came too soon as Andrew arrived at our side. It came as both of us rested our hands on Chloe's shoulders.

Her head low, her comforting words stopped as the body went limp. Chloe remained seated, Andrew and I sharing a solemn pause with our heads down.

It was Chloe's shoulders rising, her back arching which caused us to look up. The woman in her arms seem to draw a long, deep breath.

IN THE END

Chloe's looked up with a wide smile, her eyes full with compassion and joy that her prayers had been answered.

Startled, I watched as the woman's remaining eye opened. The white was red, the lens milky.

My legs forced me back as she dived headlong at Chloe's hand resting on her blood-soaked chest.

Teeth found bone and Chloe's arms shook as if electrified as she struggled to pull free.

I'm ashamed to say my instinct forced me to leap back.

I stared wide-eyed, helpless in the view of my friend's hand clamped in the mouth of a monster grinding into her flesh.

8

The sight caused my brain to crash. The woman had been dead only moments before. Fear took control over my body, but the sound and sight of Chloe's pain pulled me back as anger overtook the fear.

Without thinking, I stepped forward into the stench. Blood sprayed from the monster's mouth.

Chloe's shock had gone, replaced with a burning scream. I watched as the woman chewed on Chloe's hand like an animal.

With a swing, my right foot connected to the woman's head and I grabbed at Chloe's arm, but the grip held firm. A second kick did the same and Andrew was around the other side, his feet in on the action.

After longer than I feared, the skull gave way under the attack and the bloody mouth released.

With one arm under each shoulder, we dragged Chloe sobbing back to the

IN THE END

car and the howl of stunned reactions to what they'd witnessed in the headlights.

The girls were frantic, tears streaming, but still they took control of Chloe, cradling her hand with such care. With the light on, I shouted for calm between the heavy breaths I could barely control.

The car filled with a outburst of questions, demanding what the hell was going on, screaming out as they tried to make sense of our violence.

The words rolled into white noise, which sent my vision swimming with the memory of my foot smashing at the woman's face looping in my head, doubt at what I had seen already creeping in.

The disbelief turned to fear that despite the state we'd left her in, she might come crawling along the ground to take a second bite.

I shouted again for them to hold back and for Andrew to get in the fucking car.

With the doors barely sealed, I revved the engine, stomping the accelerator to screams of panic and sympathy for the patient who lay across them on the back seat.

The car swerved left and right, my concentration fixed hard on the drive. Abandoned vehicles flashed by in the headlights, the lines of bullets and smashed glass not overlooked.

I left the engine to roar and the pitch-black scenery to fly by the window until Andrew shouted, his voice clear and with a strange calm.

With his hand on my shoulder I let the engine dip from the red line to idle. I let the wheels coast. The inside calmed with the falling speed and Andrew pointed.

My gaze followed his finger and I saw the road ahead clearly for the first time.

Ahead stood a giant white warehouse; a dead supermarket. It was rare to see these huge buildings without their lights blasting out twenty-four seven. The mood grew hopeful in the back as I let the engine build and turned into the car park.

Two cars sat in the wide expanse of

IN THE END

tarmac, their bonnets up, abandoned by their owners.

Circling the shop took over ten minutes in the car. The place looked locked up tight, the doors sealed, shutters down across the front. Still, we hadn't spoken about what had happened to hasten this leg of the journey and I wanted to keep it that way until we'd got Chloe's wounds under control and I'd had chance to figure it out for myself.

Toby agreed to stay with the car and sit in the driver's seat with the engine running, ready to pick us up at a moment's notice.

Zoe insisted she came with us, so joined Andrew, myself and Matt as we got out at the rear of the building to examine the delivery entrance.

A small high window at the rear was smashed through within minutes, our success rewarded with an alarm we were all a little surprised to hear.

I went in, rising on Matt and Andrew's joined hands.

Inside I found utter darkness, the rage of the alarm constant and not helping to tune my vision to the pitch black.

Not knowing what I was to land on, I lowered myself down from the ledge and my feet found something solid. The porcelain of a toilet bowl I soon found out, as my foot traced its smooth edges.

Inside, the alarm was deep and high at the same time, attacking not only my ears but my stomach as well. If I had eaten in the last day, I would have emptied my guts again.

The deep blackness was so complete. Touch alone got me through the booth and out of the wider room where the darkness seemed to only deepen, the last of the moonlight shut out.

I don't mind admitting I was scared as the tone of the alarm changed. I guessed I was out into the main warehouse, but there were no lights to guide me, the emergency batteries having worn down the previous night.

Despair gripped with the last of the light as the door closed at my back and my pace slowed further. Like a fireman in a smoke-filled room but less practiced, I waved my hands in front of me in careful circles, fingers curled into my palms for protection.

My left fist caught a solid wall. So did my right and I realised I was in a corridor and not the main hall. My mood fell even further, head splitting with pain, peaking each time the claxon cycled through its infernal rhythm.

Time pressed on and I could sense Chloe's blood pumping from her injuries, her body draining with each step I failed to find some way to get her inside and her injuries dressed.

My knuckles rubbed against something hard, a cold handle.

Joy flared as I turned. The door opened, but I sank to my knees when the echo rang deeper. The echo was overwhelming, the noise pouring over me.

Tears rolled when light burst into being. A car smashing through from the outside. The room lit from the source of the attack, my hand reaching for the gun.

9

Forcing my eyes wide, the roar of the engine died back below the siren's scream. As dust and smoke continued to billow from the sudden outburst, I watched shadows rush from the new opening. Heads turned this way and that, searching something out.

The first figure carried another cradled in their arms. Chloe, I soon realised, in Toby's hold. With Lily at her back, a deep relief lifted my mood.

In the new light I saw I was in a side corridor, the group of three already out of view. Hurrying forward, I pushed the gun deep once more, my despair forgotten to the shouts of my name just high enough to register.

I saw the relief on Toby's face and a pained, pale complexion on Chloe's as she lay on the floor.

Lily knelt in a stance we'd only just seen. Chloe's face was still intact, albeit grey and drawn. Our friends huddled around, each shouting calls, trying to

IN THE END

reach above the others, but we all knew the aim.

I watched as they scattered, leaving me focused on Lily forcing blood-red rags around the patient's hand, a pool already forming beneath.

Out of my daze, I split from the scene, helpless to react to the constant pour of blood. Instead, I raced off through the spotless lanes, the tops of the rows lit just enough to help navigation.

I returned with an armful of torches, with battery packs bulging from my pockets. Back at Chloe's side, I listened to Lily's calming voice and caught sight of her hand clamped down, her fingers red with Chloe's blood.

My gaze fixed to Lily's breathless stare as she looked up.

Striding off once more, I found Toby by the medicines as he squinted in the near dark. His hands felt across the shelves. He looked up as I pushed the lit torch into his fingers.

Still I headed on and found Andrew wielding a chair, attacking a tall metal panel by the front entrance. Despite his desperate swings, the alarm still screamed out and a rainbow of weak LEDs continued to dim with each pulse of the speaker.

I lit the panel with the torch beam and Andrew turned, his face alive with fright until he saw me and he said something I had no chance of understanding.

I was off again, but I only went a few steps before stumbling into a metal cage to the side of a promotion pyramid of six-packs of lemonade bottles. My knees slammed to the hard ground as I fell.

Grabbing the torch as it slowed its spin, its beam caught on a colourful explosion of light painted on the cabinet door and I made a mental note to search for the key when I had a chance to take a breath.

Hugging lemonade bottles in my arms, I nudged Andrew on my return. Understanding my plan without the need for explanation, together we took a step back from the panel, twisted off the caps

IN THE END

and took aim.

To the scent of sweet lemons, the alarm died with a crackle to the speakers. I swear I could hear it for hours after.

We hugged and drew deep breaths. Our bodies shook as we took in the silence, only to be startled by a loud bang ringing from the back of the shop.

As we rose from our natural duck with the echo fading, we stared at each other before looking back to the alarm panel and its dark, empty reply.

Together we turned and took timid steps toward the rear wall, watching closely for anything unusual in the dark. Our pace sped as the shockwave of sound didn't repeat, slowing only as the torch found a double set of doors in the distance.

Walking through the aisles, I looked to Andrew and he urged me on with his brow.

I stepped forward as we arrived, pushing the left door with my breath held. Leading with the beam, I passed it over bundles of cardboard packaging squeezed in densely strapped bales, ready for the next delivery which wouldn't be coming.

    I searched on with the light falling on more doors either side, stopping only as it showed the square plastic yellow flash in the centre.

    My breath relaxed.

    "I think it was just a breaker for the alarm. I guess it's where the battery is," I said, nodding towards the door.

    Andrew stepped forward to take a look, but we both turned back to the main floor, searching out the raised voices of our friends.

    I followed Andrew as we ran back to find lanterns surrounding Chloe, blankets under her head and covering her legs.

    The car stood silent with the lights off, leaving just the chill of the night creeping through smashed-open fire exit doors. The front of the Freelander had been wide enough to punch through the doors, but not to get all the way through. The metal wings were caved in, wedged between exposed steel beams.

    "It won't stop bleeding," I heard

IN THE END

Lily say, loud and clear. Dread made the emptiness of my stomach feel worse.

Andrew and I knelt, taking our place in the circle. Chloe's hand was packed hard with bandages. Toby ripped open fresh packets to replace the bloody rags piling up by her side. His face was a match for his wife's, a shared look of fear I couldn't linger on.

Standing, I took deep breaths before turning to the darkness as Naomi and Zoe rose to their feet, their torches shining down at the floor.

Andrew took steps with me. Matt followed behind. Our pace was slow with guilt raging in each step, feeling hopeless.

I couldn't do anything to stop the bleeding. I couldn't look on. I knew it was time for the talk.

It was Zoe who raised it first to mouthfuls of water taken from the lane we'd drifted to.

"Well?" was all she said, but the meaning didn't need to be explained.

I turned, looked back and away towards the halo of light where our three other friends were holding vigil. We were far enough away they wouldn't hear, but still I kept my voice quiet.

"You saw it for yourself," I said, knowing full well it wouldn't be enough.

Naomi was the first to pick it open. "All we saw was you and Andrew going to town on that woman's head. What the fuck happened?" she said. Her voice was hurried, but she kept her volume low.

Andrew and I shared a look. He nodded at me and I let the words out.

"She died," I said, pausing for a moment. "Chloe was comforting her, you saw that?" I watched as nods replied. "But she came back. She bit into Chloe's hand. She wouldn't let go."

The huddle was silent.

"You thought she'd died," Matt said. "You're no doctor."

"She died," Andrew said, stepping closer into our circle. "She would never have survived those injuries. Half her face was splattered across the road, for fuck's sake."

"Mate," I said, and he lowered his head. "Look. She seemed to be dead, but you're right, she must have been alive. She must have been defending herself. Her brain had been confused with pain, I guess. It was an animal instinct. Yeah."

I looked to the floor because I didn't want to see their reaction. "I mean, there's no other explanation, is there?" This time I couldn't help but look around and watch the sunken faces as no one spoke.

"Don't say it," were Zoe's words.

"Say what?" Naomi replied.

The silence filled the gap and we heard what sounded like Lily's gentle voice singing low in the glow of lanterns.

"Zombies," Andrew said. Laughter followed from his words, but I watched his fixed expression.

Naomi and Matt's chuckles died back when they saw the rest of us weren't joining in. What Andrew had just said had already crossed my mind. It had been my only explanation, but the word grated against all common sense and there was nothing I could do to stop my mind racing to search for another explanation.

"Fuck off," Matt and Naomi replied, almost in unison. Their volume fell back as they turned and walked away, only stopping as a great rattle of metal came from the wide shuttered entrance.

Within less than a second I'd put it down to the wind. Until it came again twice more in quick succession.

10

Zoe stared. Her gaze was intent on mine. Her shoulders rattled each time the shutter banged.

After the fifth, I lost count.

Naomi was the first to move, the first to turn to Matt then back to the rest of us as they re-joined our circle.

"You're joking, right?" Naomi said, looking to the shutters then back through the group. "You're fucking joking? You guys need to stop watching shit TV."

We continued to stare forward, our eyes on Naomi. I noticed Lily's voice had calmed in the background.

"You wanna take your chances?" Andrew said, his eyes wide.

"With the fucking zombies?" Naomi replied. "Shut the fuck up. They're people, like us. People left behind in this fucking mess. They've heard the alarm and come to find help," she said, raising her eyebrows. "If it was you, wouldn't you want safety?"

Everyone kept quiet. She'd made a good point, but she hadn't been there. She hadn't seen the milky eyes of the woman, her mouth in a death grip around Chloe's hand. She hadn't had to crush the woman's head to release her friend.

"But what if it's not? What if it's the military clearing the place out?" I replied.

Naomi took a step toward me, opening her arms.

"Break open the champagne. We've been saved and can get the fuck away," she said, softening her voice, her eyes clenched.

"What if it's an invasion?" Matt asked, his voice low too.

"What? Not you as well. Do you think aliens have landed?" Naomi replied, the harsh rattle of shutters stopping the rest of her words.

"No, no," Matt said, taking his own steps forward so he could lower his voice as he shook his head. "Another country, I mean?"

Naomi's smile grew wide. "And you

reckon they're going to knock on the door?"

Our heads turned in unison. A fright ran through the five of us as Toby appeared around the corner, his head low, his gaze on his bright-red hands. There was a dark soaked bandage in his palm.

"What if it's a doctor?" he asked, his voice solemn. "It won't stop bleeding. She can't have long left."

Naomi turned and took a step before looking back, locking her gaze with mine.

"Your call," she said, raising her brow. "When this mess is over, the decisions we make will be pulled apart. Perhaps think that over before you leave them out in the freezing cold." She turned and headed back toward Chloe.

"Hey, unfair," Zoe replied, her voice upset as she took a step toward me.

"Is it?" I said, looking around the group and catching each gaze intent in my direction.

Naomi was right. Every decision would be picked at in detail, but when did I get chosen leader? If she cared so much then why didn't she put herself forward to take control? Ever since she settled into the group, she'd become a vocal part of our dynamic. She was fun, for the most part, keeping us on our toes when the things we did had no effects.

Before this shit, decisions were taken on a whim by whoever spoke up first or came up with the craziest idea. Was I now in charge because of the guy who'd run into the path of my car? Was it because I was the first to hear about the crisis? Or because I'd been standing next to Chloe when we watched the world change forever?

Was it because they thought I could handle the pressure, or did they, did *she*, need someone else to take the responsibility? Needed someone else to take the shit for doing something wrong?

I drew a deep breath. Like it or not, which I didn't, they'd given me control and I had to do something.

Feeling the weight in my pocket, I turned to the remainder of the group.

"Who's coming with me?"

11

My breath caught as Andrew volunteered with no delay. Stepping to my side, his face hung with a heavy brow, shoulders rising.

I couldn't help but raise a thin smile. Matt took a moment. He looked to where Naomi had just walked before he stepped forward, his hands still stuffed in his pockets.

Not waiting for Zoe to make a bad decision, I turned to her, clenching her shoulders and taking her by surprise, her head reacting as I leaned in.

"I need your help, too," I said, and watched as her eyes went wide. "I need you to get the others away from the door. Get them as far back in the store as you can. Find a comfortable place if Chloe's up to it."

I watched as Zoe blinked a nod and I turned, not waiting for her to process the words, react, or to come back with some headstrong plan.

The copper odour of Chloe's blood

was clear long before we rounded the aisle to see her head on Lily's lap. Toby still pushed down bandages to her hand, the scarlet pile at his knees bigger than the fresh stock to his side.

Naomi hung around where the car wedged, the collar of her long coat drawn up tight around her neck. Her white breath reflected in the torchlight.

With only a glance in Chloe's direction, I couldn't hold my gaze any longer. Her face was empty of movement, her life still draining out through the bandage.

All but a single lantern at Chloe's side fell to dark, the warehouse near returning to its original bleak state.

The steel of the car stung my fingers with cold as I leant around the thin wall and past the metal skin, peering into the night, lit more than I'd appreciated with the half-moon light.

With the coast clear, I lifted myself around the car. Climbing up the bumper, I regretted how easy it was to get past the barrier.

With Andrew climbing at my back,

IN THE END

I chanced a look back and took a hard swallow as I saw how deep, how completely the Freelander had embedded itself into the opening.

My regret retreated a little as I saw the fire door wasn't visible from the front of the building, hidden by the tall wall of the main structure.

We crept in a line along the wall, halting as we reached the corner. I turned once again, looked back and swallowed a hard breath, knowing if we didn't survive this it wouldn't be long before the others were done for.

Andrew urged me on, pushing at my back, nodding toward my pocket.

He was right. I had the gun. I should go first. I was the only one who had a hope in hell of stopping whatever was trying to get into our safe place.

The gun felt heavy in my hand and I regretted not taking a few moments to familiarise myself with its workings. Yes, I'd seen so many in films. Watched those shit TV programmes Naomi thought were muddling my brain, but never had I held one in my hand. Never had my fingers searched in the near pitch black for a safety catch or a cocking slide.

I did what I'd seen so many times before and I slid the top of the gun back. As I did, something fell to my feet with a metallic click and I caught sight of the brass bullet shining in the moonlight. The gun had been primed by its previous owner. It was already cocked, or whatever the phase was. I should have realised. I'd taken it from someone who'd died trying to defend themselves.

I couldn't see or feel a switch or a catch to the side, but to Andrew's onward urges I pushed the fallen bullet into my pocket and took my chances the gun was still ready to defend.

Peering around the first corner with the gun pointing to the ground, my first view was of my fast, white breath rising into the air, announcing both our presence and my frantic state.

My second view was the wide-open space of half of the car park and the road entrance from where we'd arrived.

Moving on, I tried to forget there was only a short distance before I would round the corner and see the shutters. Only a short distance before I would see whatever was waiting for us to come and whatever welcome they would give.

I reached the corner sooner than I'd wanted. Andrew's urges had stopped and I turned to see both him and Matt still there, their faces a mirror of my concern.

This was my last chance to turn back. This was my last chance to hand the gun over and run to the warm, safe place with the others. But I wasn't that man.

I'd come out for a reason. For many reasons.

I'd come to find for certain I wasn't in a comic book or a world of horror fiction. I'd come to prove Naomi right.

Oh, how for once I wanted her to be right.

The next couple of steps would tell and I raised the gun as I took them slow, very slow, stepping so my feet would make no sound at all.

12

A sudden rasp of the shutters pulled my chest tight as I rounded the corner. The rattle felt so much louder.

There stood a silhouette dressed in the bulk of a dark woollen coat, its head hidden and face wrapped with a scarf.

The figure leant into the metal as if listening with intent. I watched on with my breath unwilling to come.

Waiting for what, I wasn't sure.

The figure slumped to the floor and for the first time I could see a larger bundle of blankets at its feet.

My heart settled now I could see the figure who looked more like an unlucky vagrant who'd missed the evacuation, the superstore his normal night-time hangout. I surprised myself at a rising anger that Naomi had been right all along.

With my stance relaxing and the gun swinging down in my hand, I turned and a smile bloomed, the vent of tension spreading to my friends.

IN THE END

Andrew was the first to creep past my shoulder and Matt followed. I turned back and together we stood in a line out in the open, taking a long look into the night.

Andrew coughed. I looked in his direction, eyes wide, staring as he stifled the clouds of white air spluttering from his chest.

Spinning back, I saw the figure's head twitch, springing to his feet, jumping up with a vigour not matching his broken-down appearance.

Like the crazed individual I'd feared all along, the figure's arms were out and muffled calls howled from behind numerous scarfs.

My friends left my sight but I would not turn or take my attention from the monster racing towards me; the monster who didn't care for the gun pointed at its chest.

The distance swallowed up too soon. I wanted to see Andrew's reaction, wanted to know if I should blast away. Was I right to use lethal force to stop what was happening to Chloe from happening again?

But I couldn't turn so I had to make the choice alone.

"Stop or I'll shoot," were the words I shouted, despite knowing they'd be no use.

To my surprise, the figure's speed slowed, its steps becoming shallow.

Inspired by their reaction, I took a step forward, alarming myself as I did and setting a stance I didn't even know I'd taken notice of from the movies.

By now the figure had stopped and instead moved backwards, but soon fell over its own feet, stumbling, crashing to the ground with a great huff from his lungs.

He was a vagrant once more, a poor man with nowhere to call home.

Lowering the gun, confused emotions rattling around in my brain, I heard an animal scream from where the tramp had left his belongings.

The blankets had risen, but only to half the height, to become another figure, their scream high and child-like. Their face wasn't covered. Their golden

IN THE END

blonde hair not under a hat. Their cries were not muffled and I reacted, as did my fear, but in opposite directions as I pulled the trigger.

13

The trigger gave only a soft click. Swamped with thanks to the fates, I realised the bullet in my pocket must have been the last.

Empty of breath, I aimed the gun downward, looking to see if anyone had heard the tiny, metallic voice.

I was desperate to find if they knew what I'd got so close to doing. Their faces told me they had. It had been the only sound for miles.

"I'm so sorry," I said over and over, not telling what I thought I'd seen. I just watched as the girl ran to clutch the waist of our stranger.

The figure's hand rose, pulling the scarf down to reveal a young woman, her face round, stiff with fear, her arms wrapped around the child's. The kid soon pulled away, looked back up, her face strong. Her gaze caught the pistol and I stuffed it back in my pocket, holding out my hand and offering to help the young woman to her feet.

IN THE END

With breath still lifting hard to the air, she held back, keeping her hand low and making no attempt to rise until Andrew rushed forward. He didn't wait for an answer before he took her weight.

No one asked questions or put up any struggle as we helped the pair climb through the blocked fire exit and into the warmth.

Andrew took the lead, trying his best to shield the view of Chloe still laid on the ground. The circle of three friends who'd stayed stood to block any stranger, friend or foe, with crowbars and hammers held in their hands.

Only Naomi kept her grip solid on the handle of the claw hammer as the stranger's features became clear in the light.

I winced as I thought how much she would revel in the story about to be told.

To my surprise the events were not told by either of the pair. They were sisters, both too young to be anything else to each other, the woman having just left her teens, the kid only just turning double figures. Their features were almost a match, their long blonde hair and blue eyes glinting in the torchlight. It was only their height and definition in the cheeks which gave away the difference.

I overheard the whispered answers to slow questions fired their way as I knelt beside our patient. Their names were Cassidy, the eldest, and Ellie, the younger.

Chloe's body lay motionless and I feared the worst. Lily's blood-soaked fingers were no longer wrapped around the palm of the injured hand.

I dared not prompt the answer I desperately wanted, but Lily seemed to understand and told me the bleeding had stopped only moments before.

I saw the first of the shallow breaths and for the first time that day I felt a wash of happiness. Staying sat at her side, I let myself relax, letting the others scatter and gather more supplies.

After a hearty meal and with my shoulders wrapped in blankets, I felt an huge gratitude we'd found this place. We'd stumbled somewhere perfect to wait until the rescue party's arrival.

Dozing as I sat, head falling forward, I listened to Cassidy recount how their day had started.

"We got the call to evacuate in the early hours of the morning. On the phone, an automated message telling us to ring the police if we needed to verify the call. The electricity had already gone by then and the phones went dead soon after. The radio was no help other than giving the same message, which didn't tell us what the hell was going on. We set off with my parents, but soon we were in tailbacks longer than we'd ever seen around here. After hours in traffic the Land Rover gave up about halfway to the A30, so we hitched a lift on a bus already near bursting. We had to stand, huddled in the aisle right at the front.

"We came to the roadblock mid-morning. People were streaming from cars, just leaving their vehicles blocking the road so they could walk towards the head of the queue. When the driver disappeared out of his door, we had no choice. Everyone forced against us so they could rush between the parked cars. Dad was the first to spot a long line of coaches, one after another leaving the head of the roadblock. As we grew closer, we saw each already over-filled, with only two left and a long, wide line of people heading in their direction. It wasn't long before the panic started. A ripple of excitement ran through the crowds, leaving behind an urgency to get on one of those coaches.

"We tried to hold each other's hands, but it was near impossible. I ended up carrying Ellie most of the way. People were shouting. Elbows shoved out. Teeth baring like they were wild animals. We got separated from Mum and Dad as I tripped. I stumbled over an abandoned case or something. It took ages to battle back into the flow, clutching Ellie, everyone rushing, pushing with their elbows out, rushing forward like rabid creatures.

"Then came the gunshots."

14

Her voice stopped as I looked up, my gaze catching Cassidy's as I realised how much attention I'd been paying to her words.

Seeing me move, Ellie, the little sister, screwed up her face and shuffled closer to Cassidy, who accepted the arm around her shoulders under the blanket.

The night had grown colder, my breath alive in the low torch light. With my head bowed, I may have drifted off.

Matt, Lily and Toby had crowded around Chloe. Each sat on a bed of pillows and blankets.

I looked on the patient's pale face and her distant expression before breaking the silence. My voice croaked as I pulled the blankets tighter over my shoulders.

"Your parents?" I asked, trying to keep the words soft, expecting a shower of tears.

They didn't come, just a shake of the head.

"We ran," Cassidy said. "The gunfire was so rapid, the screams cutting, it wasn't a place you wanted to hang around. We ran until the noise stopped and never looked back."

"What did you do then?" Naomi said.

"Waited," Cassidy replied.

Zoe, who'd been sitting loosely to their side, edged herself closer, pressing her hands around Cassidy's free left.

"We waited for hours, but when the explosion happened and that jet, I decided we needed to get further away, find shelter, food..." Her voice cut short, the words catching in her throat.

"They're probably fine," Zoe said, telling me off with a pointed look.

I nodded a shallow reply and turned back to the dark floor.

Lily was the next to come closer to our little group, her face betraying her need to get to the questions she really wanted the answers to. It didn't take long before she leaned in, offering an open bar of chocolate in the kid's direction.

Ellie looked up to her sister and, receiving a nod, she took a row.

Lily didn't wait.

"So," she said with an unusual hesitation, "while you were out there did you...?" she said before stopping herself short.

Naomi gave a great sigh. "Did you see anything strange?" she asked, her voice loud in the darkness.

All turned to her and she rolled her eyes, but the group's attention switched back to Cassidy.

Nods ran around the room, urging on the answer.

I didn't look up straight away, but when silence was the only reply I looked up. Could we be about to find out one way or another if I was going nuts?

Cassidy's gaze fell to Ellie as she ate the last of her chocolate.

Lily lent forward, offering another.

"Then that's it," Cassidy said, as Ellie broke off the squares.

Checking she was busy, Cassidy looked around the room to take in each of our faces.

Like me, I knew their hearts would be racing, too. She held each gaze until she moved on.

"Like what?"

I kept quiet and glanced to Naomi, making it clear I wasn't about to affect the answer.

It was Toby who spoke, all turning to the dim light shrouding the vigil.

"You were out there longer than us," he said, his expression more eager than his voice.

Cassidy drew a deep breath, and Ellie gave a wide yawn. Cassidy let the child get herself comfortable as she shuffled at her side. She waited as she nuzzled down on her thigh, let her eyes close and her breath turn to a soft purr before she spoke.

"We saw emptiness," she said.

I tried to stop myself leaning forward, getting closer with each of her words.

"We saw people being inhuman."

"What do you mean?" Zoe asked, not giving Cassidy the chance to draw breath.

"We saw people dead, killed with guns. We saw people acting like animals. People fending for themselves. It's only been a day and already the mask has slipped."

As a group we leaned forward as she paused. I squinted at Naomi and watched as she sat back.

"Anything else?" Zoe asked, her voice shaking.

The silence ate up the air, plumes of breath rolling in the centre of the group, giving away our fear.

"We saw," she said, and the cloud of breath stopped, "people left for dead, so many people," she said, her voice betraying she wasn't finished.

Still she paused. "Left for dead, but they weren't."

No one spoke despite the volley of questions we each had ready.

Again, it was Zoe who broke the silence.

"What do you…?" she said, but I interrupted.

"Can anyone else smell smoke?"

15

"Shush," came Naomi's annoyed reply. "Let her speak," she said, her eyes pinched.

"No one else?" I asked, searching each of the troubled faces in the shadows. "Really?" I snapped, then gave up as all gazes were on Cassidy.

Taking a long draw of breath through my nose, I could swear I still smelt bitter smoke but put it down to tiredness when Zoe spoke.

"So, what did you mean, they weren't dead?"

Cassidy shook her head, rubbing her temple with her free hand.

"Just what I said. Not everyone was dead. Some people were laying on the ground, thrashing around." Her voice grew desperate with a sadness greater than before. She squinted as if trying to block the images in her mind.

"I wanted to help. I wanted to do something about their pain, but I couldn't take Ellie there. I wanted to. I really did."

"It's all right," Zoe said, handing over a square of tissue. "There's nothing you could have done, I'm sure."

"That's it?" I asked, regretting my tone as the words flowed, then tried to ignore the glares which returned. "Nothing else?" I said, softening my tone.

Cassidy shrugged.

"It was," she said, checking her sister's eyes, "pretty fucking unusual for us. Does this kind of shit happen often to you?" Her voice was high and her tone cutting.

I didn't need to look to Naomi to know a one-sided smile hung on her face. I let the silence linger and moments pass, listening to the gentle breath of Ellie, a slight rasp on her breath.

"What's wrong with your friend?" Cassidy said.

I looked up from the floor, watching her direct the question to Zoe.

"She's been bitten," Zoe replied.

Cassidy responded at once.

"By what?" Her voice was clearly higher than she'd intended.

There was a collective silence and I couldn't tell who was asleep and who was just pretending because they didn't want to answer.

"She lost a lot of blood, but she's okay now," Zoe replied.

"It wouldn't stop bleeding," I said. There was a sound of restless movement around the lantern light.

"Is she a haemophiliac?" Cassidy replied.

Lily raised her head. Naomi and Zoe sat up straight.

I looked to Matt and Toby, who looked alert. Only Andrew lay asleep, not joining the stunned silence as the words ran around our heads.

I was the first to shake mine.

"We'd have known," I said.

"If she'd known," Zoe replied, her eyebrows high.

"She's a nurse," I said. "She would have known."

Naomi stood.

"What's your explanation? Go on,"

IN THE END

she said, shrugging the blankets off her shoulders and stepping out of the dim glow.

Heads dipped once again. Naomi was right. What was the remaining explanation? Chloe had been attacked by a Zombie, but Zombies aren't real. There are no examples in nature, apart from that fungus that drives ants up trees before it slices through their brain. Apart from that, they're confined to the screen and Halloween parties.

Right? Only one example in nature. Is that enough?

"I know what I saw," I said, pulling a great lug of air.

"So what did you see? Tell us Naomi said, taunting me in the shadows.

Soon she reappeared and sat back down with a rectangular bottle of whiskey at her lips, offering the bottle to Zoe as she finished.

I kept my mouth still as I considered her words. She was calling me out again, questioning my sanity. Would I do the same if I was on the other side? If she had gone through what I had to free Chloe from the grip of that animal? Would I believe her without question?

No, I wouldn't.

Pulling a long draw from the bottle, I winced as the spirit burned down my throat.

"Her eyes were milky white," I said in a slow voice, the last of the fumes escaping my throat.

"Cataracts," Naomi replied.

"She was barely in her thirties," I said, trying hard not to let my voice falter.

"She was in a bad way," Zoe said. Her voice was soft; at least Zoe was desperate not to provoke the discussion.

"Half her face was missing," I replied, my voice growing harder.

Cassidy looked down at her sister.

"Sorry," I said, lowering my level. "But we watched her die. She'd stopped breathing. We all saw it."

I looked towards Andrew, still asleep. I turned to Chloe and her pale, washed-out face.

"And that smell," I repliedcatching a

IN THE END

whiff of the odour, the stench of decay. The sting of human waste.

Taking the bottle again, I cleaned my throat. Still the smell was there.

"Can none of you smell that?" I asked, and watched the group exchange looks, watched each sample the air, their noses turning up. They could smell it, I was certain.

"There is something hanging around," Toby said, but a flicker of light on the far wall caught my attention.

I stood and through a thin cloud of smoke I saw the far end of the warehouse had begun to glow orange.

16

"Holy shit," I said, almost under my breath.

Toby's words were not so quiet as he climbed to his feet, his face glowing in the reflection of the heat flowing our way.

"Get up, get up," I shouted, bending down to shake Andrew's shoulders. I didn't wait for him to stir. Instead, I ran to the fire exit and pulled the bright red extinguisher from the wall.

Running along the aisles, the heat built on my chest. It would have been a welcome relief if it hadn't been for the fumes catching in my breath.

Toby joined me, another extinguisher in his hand as we rushed forward to the glowing wall with the remains of plastic posters turning black as they slid to the floor.

At first we saw no flames and only thin smoke, but as we rushed forward, the double doors burst open. A cloud of smoke and toxic heat blasted out, forcing us to stop as we doubled over.

Glancing back, my mouth in the crook of my arm, I watched Toby back up and turned back to see flames lick around the side of the doors as they rattled open and closed, billowing with heat.

I left the extinguisher before running back to our camp, joining Toby's shouts for everyone to grab what they could and get the hell out.

Instead of leaping to the exit, the group split, among the shelves. I knelt at Chloe's side, the rotten stench powerful enough to break through the thick smoke scratching at my lungs.

Lily knelt with me, wrapping Chloe in the blankets, folding up the corners as a makeshift stretcher.

Sharing her downcast look, I took a moment. Chloe had grown even more pale, thinner as the background light grew. Her breath was barely there.

I looked along the lanes, smelling the burning plastic before I saw the contents of the shelves burning as they dripped to the floor.

I shouted, hurrying everyone toward the front of the shop as I dragged Chloe's blankets behind me and pulled her toward the exit.

Soon I was joined by the others with rucksacks on their backs, the load getting lighter with each hand adding a hold to the stretcher.

Arriving at the door, we took our time to gather fresh air as we pulled her through the entrance. Looking around, I saw it wasn't just me who was doing everything to avoid catching Chloe's sunken eyes.

Soon we were out in the chill night, with no idea what the time was but were surprised again at how bright the half-moon lit up the sky.

The mood sat heavy as I rushed into the car, revving the engine as I tried to disconnect the Freelander from the building.

With Andrew, Toby and Matt back in the burning building pushing the bonnet as hard as they could, the engine roared in their faces. Metal continued to grip and when the wheels finally moved, the

IN THE END

car stayed still and filled the air with a thick rubber burn.

The heat raged out to where we stood around the car. We all looked at the horizon, no matter what we believed had happened earlier in the evening. We saw no movement. Nothing but the casual sway of distant trees. We were in the middle of nowhere.

"Let's follow the road," I said in a whisper, picking up the front right corner of the blanket.

The others followed in silence. Heads turned left and right, darting at every sound.

At the entrance to the car park I twisted, looking back at the building and watched as the fire consumed it to the frame. Black smoke rose into the night.

Soon we relaxed, Chloe's frail weight hardly a burden. Still no one spoke, taking comfort in the views. We could see for miles.

No one said anything, not even giving voice to the terrible smell we were carrying between us.

"Stop," came Lily's voice, making

everyone jump. We all stopped together, lowering the blankets to the floor.

Lily fell to her knees at Chloe's side. She pulled open the covers to take her wrist, pressing her two fingers against her skin.

We watched on, our spray of white breath slowing, pulling coats tighter around our shoulders or raising packs higher. Each of us did anything but wait for the verdict.

Lily looked up at me, a tear rolling down her cheek. Why did she choose me to receive her deep heartache?

I raised my eyebrows to prompt the next obvious question. She turned down at Chloe's face and knelt in, putting her ear to her mouth.

"No," I shouted, my voice cutting through the night as I swooped down to push her to the side.

17

Lily fell back with my swipe, caught, wide-eyed, by Toby standing behind.

His hands grabbed under her armpits and helped her to her feet. The raised voices questioned what they saw.

Blocking out the cries, I turned, ignoring Toby's glare as I saw him only just holding back the instinct to raise his fists.

Not wanting to be distracted, I looked at the pale glow of Chloe's face. I fixed on every movement I couldn't see, my fingers curled around the gun in my pocket, looking for any change.

The study was cut short with a sharp jab to my shoulder and I turned to see Naomi, her fist still raised, ready for me to open my mouth and say the wrong thing.

"Fucking prick," she said, her words just as sharp as the knuckles on her hand.

Turning away, I swallowed down my growing anger as I looked over the group.

Zoe was at Naomi's back, her eyes filled with terror and on the verge of tears; Cassidy was backing off, looking down her nose, Ellie buried in her side.

Andrew was with me, a nod in my direction. He was the only one who'd shared my witness.

I didn't catch Matt's expression. My gaze had already fallen, my eyes wide again. I watched as Lily, back on her knees, lowered her head to Chloe's face.

Toby stood to block me.

I turned away, stepping from the blanket. After three paces, I heard the intake of breath and I turned, a commotion lighting the centre of the group.

The first I saw was Cassidy dragging Ellie backwards, running and falling into a hedge.

Andrew stood still, gripped on what I hadn't yet seen. Despite my need to see what I'd feared, my vision filled with Naomi and Zoe clutched tight together.

Zoe looked to the ground, screaming. Naomi stared back, her eyes wide, her mouth wider, her skin more pale than I ever imagined.

It was at that point I knew she understood what I'd been saying all along.

I turned to the centre. Time didn't slow, but still I took in all the detail.

Chloe rose with her mouth attached somehow to the side of Lily's face.

Toby was in there too, his hands between them, pulling. He was grappling to pull the pair free.

Matt shouted, cursing, unable to do anything to his partner who'd clamped her mouth deep onto our friend's face.

Blinking for the first time, I was powerless to help. I was an onlooker, like Andrew, looking on, unable to do anything. We couldn't attack our friend. I didn't have it in me to repeat the violence I'd raged on Chloe's attacker. I couldn't repeat the same on Chloe with the slice of doubt Naomi had planted.

We weren't doctors. Maybe Chloe wasn't dead. Maybe it was a condition she would recover from, no matter what the made-up TV said.

It was as Chloe's arms raised and her mouth let go that I acted.

With Lily falling to the red-soaked blankets and clamping on Toby's hand to his screams of terror, I knew I had to do something.

My hand ached. My knuckles were white as I gripped the gun, pulling it loose from my pocket.

I held the weapon out, screaming for Toby to move the fuck away.

He looked toward me, his face twisted. With the help of Matt at his back, he managed to pull his arm away.

With teeth tearing flesh, he was free and falling backwards on top of Matt as they tripped over each other to the tarmac.

I took a hard swallow and pointed the gun. As I did, the woman, the friend who could no longer be called Chloe, stood as if alive.

There she was,, bringing a flash of doubt into my mind. The flash passed and I pulled the trigger before the empty click reminded me I hadn't pushed the bullet back in.

Stepping away with my gaze fixed on her blood-dripping face, she walked forward. Her eyes were open and milky white, fixed in an expression of interest, sparking electricity up my spine.

I stepped back again, my pace much slower than hers. I found the bullet as I fumbled for how the hell to release the magazine.

She was closing too quickly.

I found the release and the magazine clattered to the floor, the sound dulled by wheezing breaths rasping from the thing's lungs.

I launched the gun, which struck its head, but despite the jolt, it continued forward. With breath like a mortuary, it was soon close enough to touch and I watched her fingers clawing out.

The bandage had fallen from her arm and I saw the deep bite marks were dry, her hands cold and waxy as they gripped around my throat.

I stumbled. Falling backwards, my senses overloaded with an explosion of red light.

18

My vision turned red. My ears rang. I lay rasping for breath as if a great weight clung to my chest, the last few moments removed from memory.

Nausea raced up from my stomach. Nerves rattled as if all lit in the same moment, my body invaded by an alien sense.

Reality flashed back and understanding took hold. I was back in the moment.

Despair sank into my bones until, without warning, the stifling mass released.

My first thought was death, but my nerves seemed to calm and the nausea lifted. A peace surrounded me until I felt hands rushing over my shoulders and fingers tracing around my neck, forcing the turn of my head either side.

The bright red fell away. Blinking as hands gripped the straps of my rucksack and words pushed through the bells in my ears, a shadow moved across my

IN THE END

field of vision.

Before I could concentrate on the sounds, I was on my feet. Andrew's arms wrapped around me, pulling me close.

"You're okay," he repeated.

I wasn't sure if the words were just for my benefit.

Releasing his hold, he still held my arm, his fingers gripping my shoulder, the other on my hand.

We walked, his pace pulling me to a slow trot. By now the darkness had replaced the blinding red and I saw shapes on the horizon, blurred and unmoving. The cold took hold again. I could feel my face cooling.

About to turn and ask what the hell had happened, he dragged me to the side of the road, pushing me through a hedgerow. My face scraped against thorns, his hand to my mouth as we came to rest.

All I heard was our fast breath and pulling away his hand I nodded, keeping my voice quiet.

As my breath slowed, I tried to tune out the constant tone and listened to the nothing in the air, the stench still hanging in my nostrils.

We waited, listening to the rattle of the leaves with each gentle breeze. Listening for what I feared.

Spying out between the thick growth, all I could see were the stars more vivid than I could have ever thought.

How much time past before I spoke wasn't clear, but it was long enough to know we were safer than we had been moments ago.

"What happened?" I asked, hoping he heard my voice. I could barely hear myself.

"What do you remember?" he replied, his words just as quiet.

"Chloe," I said with a pause.

"Coming for me." I watched as Andrew's shape gave a shallow nod. "The gun was empty."

"I shot her with a firework," he said. "I thought you were toast," he added, leaning in with a tight grip to my arm.

"You got the locker open?" I asked, remembering back to the store.

IN THE END

His weak shape nodded.

"What are we hiding from?" I said. "Toby?" I added, as his arm in her grip jumped into my head.

"No," Andrew replied. "There were more of them."

I let my breath settle, new fear spiking the blood in my veins, my hand diving for my pocket and finding the stiff cold of the bullet.

"The gun?" I said.

Andrew reached somewhere I couldn't see and rested the cold metal in my hands, the magazine home in the base.

I squeezed his hand in reply and closed my eyes, trying to remember films and cop shows. Soon my fingers found the release once again.

By touch alone, pausing my breath with each loud click, I fed the lonely bullet into the magazine and carefully pushed it back, just in time to hear a rustle of the bushes at our back.

I felt Andrew's surprise. The noise was behind us, not on the road.

No words came, but I could swear

the stench of rotten flesh grew stronger.

Andrew rested his palm on my chest, a signal to stay still and make no noise. It was a signal I didn't need.

The rustle grew louder and I swore I heard voices. I turned towards Andrew, but I couldn't see his response.

The noise was growing.

We had choices to make. Shoot first, or run.

I pulled back the slide.

The motion from the bush reacted, gaining ground as the device clicked the bullet into place.

I pushed the weapon out towards the noise and rested my finger on the trigger, only stopping as I heard footsteps scraping along the road at our backs as well.

19

With adrenaline rushing, fear pulled me in both directions. Was it the feet scuffing along the tarmac, a beat skipped with each misstep? Was it the shudder of the bushes so close and with a speed I knew I couldn't match?

I had no time to think. I didn't move. What if it was an injured friend on the road, running from a danger I already knew too well?

What had Andrew seen for us to dive into this hiding place?

We were blind to all around, with only our ears to lead us in the right direction. Was it an animal in the bushes, a stray dog not fed for over twenty-four hours?

How long would it take for a pet to undo hundreds of generations of breeding? I'd rather tackle a hungry animal than something which would kill me and make me live again.

What if it were one of our friends? I'd had no chance to question what had happened. Alive or dead, I needed to know.

Zoe's face came to mind, even Naomi's slid past in the gallery of images. Toby was gone, or soon to be.

Matt. I didn't know how he'd fared. Lily. She was past the point of no return for sure. Was it a blessing they'd gone together? How long would it be before they turned into those things?

Toby wouldn't be dead yet. Lily either. Unless they'd bled out.

I thought of Cassidy. Her blonde striking hair and blue eyes. Then Ellie, her shorter mirror image.

I thought of Leo, Daniel and Max. A sudden hope sparking they may have made it. They'd left earlier than the rest of us; perhaps there was a chance for them.

I thought of the old man's head crashing so hard against the windscreen; the shattered glass was something I would have to live with for as long as I survived.

Was he one of them when he'd died? Is that why he was in the road? But there hadn't been that smell, the odour of decay.

No. I couldn't let the thought calm the guilt. He was alive before, but what was he now? What were any of them now? Were all of them out there in the bushes or on the road?

Or was it our friends, searching in the dark? Scared, like us. Like me.

Andrew was no help. I couldn't see past the leaves at my face, my ears full of the rustle of life, the scrape of soles against the road.

Andrew knew why we'd dived into the bush. He'd said there were more, but not how many. The roadblock was not so far away. I had no real idea of how far I'd driven in my race to get away from where Chloe was first attacked. From the place when this became all too real.

Now I'd wasted too much time. They were on us, so close. Somehow they knew where we were.

Finding Andrew's wrist in the dark, I gripped. He reflexed in response.

I tapped left, trying to indicate towards the noise in the bushes, but he twisted right, showing the opposite direction.

Did he mean it was not the way to go?

I indicated left once more, moving his hand with a jerk.

His arm was limp. The noise was too much, the scrape of the feet too close. The rattle of the leaves was like drums in my ears.

I took Andrew's lead, or what I thought he'd meant and leapt right, the breath of cold air feeling great on my face. I held out the pistol in my hand.

I'd made the right and wrong choice, depending on how you felt about what I stood in front of.

My feet were on the hard surface of the road, my vision clear, the first rays of sun climbing the horizon.

I hoped the gun worked this time.

20

In front of me stood someone I'd not seen before.

Still, my finger wouldn't commit on the trigger. I'd made too many recent mistakes already.

She was mid-twenties with brown hair tied high in a bun. She wore an Aran jumper with a black hole over her breast with dark, dried liquid. Somehow, I knew it would look a different colour in the sun.

Underneath was perfect skin, not the wide-open wound I'd expected to see, seeping with blood.

The right of her face looked perfect in the first light of day. I didn't want to look at the dark sunken hole where her left eye should have been. Skin on the left of her face was tight, drawn over skeletal features. Her mouth hung wide.

The wind blew her stench across my nostrils.

I pulled the trigger and the gun exploded.

At first I thought my hand was on fire, afraid the shot had ripped through my flesh as the gun shot backwards.

When she dropped to the floor, I looked at my hand to see it was still intact, the gun in one piece. Just a ring of pain was left in my ears.

My legs carried me forward and I stood over her body. Now both her eyes were missing. Her mouth was closed. She was at peace.

The rustle in the bushes grew but I didn't turn or flinch as I looked up to the horizon. The sun was beautiful as its amber rays followed the curve of our little planet.

Andrew joined at my side. I glanced left and saw another, then two more. Zoe, Naomi and Cassidy with Ellie tucked up to her hip, almost hidden.

Each joined in the line and stared out. We shared that silent moment of hope as if today was the day when maybe the world would make sense again.

One of the girls was the first to pull in a sharp breath. The others followed,

IN THE END

their hands reaching for their mouths, almost in unison as we saw a figure running towards us on the road, a dark outline against the growing light. But he wasn't alone.

Horde was the only word I could find to describe what we saw. On the horizon came a mass of figures with unnatural movement. Their speed was less than the runner's, but not slow enough for my liking.

"Go," I said, turning to the line. "Go.".

Cassidy and Ellie were the first to peel off and break into a jog, then Zoe and Naomi, sobbing for the shattered dream of hope we'd just shared.

Andrew stood on the spot.

"Go," I shouted.

"Fuck off," he replied, panting through a half-hearted smile.

Together we held our ground, the runner closing. I shifted the warm gun in my hand to use as a club.

Andrew stood with a lighter held tight in his fist, the stick of a giant star-covered firework in the other.

After a minute we saw Matt's face, his roman nose appearing first as the light climbed.

Andrew and I swapped a glance with wide grins. I heard the click of a lighter at my side, the fizz of the fuse.

With my hand out, I grabbed at Matt's spread fingers. The rocket flew through the air, racing toward the crowd, their horrid stench already here.

I had Matt's palm and let myself relax at his warmth. We were already running, making good ground towards our friends as the firework exploded at our backs.

We almost clapped hands in a high five, turning to watch the middle of the pack stop. Wetried to ignore the wave of double dead bodies forming over the mound.

Andrew couldn't have been carrying enough fireworks to take the whole pack on, but we had pace. Above all we had pace, although the girls were already beginning to slow.

Still running, I watched as Zoe stopped first. She turned our way, then

Naomi too, despite my waving hands and shouts urging them on.

Cassidy was next and Ellie tucked in. They'd turned and were jumping in the air, arms waving. They were screaming at the top of their voices, no longer worried about the horde of things running our way.

Before I could slow, I heard the definite sound of helicopter blades cutting through the air.

21

Tears fell as I came to a stop. With my hand reaching for my mouth, my lungs gasping, relief stunned my nerves. I wasn't going to die anytime soon. We weren't going to die the same terrible way as our friends.

I saw the helicopter as a dot on the horizon, but still it was clear they were heading our way. It followed the road. They couldn't miss the horde who took no notice. They wouldn't miss us. We were saved.

With the chopper looming, I walked backwards. The stench reminded us these things were gaining and would still run us down if we didn't pick up the pace. We needed to get away so the crew could land safely.

Matt slowed, waving his hands, not moving much from his position. The rest of us turned and hurried once again.

The beat of the rotors grew. With each step my legs felt lighter, my mind clearing, joy rising at the thought of a safe escape and getting answers to those questions circling around everyone's heads.

We'd lost friends along the way, but hope surged that we'd see Leo, Daniel and Max on the other side.

The tone of the engines changed and a jolt of rapid gunfire broke out.

I slowed. The others did too. Ellie tucked back into her sister's side. Naomi and Zoe linked arms tight as we watched a line of fire rain from the side door of the camo-green Merlin helicopter still heading our way.

A figure in a helmet steered the door-mounted gun, bullets glowing red hot as a dark mist rose from the crowd.

I took steps back. The horde continued moving forward, despite their numbers shrinking before my eyes.

The others followed; even Matt started to move as the gunfire paused and we watched the walking bodies ignoring their slaughter.

After a moment, the gunfire took up again with a wild fever, but soon fell as the numbers on the ground thinned.

I slowed, the gaps between blasts growing as the crewman took his time, the crowd shrinking with each burst.

We watched as a ball flew from the side door. An explosion tensed my shoulders as a spray of debris reached high in the air.

Backing off, the action gained ground. The helicopter was circling, chasing individuals limping as they finally started to scatter. More grenades flew from the doorway, explosions rocking me back as I stuck my fingers into my ears.

We backed off further and Matt had too, but he was still a few hundred metres away. I pulled my fingers from my ears and turned.

I breathed a sigh of relief, for the first time not gagging at the foul smell.

We were safe. They were dead. Again.

I hugged Andrew at my side, walked the few steps and met Zoe, then Naomi, taking them in my arms. I felt the stress release with each squeeze, even sharing a smile with Cassidy as her sister hid

IN THE END

away.

The sound of the chopper grew. The long machine gun had relaxed, pointing down.

I took a few steps to Matt but stopped as the chopper came closer, flying over our heads as they continued to follow the road.

For one fear-filled moment I thought they would race on along the highway, but I relaxed again as it rose higher, sweeping to our side in a long arc and circling the field to head back our way.

I pushed my hands in the air, the others joining as we waved. We wouldn't allow them to mistake us for people who didn't want to be rescued.

Andrew said something in my ear, but I missed the detail. Instead, I watched as the helicopter twisted, turning through ninety degrees.

I watched, still waving high as the machine gun turned. My stomach squeezed as fire rushed from the muzzle and Matt fell, a red mist following the bullets ripping into his shadow.

22

The spray of bullets glowed against the fading darkness, its path grinding onwards past Matt's slumped body as it kicked up great mounds of tarmac.

We stood in a line, gripped as another version of death raced in our direction.

"Run," I screamed.

Everyone seemed to wake and turn on their heels, but I held my ground, waiting for their reaction.

Andrew ran across in front of me, his plan clear: to separate from the group to force a choice of who to shoot first.

Zoe and Naomi clung to each other as they moved, but soon let go to gain speed, running along the straight road.

Ellie's short legs weren't pumping so hard. Cassidy slowed too as she scooped her up.

I wouldn't let them be the first.

I raced on, catching them with no effort and grabbed Ellie around her middle whilst looking at Cassidy as her eyes widened.

She released her grip. Ellie squirmed as if I was the Child-Catcher from her nightmares, only calming as I threw her over my shoulder and she saw her sister running beside her.

"Get off the road," I heard Andrew scream, his voice already distant.

I swerved left, seeing sense in his words. Cassidy followed too. I couldn't keep track of Zoe and Naomi, my focus fixed forward at the grass at the edge of the road. I tried to stop my top-heavy weight from falling on the uneven ground.

At our backs, the machine gun had stopped screaming, but the engines were so loud, the tone deep as it changed pitch.

I glanced around to see it turning for the chase. The only chance we had was to run and hide.

An explosion rocked me, taking all my effort to recover from the stumble. Ellie let out a yelp, but the madness sounded further away than I expected.

My stomach felt empty as I realised they were going after one of my friends.

The sky brightened with each wide step. The grass led down a valley at my feet, the light horizon filling me with hope.

In the dawn light, a wood of dense trees stood a few hundred metres away. Somehow, I found more inside me and picked up the pace, ignoring the scream of pain in my legs.

The machine gun lit up the air and I winced as an explosion followed, lighting the sky with a flash. It was the obvious pop and fizz of a firework.

We were at the treeline and I let Ellie down. With my arms throbbing with relief, I stared as she jumped the few steps to Cassidy, grabbing around her waist.

I followed as they turned to stare at the attack. The helicopter had followed the road. The pit opened wider in my stomach as I saw it must have been Zoe and Naomi they'd chased.

I closed my eyes and let my breath settle. I said a Godless prayer in hope

IN THE END

they'd split up to halve the chances.

A breath pulled at my lungs as I watched a thin silver line appear from behind the chopper, the air popping with a blue glitter explosion at the tail rotor. The helicopter didn't react, a line of fire bursting from the door at its original target.

I wrapped my arms around myself. I was cold, but not the kind the sun would solve. The chill came from not being able to change the next few moments.

Cassidy stepped near, leaning next to me. She looked up, her face warm but concerned.

"Thank you," she said, glancing at Ellie as she hid behind a wide tree.

Cassidy's arm went around my shoulder and I leaned in.

Another firework raced from the ground, its launch closer than before. The chopper rocked to the side as the red explosion hit the rear of the fuselage. The darkness wouldn't tell if he'd done any damage, but it didn't seem to matter.

The line of bullets cut off and the

chopper raced forward, turning to aim its guns. As it turned, another rocket raced, then another at its back. One after the other, five or six rounds burst from the ground.

Andrew was giving all he had as I silently urged him on. I hoped by now he'd turned and fled, running to find somewhere to hide.

The air popped as each glitter ball exploded without harm, the chopper out of range, out of danger as it tracked back.

I pictured the gunner looking through his visor, one eye closed, taking time to centre his aim. A long blast exploded from the muzzle. The chopper hung still for a moment before turning, tracing the route to its last hunting ground.

I turned to Cassidy and took her embrace. Not able to hold back the tears, I sunk to my knees.

23

A crackle of electricity cut through the air. Through tears, I turned up to the hazy sky. Shockwaves rattled through our bodies as a furious explosion of light erupted from inside the helicopter.

Clambering to my feet, I ran, my vision fixed as the aircraft became unsteady. Smoke circled, whisked away by the speeding rotors.

Stumbling, I looked to the ground. I jumped to recover, looking skyward as quick as I could, watching the body of the chopper spin. My feet took me right, turning as the path of the rotating craft sped through its turn.

My gaze fixed forward, seeking any sign of my friend. Or what was left.

The grass grew thicker and I slowed to raise my legs high over the uneven ground. It was hard going and not just because my attention was elsewhere.

Out of the corner of my eye I saw the helicopter falling to the ground a few hundred metres away with a second explosion. The tail caught and the spin changed direction in an instant, sending the craft over on its side, the rotors crushing down and shattering, debris shooting off in all directions.

Falling to my hands and knees, I linked my fingers over my buried head. Tucking into a foetal position, shrapnel fell to the grass. The burn of oil and hot metal fell all around.

With the last of the debris, I stood, giving only a casual glance over to the wreckage as it rocked to a halt and ended its final barrel roll.

"Andrew," I screamed and paced forward again. My gaze searched the dense grass.

I soon saw the road and its surface mottled to shreds, broken with lead still steaming from the small craters.

"Andrew," I repeated, my voice breaking. Crunching loose tarmac on the road, I stopped, turning and letting my voice sing out into the surrounding nothing.

I saw him over the verge, climbing to his feet. Rising from the tall grass, I

IN THE END

ran toward the wide smile on his smoke-blackened face. His hands were out, red and burnt, his near empty pack hanging in the crook of his arm.

I ran, bounding over the verge, skidding down the side, jumping the shallow ditch and grabbed him as he sucked through his teeth at my embrace.

He pressed his elbows at my side; it was all he could manage as he winced at my grip.

"You suckered them in," I said through laughter. "You sneaky bastard."

"Saved the biggest for last. The Brimstone. You should have seen the size of the fucker," he said.

I could hear the grin in his voice, but it turned to a wince as I hugged tighter.

Drawing back, I took notice of the sun above the horizon. I watched the sky free of cloud, the blue softening with every moment.

Brushing the loose dirt from my fingers against my jacket, my hands came away with blood. I looked down to find the fabric of my jacket unbroken.

I knew it wasn't mine when I caught sight of the hole in the side of Andrew's dark woollen coat.

"Shit," I said, showing Andrew my hands and pointing down to the hole.

His eyes grew wide. With his hands still out in front, I caught the smell of charred flesh in my throat.

With great care, I pulled the bag from his arm as I tried to keep it from the rawness of his hands. Unbuttoning his jacket, he winced with every movement.

Peeling the coat back over his shoulders, I held my breath as I saw the thin brown jumper soaked red underneath. I tried to keep my expression straight. I knew, despite not looking, that Andrew's gaze was fixed on mine, keen for my reaction.

Pulling up the jumper, the t-shirt too, I folded up the layers dripping with fresh blood, drawing a sigh of relief as I saw the line traced down the side of his skin.

"It didn't go in," I said, the words breathless.

IN THE END

He relaxed, tensing again, air sucking through his teeth with every movement.

I took a second look. The bleeding had already slowed.

We were safe. A calm air settled.

We'd survived another moment of terrible history, but the joy was short-lived when a high, animal-like scream cut through the air.

A young woman's desperate voice, calling for help.

24

I turned, looking toward Andrew. His gaze was already urging me away, his hands shooing me off despite his visible pain.

Shrugging the weight of the rucksack from my shoulders, I broke into a sprint.

I slowed only as the tall grass pulled at my feet and I tripped over the uneven tarmac.

The frantic scream came again, cutting through the air in a blood-curdling call.

Despite searching the horizon, I still couldn't see anyone or shake the possible outcome. I pictured Zoe slain, blood soaking to the ground, a line of scarlet ripping through her legs. Her gaze fixed, desperate on mine.

With my next few steps, the face in my mind had changed. Naomi's wide blue eyes glared back as I looked down. She sneered down her nose, telling me it was all my fault.

IN THE END

I tried to tell myself the pain in my chest was no less when it wasn't Zoe I pictured.

I couldn't take my eyes off the utter destruction of their legs, even though it was all in my mind. With my feet rolling on the brass of a spent cartridge the size of a finger, the image disappeared.

I told myself the damage was done and tried to force away all thought. But guilt surfaced as I hoped it wasn't Zoe I was about to find, or Naomi standing over her body, screaming for a miracle. Heartbroken.

The shrill call came again, the only sound for miles around, growing louder each time. Still, I couldn't see my destination. All I knew was I was heading towards the crash site, the grass churned up where the rotors first hit.

Half a blade jutted from the ground, a jagged, razor edge cutting through the breeze.

I caught movement to my left from the tree line.

It was Cassidy, her sister dragged along in hand. They were closing, racing forward for the same reason.

Turning, I saw Naomi, the pit so wide in my stomach I thought it would split open.

She stood in a dip in the ground, the shake of her body plain to see, even from my distance.

She raised her arms in a frantic wave, but turned back, shaking her head with tears tumbling down her face.

I turned toward Cassidy and held my palms out, looking at Ellie.

"No," I said, my voice grave.

Cassidy took one look to her side and understood.

"Ells, wait here," she said.

Keeping my pace, I listened as Cassidy repeated, this time with the sharpest edge I'd heard.

I was moments away and through wet eyes I saw a body laying on the ground.

She was dark, charred beyond recognition, her body swollen, head ballooned. Her arms were bent at all angles, legs wild in all directions. She was moving, swaying as if finding comfort in the motion.

I'd known her for half my life. I didn't know if I could watch this happen.

A few more steps and I heard a low, rumbling moan. The pain in my stomach boiled to anger. Fear raged.

I sniffed the air, taking in the oil and burning chemicals. There wasn't the hideous odour. She hadn't died and come alive again. She was living, at least for now.

Movement caught in the right of my vision and as I arrived at the body, wiping my eyes, I saw Zoe coming down into the valley. It wasn't her laying on the ground.

The swollen, bulbous head was a helmet. The swollen body was someone else dressed in a charred olive flight suit.

My pain fell away. My tears cleared as the body snapped into focus and for the first time I saw him for who he was. The guy who'd saved our lives, then tried to kill us instead.

25

"Why are you crying over this piece of shit?" I shouted, sneering down in his direction.

Cassidy drew up by my side, Zoe at Naomi's, linking their arms and tucking into her like Ellie had done before to her sister. Their eyes were fixed with something like grief.

The muscles in my chest tightened as I fought for breath. "I thought it was you lying there. I thought one of you was screaming because the other was in such pain, or dead. Not this murderer," I said, turning as I took a deep breath, pulling back from the urge to spit on the pained body.

I felt Cassidy's hand on my arm and I turned towards her. Her doe-eyes stared, her fingers squeezing. She was trying to urge me to relax, but I couldn't stand here. I couldn't weep for this man. This killer.

I turned to Naomi, aiming my venom in her direction.

"Do you realise who this is? What he tried to do? What he did to our friend out on the road?" I shouted, my hands waving intent.

"Andrew?" Zoe gasped.

I let a pause hang in the air, but guilt brought my voice.

"No, he's back there," I said, my volume lower. Taking a step forward, I raised my hands, thumb and forefinger nearly pinched together.

"This close. He was this fucking close to death," I said, pushing my hand out. "This close to another fucking funeral when this is all over." I took another step, my feet within swinging distance of an olive leg bent at the wrong angle. "Why are you crying over this?" I repeated.

Zoe stepped in front of me, stopping me from doing what she read as my intent. Her hands rested on my chest,, her eyes wide, calming. At least trying to be.

"He's human," came Naomi's weak voice through a sniff. "Acting on orders."

I couldn't help but step to the side,

stepping around Zoe and moving to stand over the rocking body.

"Orders to kill us," I said, giving each word the slow, careful thought they deserved. "We're the innocent. We've done nothing wrong. We're no harm to anyone."

I thought of the old man again. That was an accident and if anyone dare say otherwise…

"Orders to kill the infected," Naomi said in a weak voice. "Or those carrying maybe? They were trying to save the rest of the people. Our people."

"Are you saying what Andrew did was wrong? Was he wrong to save your life? Our lives?"

"No," she said, turning away.

I watched her walk up the side of the small valley.

I turned to Zoe, wanting to see what she would do. I wanted to see if she would stay or go.

Her stare fixed on the sway of the body, the gentle moan which had grown quiet. Zoe looked up, regarding my face for what seemed like a long time.

Something went weak as I watched her inner torment play out on her features and I melted inside. I gave her the out.

"Someone needs to get Andrew," I said.

Zoe nodded, then jogged after Naomi to wrap her arm around her shoulder as they disappeared over the crest.

"Cassidy," I said, sweeping around to catch her eye. Hers, too, were on the man lain on the ground.

"It's Cassie," she said, her voice stern, her gaze not leaving the man. "Call me Cassie, please."

I nodded and she turned, then paused, nodding toward me then back at her sister. "Someone needs to take care of him," she said, walking away.

"Guess that's me then," I said, although there was no one to listen.

My chest relaxed. My breath coming easy, long and deep.

I took my first proper look at the man. The straight line of the charred flight suit. Utility pouches around his stomach were open. A first aid kit spilt out as he rocked. A holster was still tight around his left thigh. A pistol peered out.

I was amazed how much the mind can play tricks. To have thought it was Zoe lain there seemed impossible now.

I turned and saw no-one in the valley. They were gone from sight. They'd left me to decide, to take the hard choice. Put him out of his misery or take my revenge and leave him slowly to die. Leave him defenceless, meat for the real enemy.

It was my choice and I wouldn't let them hold it over me. This was a new world. The old laws no longer made sense. We were in the new frontier, governed only by the law of the jungle. Survival of the fittest.

Did mercy still have a place?

Although I'd been watching the steady rise and fall of his chest all this time, it was only now I realised it had stopped. The decision had been taken away.

With gratitude, I dropped to my

knees and undid the Velcro of each pouch, taking the first aid kit, a survival tin, and two magazines for the gun.

The body twitched and I stepped back, watching on as the chest deflated, gas belching from his mouth and the other end.

I paused, a thought sudden in my head. What if you didn't need to be bitten to catch whatever it was? Was death enough?

My pulse raised as I set about working the Velcro of the holster. Then I caught that smell again.

"Give me a fucking break," I said, almost shouting.

I looked up, not knowing what I'd see. Ihadn't expected another olive-green flight suit standing over the edge of the valley. His face was red with blood and he swayed as if dizzy.

In his hand he held a pistol matching the one I was moments from gripping, the gun waving from side to side, but pointing in my general direction.

26

COMMANDER LANE

The first sign was the internet going down, the Skype connection to my wife lost in an instant. Her face was frozen in perfection, despite the wide yawn.

With the sudden halt to our conversation, we'd have to decide later what we'd get up to when my shift finished tomorrow. How we'd celebrate New Year's Eve a day late, just the two of us. The twins weren't children anymore. I had to keep reminding myself they were nineteen, back from Bristol University for a month. Tomorrow, like tonight, they'd be at a house party, living life as young women should.

I had to stay awake, part of being on call, but Bethany kept her eyes open with matchsticks because she wanted to stay in my time zone.

The second I knew was when my petty officer found me tucked in the

IN THE END

corner of our mess room, relief on his face. With politeness he told me he'd been hunting for me for too long already.

A shout had come in. He didn't know if it was a training exercise or something more real. All he knew was we'd been ordered to the apron with a briefing on route.

A situation like this wasn't unheard of, but unusual enough to note. We were given a clear flight path to RNAS Culdrose, the only other Naval Air Station in the UK.

The third sign something had gone to shit was in the Land Rover on the way to the aircraft. I saw the point five machine gun bolted down in the doorway.

Leading Hand Spicer was already aboard, his feet straddling the machine gun. Lieutenant Commander Stubbs sat in the seat next to mine, all but spinning the rotors.

Despite being an operational unit on call, we weren't search and rescue. Those days were gone. We were there to support coastal tactics. To help in a national emergency. To defend the country. But in reality, we just drilled until everything was muscle memory.

Never in my seventeen years of service had we exercised on New Year's Eve.

All that said, the weather was clear, cold and cloudless. I'd want to be up in my Merlin rather than trying not to fall asleep in the mess any time. Plus, I'd have a great view when the hour struck.

Still not briefed and following the set route, we were flying over Plymouth when the ground just went dark. I'd never seen a power cut from the sky before, the ground just shades of black. It reminded me of the bleak Afghan countryside. Each moment I expected tracer rounds to light up the night while I hoped they weren't aimed in our direction.

The power was still out by the time we landed at Culdrose half an hour later. My mind kept asking if being scrambled and the power going out were connected.

We had seen the naval station

IN THE END

from miles away and could make it out from the depths of the darkness. It was apparently the only place on the horizon to have decent backup generators. The clear weather and half-moon helped; so did the apron awash with blinking anti-collision lights.

Headlights from trucks and Land Rovers ran around the base, a convoy leaving through the main gates. The only other lights in the dark night. If this was an exercise, then everyone in the Royal Navy seemed to be playing their part.

We finally got our orders as we touched down. We were there to transport VIPs, but we had to wait. We had to stay in our seats and keep the rotors spinning. There was no mention of the reason why.

I stared out from the windows, shivering after being told in no uncertain terms not to stow the gun so we could pull the door closed to let the heat build. I was pissed because I could have been up in the air or back at the mess stealing forty winks. There was no enjoyment in waiting, but it was part of the job.

Crates were loaded, ours one of thirty choppers sitting on the tarmac. This would blow the fuel budget alone and would cost us another exercise or two. I just hoped it wouldn't cross over into tomorrow. The roster only had me on shift for five hours more.

Stubbs had his eyes closed, within seconds pulling his usual trick. He was an ex-marine and could fall asleep with the flick of a switch.

Spicer pulled up from around the machine gun and leaned through to the cockpit. We'd been crewed together for almost three years, which was unheard of in the service. Stubbs, in the seat next to me, had been on the team for just a few months, but we hadn't bonded in combat.

Spicer was the only rating on the crew. We'd shared a full tour of Afghan and had become friends, despite his rank. Living in a tent twenty-four seven, flying every other moment and putting your lives in each other's hands every day kind of did that. I'd got us out of situations so many times with my

IN THE END

hands on the stick. He'd shot our way out of trouble more than I could count. I couldn't do his job; I didn't have the balls to pull the trigger.

I remember those first few shots in anger. Remembered how he'd changed, withdrawing for days. But he'd pulled himself out with a little help of our ribbing and a reliance on his drills and training.

I told him of my plans for tomorrow, today now. A meal and a few glasses of wine. He told me of his night of movies. His two young daughters, twins, too, cradled in his arms.

I told him to stop being such a sappy twat, before quickly shutting my mouth and elbowing Stubbs in the ribs as three Land Rovers pulled alongside.

There were only three passengers, the other two Landy's full of Marine escorts with full kit, as if they were about to set out on a week-long expedition.

A commodore, rear and full admiral shuffled into their seats. The guards were acting like we were back in

Kandahar, not on the Lizard Peninsula. We could have taken the escort too, but more trucks arrived and filled the rest of the load space with nameless document boxes and weapon crates.

    The fuel tanks were topped off, the bird heavier than I'd felt her for a long time and we left within an hour, although it felt like we'd been sitting there for much longer. We lifted, being none the wiser, but that wasn't unusual either.

    Keeping questions to ourselves, we were like cadets again with these bigwigs in the back. I had a promotion board assessment in two weeks' time. Captain was on the cards and a wrong word now could scupper the chances. It was still all about who you knew in this world and I hoped the new rank would mean less night shifts, in peacetime at least. I was getting too old for the night-time work. Not the shifts themselves, but the time away from my family.

    Lifting from deck and out into the darkness, it was clear to see the power hadn't returned. The only lights were those moving along the roads, most

IN THE END

heading north in the same general direction as us. The ground was a tapestry of red lights snaking around like spidery nerves.

Passing Plymouth, the power cut had worsened. We hit Exeter before we saw streetlights and buildings lit. The M5 motorway was at a standstill, both sides of the road full of cars trying to go in the same direction. There were six long lines of static tail lights.

We settled back down on the ground at Yeovilton, ours among only a few of the line of Merlins which stopped. The rest headed onwards. They were going to London, but only at a guess.

By now it was clear there was a mass evacuation. We were an air bridge, a quick and easy way out for those higher up the ranks.

I tried to keep my thoughts away from my family back home.

None of us were surprised when we were sent back into the air, to return three more times. The base was more empty with each arrival.

Landing for the fourth refuel,

we were relieved but confined to our quarters, not allowed to leave the base.

I tried Skype the moment I got into my bunk, but nothing was going through. There was no connection. I tried the phone. All the lines were out, but only the externals. I rang around and quickly found they'd been disconnected. No contact was allowed with the outside while the operation was underway.

A senior officer's voice cut into the call. I hung up and tried to take his advice to get some rest. I was dog tired.

A fist woke me as it hammered on the door. It was Stubbs. We had five minutes to get to the operations room.

I tried Skype again, but still there was no connection. I didn't bother with the phone.

We arrived in the ops room to find it packed full, the admiral from last night still in his fatigues, looking like he hadn't had a moments sleep.

Like the rest of the ops room, his eyes were red, sunken and slow moving.

He finally told us what the hell was going on.

27

Every other word told us they were making most of this up, their guesses based on the limited data the government had gathered in the short space of time since the world had gone to shit.

The cause of the power cut was an educated guess, thought to be an explosion at a distribution site. Most of us standing here had seen for ourselves the electricity was out across the entire Southwest. The details were hazy because they were in a hurry to tell us that a surge of power from the unbalanced grid blew out the protection to an MOD containment facility in Truro. Think Boscombe Down, but on steroids. The admiral's exact words.

The upshot was the release of a contagion. A virus or bacteria. They didn't know which and none of us were doctors. We couldn't tell the difference. All they knew was it was important enough to trigger a huge evacuation the like of which had never been seen in a western country.

Protocol was out the window. Shouts came from gathered officers. People wanted to know what the contagion did and why there was such a panic.

When the responses didn't come, more questions fired their way. Should we be worried about our families?

The admiral cleared his throat and looked at his notes, but we all knew he was buying time for hard answers. And they came. The contagion acted fast, infecting as it blew through the air.

"What about us?" came a cry from near the front.

"You're all fine. We would know by now. The contagion is too heavy to drift at anything greater than a few metres off the ground," he said, and a rumble of discontent rose again.

"And we predict with great certainty the exposure was nowhere near Culdrose when the air bridge was in operation." His words didn't help the muttering. No one bought his bullshit.

Still, he told us the contagion was

IN THE END

already changing. It was no longer airborne. The cold had killed that element off but it was still spreading by contact alone.

He told how the infected would become empty, unable to converse and barely able to control themselves. The pathogen attacks the hormones, sending adrenaline, testosterone, and cortisol flooding around the system. The mix sends the victims into fits of irrational anger.

Then came the answer to the question no one wanted to hear.

There was yet to be a cure.

Everywhere I looked I could see puzzled expressions, their fixed stares not changing as the admiral continued to tell us the evacuation went long into the night, stopping as the first signs of the virus showed up in the lines.

"What happened to those people who didn't get out?" I said.

All eyes fell on me, then back to the admiral.

He let the pause fill the space until he was forced to answer by the rising discontent from the audience.

"It is our understanding all those not infected have been successfully evacuated."

There was an uneasy silence across the room. No one questioned it. No one wanted it to be a lie. Before we could find the courage, we found out the reason we were being told.

They were sending us back into the exclusion zone.

We didn't need convincing. We were more than willing to go behind the line and take the only action we knew would stop our families from suffering.

It was night again as we stepped outside. The chopper was heavy with ammo, stacked rifles and a general-purpose machine gun.

We took to the air. After half an hour, we began cruising around our allocated sector. The place was really dark. Night vision picked up a few glowing white spots of light, but nothing like we were looking for. It looked like the admiral might just have been right.

We flew for the four hours our load

IN THE END

would allow, with the worst sight being the fires, the sky glowing orange.

We were glad to refuel with no shots fired, and glad to take a quick break, even if just to reassure ourselves the air station was still working. Our houses were fine, too. A short trip showed the lights still on and served as a reminder why we were doing this job.

We stayed at the base for another couple of hours. We reported the fires, but not much else. We were told the other crews had come back the same. We were soon back in the air, lighter this time without half the ammo and the grenades. It gave us maybe an hour more in the air.

We were two hours into the second run and the time had gone much like before. The green of the night vision straining our eyes, we caught the first signs of what we hadn't wanted to see.

In the middle of the road were two figures fighting. None of them took notice as we flew closer and watched their anger rage. It was clear one of the pair was stronger than the other; only the weaker one took notice as we flew over.

Turning back, I set into a hover, letting Spicer take a good look. He climbed onto his front as he called for me to get us closer. He wanted to see for himself and reported as the infected person bit down into the other's arm.

I had Spicer repeat over the radio and he did, adding detail. The stronger one was biting and ripping flesh with his teeth.

I put space between us and Spicer let a single burst release. The chatter of the gun took me back to Afghan and those days I had such mixed feelings about. But as each round flew from the machine gun, I knew we were closer to keeping our families safe.

After another hour of flying and knowing what we were looking for, we were still taken back as we came across a slow-moving glow of heat on the horizon.

With the first signs of the morning at our backs, we each removed our goggles and saw what could only be called a herd. There were tens of people, maybe a hundred. We couldn't take a more accurate count. They were walking, stumbling, falling into each other. It was clear these people were in pain.

Stubbs reminded us in our ears that there was no cure.

We had a job to do. We had to protect our own.

I called it in but knew what the response would be. I'd already turned the airframe side on, thinking of my kids and my wife as Spicer racked back the slide and began destroying the crowd.

28

At first it felt like an RPG strike. In Afghan, we'd been told of a Chinook pilot who'd survived such an attack, the grenade exploding moments before its target. The door gunner had somehow hit it mid-air, but he'd paid the price. A scrap of shrapnel from the launcher had shredded his neck after missing his body armour. Dead, because he flinched left, not right.

It was only as I swung us around that we saw the fireworks rising from the ground. I set about searching for the target, the air between us filled with colourful exploding sprays.

I swung the door side-on for Spicer to take his aim. It wasn't long before I heard through my ear that the poor infected bugger had been laid to rest.

What happened next is still unclear. Turning us away and heading to sweep up the remains of our last targets, there was an explosion in the rear and the world went black. Another explosion

IN THE END

came soon after. There was no way Spicer could have survived.

The next few moments hardly registered. My world rolled around as if I was in a tumble dryer. Then, hit in the face, I was out cold.

I woke upside down and couldn't move my neck. I must have blacked out a second time as I released my straps, not realising the outcome. Crumpled in a heap on my head, I struggled to my feet. I couldn't hear anything but a deep ring in my ears.

Stubbs was dead with a length of metal sticking from his right eye, his arms hanging down from his side. Blood poured in a steady stream.

The upside-down cabin was mostly empty. Spicer was gone, the mount for the MG still in place on what was now the roof. The weapon itself was nowhere.

Stumbling out of the door, I saw the scattered contents of what had been inside. My gaze followed the path where we'd rolled, staring at where the grass was crushed and mud churned.

The world swam before me. Nausea

rose and fell in waves. My feet wouldn't place where I asked, as if the wiring in my head had been swapped around.

The sleeve of my flight suit came back red as I wiped it across my face, distinct against the olive green. I touched my forehead and watched in slow motion as blood ran down my hand.

Letting go, the warmth trickled down my face, spreading like warm chocolate from a fountain.

Soon, parts of my senses returned. I recalled how I'd come to stand with the world upside down. Thoughts turned to the reason I had a gun strapped to my thigh and remembered we hadn't taken care of all the infected.

With my head swaying under the weight of my helmet as I bent down, I slid the Glock from the holster, pulled back the slide and took my first steps onto the solid ground.

First things first, I had to find and pay respects to my friend.

29

LOGAN

"If you can understand me, don't move a muscle," the man in the olive-green flight suit shouted, blood spraying from his mouth as I crouched by his dead partner. I listened carefully to the words he overstated as if he was in a foreign land.

With the rest of my body still, I let my fingers creep forward to touch the cold of the pistol still sitting in the dead man's holster.

With my gaze fixed on his scarlet face, I watched his unsteady walk as he swayed forward in slow, careful steps. I caught sight of the Union Jack on his chest pocket and I couldn't get my mind around the way he was acting.

He spoke with an English accent from the south, Kent probably, but he talked like he was part of an invading army. Did he know we were on the same side?

I had only seconds to think. I could slide the gun free and take a chance he wouldn't react in time. I could leap away, scrabble up the side of the valley. He was in no state to give chase. His aim would be terrible, but I couldn't discount luck. He was a trained killer and any hit would be bad news, with no chance of a hospital visit before the infection set in.

Or I could just kneel here, let him take charge, talk myself out of him finishing the job while I hoped the others came back. Maybe Andrew might have another rocket up his sleeve.

I couldn't do either. I had to take charge. I was where they'd put me and I wouldn't let them down. Anyway, they wouldn't come running if they heard a shot. They'd left me to take care of the suffering on my own, whichever way I chose.

Raising my hands in the air, I saw the moment the guy clocked his partner laying still on the ground. I watched what I thought was a flinch, but then he stood tall, pushing away the emotion.

IN THE END

"I said don't move," came the bloodied voice.

I was already standing, thankful he hadn't shot me yet. I knew the more time that went on, the more my chances extended. What else could I think?

Naomi's words came into my head. He had orders to protect and to stop the infection.

"I'm not infected," I blurted out, losing the battle to keep calm.

The guy didn't react, other than to slant his head to the side.

"What's your name?" I said, moving my right foot an inch forward.

"Stay where you are," he replied, blood dripping from his chin in a long string.

I held myself still, focused on his face. He had a gash along the length of his forehead, blood still washing down into his mouth. If I could last long enough, this guy would bleed to death.

Movement caught in my vision from below. I stepped back, my earlier question answered.

* * *

COMMANDER LANE

"If you can understand me, don't move a muscle," I shouted. I overstated the words in case some stunted intelligence remained in the figure I could just about make out. They were crouched over a mound of earth as I struggled to clear the blood from my eyes. Each time I could finally see, a blanket of fresh darkness smeared across.

The figure wasn't moving, but still I stepped forward. I couldn't wait. I needed to shorten the odds. My aim last month was only just good enough to get my licence renewed without the world clouded, swaying side to side.

He was watching me, focused on my actions. Each time my view cleared, I expected to see him jumping forward, racing to chew my face off.

I was dreading the moment I would have to shoot. The moment I would find out if I could live up to my friend's bravery.

Instead, he watched, his movements

IN THE END

slow.

I shouted again and he stopped. He understood language, or maybe it was just my tone and now he looked like he was mouthing words.

Was he talking or growling? I couldn't tell. My hearing was still just a constant ring.

I moved forward; there was still a lot of distance to cover. If he had any sense left, he would have run and not stood staring back, moving his mouth around like he was chewing gum.

"Stay where you are," I said, holding up the gun.

He'd jumped forward as my vision cleared. As it blurred all too soon, my mind told my finger to pull the trigger.

The words repeated over, but. I wouldn't comply.

With the next snapshot my adrenaline spiked higher. The guy had stepped back and out of shot.

My gaze turned down to the mound. Had it moved? Was it twisting around?

30

LOGAN

We were in the woods when Lane woke. That was his name on the badge on his breast pocket. A good hour had past since we'd dragged his body from beside the road. I'd taken his gun as he slumped and I dealt with what had become of his partner.

I'd been mistaken. When the body at my feet moved, his arms and legs loose, his eyes white and teeth bared, it was the first time Lane had seen him.

He knew what it had become. I'd watched as Lane wiped at his face, blood rolling down his forehead and into his eyes as he took his first look. It could have been the loss of blood, or the shock, but he collapsed in a heap.

Andrew arrived, held under Naomi and Zoe's shoulders soon after, questions on their faces. I pressed a bandage on the face of the guy they were yet to meet.

We agreed making camp in the woods was needed and, moving Andrew and Lane, we did just that. Naomi and I made a fire after a five-minute walk in.

She waited until we were alone before she apologised and I told her with a thin smile there was nothing for her to apologise for. I wanted her to have been right too. I returned with an apology of my own for my heated words only moments before.

With the clear air and warmth more than welcome, the two pistols were split between myself and Cassie, who took guard as the rest of the able-bodied scavenged what we could from the crash site. None of us had the courage to visit Matt to gather what he'd stowed in his pack, to check if he was resting.

We sat around the fire getting warm, patching up the two injured members. Naomi gave me glances, a slight smile each time she tended to our air force man.

We were okay, I thought, and I tried to relax by the fire. Tried not to flinch at every sound in the woods, every crack of twigs or whistle of wind. I took comfort we were deep enough inside. We would hear anyone, living or otherwise, approach from far out.

"I'm sorry," were Lane's first words, stopping to take a drop of water offered from Naomi's bottle. He looked so much different without the scarlet mask; our age, maybe a little older. Weather worn, face down-turned.

"I'm sorry," he repeated, his look falling on the gun resting on my lap.

Our gazes caught and he said the words again.

"You didn't know we weren't infected," I said, sharing a look with Naomi. "But now I need you to tell us everything."

And he did.

"They lied," I said, trying to hold back the anger I didn't mean for him.

"Or they didn't know," Naomi added.

Lane stared back, no reaction to the words.

"It's still spreading in the air. No one touched your man," I said.

"Spicer. His name was Leading Hand James Spicer," he replied, looking down at the ground.

"And your name?" Zoe asked, her voice soft from the other side of the fire.

"Commander..." he said, cutting himself off, looking down. "Connor Lane."

"Well, Connor Lane," Andrew said, leaning up at my side, the pain stretching out his face. "Welcome to hell."

Zoe snapped his way and Andrew relaxed back, letting the air suck through a tense smile.

"So what do you think, Commander Lane?" I said, looking him in the eye.

"Connor. Or Lane, please," he replied. "I've already told you."

I shook my head.

"You've told us what you've been told, not what you think."

He kept his gaze on mine for a moment, then looked around the group before staring deep into the dancing licks of the fire.

"I think we don't know shit. I think they're making it up as they go along. Spicer wasn't bitten," he said, his face hard as I watched his effort to control his breath. "But still, those eyes."

I nodded and filled the space when he stopped talking.

"We've lost three to bites. They bleed out and die, then…," I said, but couldn't continue.

"We all know what comes next," Naomi said, as we shared a nodding glance.

"I'm sorry," Lane said as he turned my way.

"I think death is the key factor," I replied. "I guess, what else matters?" Following every other face, I turned and let the flames hold my attention.

"So what next?" I said, after what seemed like an age of listening to the wind in the leaves and the crack and pop of wood in the flames. I looked at each face reflecting the question.

Lane was the first to speak.

"We should wait here. They'll come and rescue us. They know where we are, there's a transponder in the helicopter. Even if it's damaged, they'll have our last position."

I watched as faces lit up. I didn't want to be the one to let them down, but I couldn't keep my concerns to myself.

"They'd risk another crew for someone who's already infected?"

The faces around the fire fell.

"I'd like to think so," Lane replied, still sipping the water.

"I'd like to think so, too," I said. "But what if they come? They were in the same briefing, right?"

Lane nodded.

"They see you, then fine. Hugs all round. They see us and open fire." I waited for someone to argue. "Tell me why they're not like you."

Lane took his time.

"We don't decide," he said, his gaze floating around the group. "We call it in and they sign off."

"Exactly," I replied.

Zoe was the first to react with sobs from across the fire.

"So, what do we do?" Naomi said,

standing and moving around to comfort her.

"We get warm. Rest up. Take stock. It's still early. But we need to get on the move, find somewhere warm and secure for tonight," I said.

"Then what?" It was Naomi again.

I looked to Lane, nodding back in my direction as if he knew what I was going to say.

"We keep moving north."

Lane continued nodding as deep as his bandaged forehead would allow.

"Then?" Naomi said, leaning in.

I drew a deep breath, all heads turning in the same direction toward the road at the heavy crack of twigs, the damp leaves rustling.

I palmed the gun and rose to my feet, looking around.

"We see if civilisation lets us back in."

31

I returned to camp, no shots fired. The noise was from a deer or smaller, at least something alive. I was sure zombies never hid in the movies. Right?

Cassie stood by the fire, the gun in her hand and looking at me, nodding as I forced the corners of my mouth high. Ellie was asleep close to the fire; Cassie's every other glance checking a stray ember hadn't caught her clothes.

Andrew lowered himself down as he saw me arrive through the bushes, pain still drawing his features out. He needed to rest but staying here wasn't a long-term choice.

The same went for Lane, but our need for tonight's shelter was so much more important. We had to find somewhere we could keep warm, somewhere we could barricade before we slept.

I needed sleep bad, the corners of my eyes screaming out for rest.

Watching me sit, Cassie stayed on

her feet and took nervous steps. It was clear she wanted to be on the move. I understood.

Beside me was the pile of supplies. Between us, we'd done a pretty good job getting what we did as the Tesco burnt to the ground.

Twenty tins of fish; couldn't stand the stuff. My old self didn't anyway, but they would be much better than digging grubs from the bark of rotting trees. I'd give anything for a bigger supply, enough to eat until we got home.

Home. The first I'd thought of the place since we'd set off on the journey less than a day ago. Was it only twenty-four hours since our world went up the creek? My parents faces crashed into my head. Their imagined thoughts given words. What must they be thinking when they saw the news? At least I didn't have a wife worrying where I was. Didn't have kids panicking when they heard what had happened in the South West. None of us did.

My mind lingered on the thought. Between us we had two who couldn't;

IN THE END

I put my hand up in my head. It had been the death-nail to my one and only relationship. Four who wouldn't and the rest where it just wasn't the right time or hadn't met the right someone. Maybe that's why we'd stuck together for so long and hadn't drifted apart when kids and exploding families separated our lives.

A twig snapped; a spray of sparks spat from the fire. Each gaze fell in the direction of a loud noise, shoulders relaxing as the light-show drowned in the daylight. I was thankful for the distraction.

Water was our main issue. We had chocolate, first aid kits, pain killers galore; antibiotics we'd tried to push down Chloe's throat, left over from the chemist. A whole spectrum of other medications in prescription bags which had sat on the shelf, never to be collected. Maybe some of them would come in useful; although we'd need to find some sort of medical book first. Toothpaste, tooth brushes, but only four bottles of water, two litres in each.

Three, I corrected as Naomi rested an empty bottle at her side. I discounted the bottles of Jack I knew she'd kept out of sight of the pile.

"We need to start rationing," I said. No one complained or suggested an alternative.

We had an SA80 rifle from the crash site, the only surviving equipment. It was battered and scraped, could be bent, I couldn't tell. We'd have to wait for Lane's advice when he was better, but long before the need came at least.

Naomi's gaze twitched upwards, then Zoe's followed. A crack sparked from the fire for a second time.

Zoe's gaze fell, but Naomi stood, releasing her grip from Zoe's shoulders.

Lane had his eyes open towards the sky, then looked to me, already raising himself on his elbows.

The sound was unmistakable, rotors pounding in the air.

I stood, helped Lane to his feet, looked twice at the pistol then pushed it into my jacket pocket.

With his arm around my shoulders,

IN THE END

I supported him to his full height. Steadying his balance, we took the first steps out of the circle. I turned, hearing Cassie at our backs.

"Stay there," I said, nodding to the pistol in her hands. "Keep watch."

Her footsteps stopped as we built speed, the sound of the chopper loud and constant. They were hovering. I pictured them over the wreckage, the gunner peering down, searching the surroundings for their men. They'd see one, a hole in his head. They'd have flown over the carnage across the road.

We were getting close. We just needed them to stay a moment more before they would see us and we could roll the dice, hoping they saw their comrade before they saw me.

The second noise was one we'd heard before as well. The pitch of the engine changed. We'd already slowed. Then came the scream of the machine gun from the door and the snap-snap of bullets hitting the tree-line.

"Infra-red," I heard Lane murmur, but they weren't shooting at us. Their aim was on the four dead bodies walking into the trees in our direction. Their torsos and legs were a pulpy mess of small explosions with limbs missing, eyes white and mouths hanging open, each circled with dried blood.

Lane relaxed his arm from around me. I was about to fire the pistol when Lane pulled me down. Snaps of lead hit the ground too close, tracing our outlines, or so it felt.

The helicopter withdrew as I'd buried my head and the footsteps dragging behind us silenced.

I lifted, relief battling with the disappointment, but instinct ducked me down as a gunshot burst from the direction of the camp.

32

I didn't stay down long, leaving Lane to get to his feet by himself while I ran. My shoulders rocked forward as another shot echoed through the trees, the bang followed by a chorus of vicious screams.

A third shot exploded as I raced closer to the source and I heard the trample of feet running, Lane behind me, his face contorted with pain as he followed.

A fourth split the air and I sped up while fumbling for the gun. Its cold, not quite metal, reassured me little.

My first sighting was of Zoe, tears streaming down her face. She was running, pushed at her back by Andrew. Both were heading my way, their faces alight, eyes wide.

On seeing me, Andrew held his hand out to take mine, waving me from my course, trying to turn me as he saw my approach.

Shaking off his hands, his worry, I

pointed to my right.

"Go that way," I said, breathless.

Andrew understood. He'd heard the machine gun only moments earlier and, missing with one last attempted grab at my jacket, he veered Zoe off the path and into the untracked route, darting around the trees.

"No," I shouted. "I'll catch up. Get her safe. Take Lane." I didn't look back, didn't check if they'd taken my advice. I had to keep running, had to get everyone safe.

Another shot sent me stumbling as my foot caught a root, the gun falling from my hands. Down on my knees, I scratched around in the leaves.

Before I was up, Naomi was running toward me. In her arms, Ellie fought, whipping her body round to get free.

I pointed the way I'd sent the others and was running again, the smoke of the campfire strengthening with every step. A first trace of rotten meat.

The camp came into view, as did the maelstrom of movement and the crowded expanse of bodies standing,

IN THE END

clawing forward.

I loosed off a round into the mass. A head shot. One went down. I had just enough time to see at first sight he looked almost like he was still all there; only his pallid, cold complexion told me there was no real life behind his clouded eyes.

He was in the front line of the pack, my eyes adjusting to see the three and four body-thick group squeezed between the trees, meandering forward with cumbersome pace.

Cassie was to the side and on her back, her face and hands bloodied as she struggled to push a double-dead body from her front.

I couldn't tell if she'd been hit and I shook away a thought flashing past, a thought I couldn't bear to hold on to. I retrained my aim from her as she rolled the limp, dead body away.

How the hell did they get to the camp without being noticed?

My thoughts were shattered as she fired off a shot and the fifth body lay dead, dead again on the floor with its face blown away.

As she tried to get to her feet, the pack parted, split, and out jumped a woman, once a woman; I could only guess from her shape. Her clothes were tattered, barely there. Her skin darker, greyer than any I'd seen. Her eyes were clouded red, not white like the others. She launched herself to the ground where Cassie scrambled.

Another shot went off. Mine. Although it felt like someone else had control. The bullet missed. I watched as Cassie dropped her gun.

She was using all of her strength to grip the neck of the thing as it scraped at her hands, its teeth snapping open and closed. Its face was long gone, along with its hair, leaving only a ripped and bloodied scalp.

My second shot didn't miss, but the attack still continued with a ferocity getting the better of Cassie.

I ran, jumping the fire, pulling up a burning log and threw it into the crowd. Pushing the gun to the thing's temple, I let the bullet explode its head.

IN THE END

The creature went limp. I popped two wild shots into the crowd, some of which were on fire, but none had reacted, none seeing a need to put out the burning flames on their bloodied clothes.

I grabbed at Cassie's scarlet hand but my grip slid off. Instead, I clawed into her shoulder fabric, dragging her to her feet while emptying the rest of the magazine into the crowd.

We ran with the smell of cooking flesh receding. Our hands gripped into each other's as tight as they could, pulling up, tightening further as one or the other of us slipped in turn.

We kept running, only slowing as we passed the helicopter's victims, bursting into the open air and out from the woods; slowing just enough to twist around, to figure out where we were. To scour for danger. To find our friends.

We saw the crash site with smoke still rising. We saw the road but could see no one standing. It gave us little relief when we didn't see anything running toward us. We couldn't see our friends, but then I remembered I'd sent them in a different direction.

"Tell me you saw that?" Cassie asked through fits of breath.

I didn't answer straight away. Still holding her hand, I pulled her along the edge of the trees, hoping I was heading in the right direction.

"I saw it," I said, only just able to get the words out.

"We didn't hear it coming. It pounced out into the open, then stood there looking around. We were all just staring back. No one moved until it jumped at me, screaming like a demon from a horror film. Oh my god," she said, her voice cracking as her bloodied hand went to her mouth.

We jogged on. I couldn't deal with this right now. I'd seen what I'd seen, but still I couldn't think about what it meant.

A pained animal call came from behind us. It sounded like something was injured and sent a chill along my spine as my body urged me to run faster.

I remembered the gun was empty

in my hand, remembered the two magazines in my jacket pocket and undid the zip as I let go of Cassie.

"The noise you heard," I said, slowing so my fingers could get at the depths of my pocket. "Was it like that?"

"No," she replied, matching my pace and turning to catch what I was doing. Her eyes widened, colour draining from her face as she looked past me. A shrill, demonic call ripped through the air.

I didn't need her to say a word. I knew her answer if I asked the question again.

33

I didn't twist back, didn't turn, but still our speed had slowed to barely a jog.

"Run," I said, keeping my voice calm. I knew if I let the panic in it would take control. I needed to slide in the magazine, not let it fumble to the ground.

"Run," I repeated, as the gun gave a gentle snap, my palm driving the store of bullets home.

Still she hadn't sped, her gaze fixed over my shoulder as her complexion drained.

"Run," I shouted, letting my voice have the full volume it needed. My hands pulled back the pistol's slide.

Cassie looked at the gun and turned forward, her speed building as I fought against my instincts, somehow managing to slow to a stop and circling to point the gun out as far as I could.

My arms wavered as, the length of a football pitch away, I saw what appeared

IN THE END

to be an animal running on two legs. Its back was hunched over, its arms out and fingers hooked like claws.

Even from the distance I could see the remains of clothes, tattered, dark-stained rags dragging in the air as it raced toward me; it was once human.

Unlike what I'd seen attack Cassie, this had a face. He was once a young man, now a beast with gaunt, tight skin, grey features curled up. Snarling, running at the pace of a leopard on the plain. Its bared teeth snapping open and shut.

Holding my nerve, going against all my instincts, I kept my finger from pulling, from emptying the lead into whatever was charging.

I was thinking ahead; if there were three of these things, there could be more. I had one gun and two magazines, with no idea how many bullets each held. We would need all the brass we could muster if we were ever to get to the other side of the exclusion zone.

The thing had already covered half the distance and still I held my nerve with my finger twitching against the trigger. My heart pounded so hard I thought at any moment it would get too much and I'd be on the floor in a heap. I knew my best chance would be to wait until it was at least half the distance closer.

Time was going too fast with so much running through my head and now I could hear something in the tree-line. Something else racing me down, but I dared not turn my attention away. Whatever it was it couldn't be bigger or scarier or run faster than this hungry-eyed beast who would try its best to eat me alive.

I shook, unable to take back control, but somehow I was winning against my instinct screaming at me to turn and run. Those things we'd first seen yesterday were slow and easy to outrun. You could smell them a mile off and were simple to out-fox, but still frightening as hell, their existence incompatible with how the world worked.

Then came this beast running towards me; it was almost at the point

IN THE END

where I would see if I'd made the right decision. It was like the king of these creatures and threw the new rule book out the window, then leapt after it, ripping pages, eating the words and savouring every mouthful.

I let the first shot fly from the muzzle earlier than I'd planned, proving me right as it flew harmless through the air.

Resetting my arm and relaxing my stance, I closed my left eye and pulled again. As I did, the creature jumped high, leaping like a gorilla on speed, clawing its fingers as it sailed towards me.

Lifting my arm in an attempt to track its movement, I shot again, but with each bullet I knew the angle of my arms hadn't caught up enough as it punched through the air.

Again and again I pulled back the trigger, the gun exploding each time, rearing back in my hand. One shot hit. Its body deflected, sending it spinning to the right as I caught its shoulder, but there was nothing going to stop it falling on me with its full weight.

    Still, I fired and fired again. Its body, a projectile itself, crashed against my torso, sending me sprawling to the ground and crushing against my chest.

    As my back hit the ground, I caught sight of a dark, hunched shape lunging out from the woods, leaping just like this creature had. My head hit hard against what felt like a rock, stars burst across my darkening vision. The weight on my chest was no longer noticeable as I felt powerless to stop my eyes closing.

34

My eyes had closed, but just for a moment. The chaos of a pitched battle, yelps of pain and beasts locked in combat pulled me back.

I heard two slathering, growling creatures. I heard blows pounding, rending flesh from bone. Twisting, flushed with relief the abomination was not at my throat, I looked down to make sure my entrails were not on view through an open belly.

I was intact.

Leaning to the left, I cursed bruised ribs and saw the tangled battle. A dark, crazed hound was at the throat of the creature I'd stared down; the creature who'd tattered my plans. My aim leaving me when I needed it the most.

I rolled, finding the gun underneath me, swearing as it dug into my crushed chest. I rotated back, pulling it up from my side, its weight more substantial than it should have been.

Still leaning, I pulled the trigger.

Repeating twice more. The body of the creature rocked, blow after blow crushing into its head. The shadowy hound flinched with each round, but still it ripped at the throat, locking on for one final rend of flesh before it released, coughing up what it hadn't meant to swallow. A sensible creature.

I could feel myself passing out. I closed my eyes, but knew I had to stay awake or be at this rabid creature's mercy. I was on my back, looking up at the clear blue sky, the gun still pointed across the ground. I could feel the animal slowly stalking forward, its paws light on the short grass.

Letting the pain calm, I rolled to my side, outstretching the gun. The first I saw was the still body of the beast which had terrified me as it pounced, its head a pulp.

I'd hit with all three; its neck wide open, muscle, tissue and veins out for all to see. Thick, dark blood crept out like treacle.

The slow step of the hound pulled my gaze from the body. As I caught its shape, it took another step forward with its head bowed, eyes on me. Its long teeth bared, sticky blood mixed with foam, white saliva dripped along it lips to the grass.

The gun was still out and I straightened its weight. It was heavier than ever but I knew the opposite should be true. The dog, a pet before today, had saved my life, but looked like it had done so to take me for itself.

I'd had animals as a child; dogs, hamsters, no cats, but not while I'd been an adult, convincing myself I didn't need a companion.

My heart sank as I thought of the rabid, demonic animals joining the list of things we would have to fight and compete with if we were going to survive the next few days. They weren't spared the same fate as their owners, no immunity from this horrific disease making us fight for our lives to get out of the South West.

I locked gazes with the animal and stared as it inched forward. I knew what I had to do. So many lives had been lost and it was dead, after all, but pulling the trigger was one of the hardest things I'd done.

I closed my eyes and nothing but a hollow click came. The gun was empty. The world had made its choice.

I had no fight left. A melancholy weight fell over me but somehow a brush of wind blew it away. I had to go on; there were people depending on my survival.

Dropping the gun, I took up on my elbows, edging at a snail's pace towards the tree-line, pain radiating from my chest, sending stars across my vision with each tiny movement.

The soft footsteps were close. I knew it was waiting for me to drop, but there was nowhere to run. Even if I had the energy.

I was on my last calorie when my left elbow slipped, back dropping to the ground, my eyes falling closed.

I let the breath push out from my lungs and hoped it would be quick, grateful for the end of the worst twenty-four hours of my life.

35

JACK

The first sign was the heavy knock at the door, Rusty's bark booming as he barrelled down the stairs.

My room was dark, but I couldn't tell the time, the red numbers on my Spiderman clock not there. Still, I knew it was late. The music from downstairs had stopped; my parent's friends gone as the wine ran out.

Outside was an eerie brightness, but our narrow lane didn't have street lights until you got near town, I climbed from under the covers to investigate.

Standing on my toy box under the window, I saw a long white coach, the headlights marking out the lane stretching past the house.

We were the only house for a quarter of a mile.

The coach was full of people staring back as I peered out the window. Their eyes glazed, half asleep. Maybe they'd just got woken too?

The second sign was Mum bursting through the door, her hand reaching to the switch. It clicked, but the room stayed dark.

Still, I could see she had my school bag and told me to pack essentials, then repeated as I glared back.

"Pants and socks, warm clothes," she explained. "No toys," she said, adding, "don't be scared," as she left.

Scared? I didn't understand what she meant. The last five minutes had been the most interesting thing to have ever happened.

I grabbed the top three comics from the shelf. Pushed them to the bottom of the bag, then emptied my drawer of pants and socks, throwing in two t-shirts, stuffing a pair of jeans after.

Apparently, I was supposed to know I had to get dressed too. Adults need to say what they mean!

I was only half-dressed when my mum was back again and practically dragged me down the stairs to where

IN THE END

Dad was half asleep with my sister, Tish, in his arms, his breath sweet and sickly.

At the front door was a solider, dressed just like Action Man Paratrooper, but his gun was smaller and strapped to his waist; the first time I'd seen one in real life.

The night was getting better.

He smiled as I stepped past, ruffling my hair. If my mum had done it I would have given her such a hard time.

We nearly took the last of the spaces on the coach and it looked like it was mostly families on board; the kids were asleep, the dads staring through the misting windows. The mums were either crying or trying not to.

There were grandparents, too. One granddad was pale white and with every other breath he rattled the windows as he coughed. The only free seats were at the back.

We took the furthest row, leaving the last two seats empty in front of us. As we sat, I was desperate to get moving, desperate to see where the surprise would end up.

Mum made us sit either side of her. Dad to her left, his lap piled high with filled carrier bags. The inside lights turned off as we pulled away. It was nearly pitch black, but it didn't stop Mum rearranging. She was a constant sorter and could rearrange an empty room. I watched as she took my bag; could just see her looking down her nose as she saw how I'd loaded my pack. She pulled the comics and threw them on my lap, pushing in bottles of water and cans of something. She'd obviously forgotten to make a picnic.

The lights were back on as we stopped and the soldier stepped out. We were at the neighbour's. They'd only just moved in, Mum was saying to Dad, their house bright with candles flickering in the windows.

I took the chance to read my comic. A classic Wacky Racers my granddad left me when he'd died, with a little note to make sure I kept them in the plastic sleeve. I would be thankful when I was older. I don't know why.

Outside there was loads of noise. A

IN THE END

woman with a cigarette in her mouth and a small dog in her arms. It didn't look like they'd been woken from their beds. She was arguing with the solider, arms waving back and forth. Why she wanted to bring a dog on a trip, I don't know. Unless it was the seaside, of course.

"Mum," I said, but didn't wait for her to turn my way. "When are we going home?"

"Don't worry, dear," Mum replied, her hands still diving in and out of bags. She always used the same tone when I wouldn't like the answer.

"Rusty?" I said and looked to my sister, forcing her finger to her mouth as she looked back. She didn't know.

Stuffing back the tears, I didn't want to start Tish off and turned to watch the woman still shaking her head. She would freeze if she didn't get on soon, just dressed in a short top with thin straps. It was the middle of winter.

In the end, the dog was returned to the house and she came back with her friend who had more sense and was wearing a coat.

The old man was coughing again, but it sounded like he was getting better. The coughs were more gentle, quieter and whoever he was with, a woman about his age, stood and asked if there was a doctor on the bus. Everyone seemed to ignore the question.

The neighbours were soon swaying down the aisle, filling the air with the smell of garlic bread and strawberries. It was a strange mix but made me a little hungry.

The woman whose husband was sick shouted to the driver as he closed the door. He looked kind of sad in reply, shaking his head and said there were doctors where they were going. Lots of them.

The lights were left on at her insistence and I tried to block out her sobs but was thankful she didn't do it as loud as my sister.

When the tears weren't getting in the way of my concentration, it was the neighbour talking like she was alone with her friend, or if everyone else was joining in the conversation. They woke

IN THE END

Tish with their laughter.

I stared at my sister, looking to see if when she finished rubbing her eyes she was going to spit the dummy and make us all miserable with her own shrieks of pain, but instead she just kept pointing at the woman, shouting Mickey.

That's when I saw the tattoo on the woman's neck; Mickey Mouse as the apprentice from Fantasia.

Right on cue, the woman erupted in a chesty laugh, just like Muttley from the comic in my lap.

I was still smiling at the coincidence when a scream ripped through the coach and we shot forward, the soldier slamming on the brakes. It was the old woman again; she was screaming her husband was dead.

I felt sorry for her, but I don't know why we had to run off the coach.

36

Tish wailed. The soldier screamed.

He waved the gun in his hand, shouting for everyone to get off the coach.

Confused, I turned to my parents, but they stood, peering over the seats and watched as everyone rose. I stayed where I was, the aisle already blocked.

The coach had come alive with movement. Everyone was awake and pulling on coats, grabbing their things.

Mum pulled up bags from the floor. Dad tried to make himself taller to peer over the crowd, but no one seemed to move down the bus.

Screams took up from all around. A wave of motion radiated towards us. I saw five or six people who had been pushing up the aisle now backed up, the last of them on top of me.

Mum was screaming, as was everyone, her hands flapping, looking to Dad for answers. I turned back to the aisle and saw the neighbour with the tattoo.

For the first time, she wasn't laughing, instead pushing her way past the guy who was about to crush me. I thought she would clamber over to get to the window, but she looked down and gave a slow smile before leaning over and swinging a stout bottle she'd pulled from under her arm.

Ducking when the window shattered, I almost said a bad word as the glass showered down. It was my only answer to the craziness but I stopped myself as I felt the rush of cold air.

She hoisted me up, her hands in my arm pits like I was five again and angled me through the window.

I watched as people turned toward us and pushed at her back, their faces screwed up as they tried to get past her.

Without realising, I'd scooped my bag up in the crook of my arm and was out the window and into the darkness quicker than I'd expected.

Dad lowered Tish into my arms. The screams roaring from inside were louder than her wailing like she was under attack.

I stepped back from the bus as more people appeared from the sides to climb out of the missing window, but the lady who'd helped me, the one with the tattoo, she'd disappeared.

Other faces, other families took her place and were climbing over the back seats, hands out, pushing others aside.

Seven or eight people were out by now, each running or limping down the road until they disappeared from view. The screams were fading, but my sister's weren't. I felt like my head would explode, then Dad appeared at the space where the window had been.

His eye dripped with blood and it was obvious he couldn't see properly, his hands reaching for the edge of the windowsill, knocking down cubes of glass to join the rest under my feet.

"Dad," I shouted and a great smile grew on his face. He turned his leg over the side of the sill and he fell to the road with a great oomph of air.

I rushed over and helped him to his feet. He was blinking more than normal, blood pouring down the side of his face.

"It's okay, baby," he was saying over and over as he got to his feet, then held his hand against her chest.

Tish seemed to quiet at his words. Her eyes were still dripping wet, the dummy hanging around her collar from the string tied to her top button hole.

I pushed it back in her mouth and she sucked at a furious rate.

"Where's Mum?" Dad said, squinting as he slowly moved his head.

I felt myself gag on the words, tears coming as I did.

"She's not out yet," I said, comforting Tish when all I wanted was for someone to do the same for me. "Mum," I said, my voice strained, an explosion of panic gripping my insides.

Dad's eyes were wide even though I saw it hurt so much. He was looking up to the gap and grabbed up high onto the edge of the sill, but couldn't pull himself to any useful distance. He let his arms drop and streaked blood from his eye across the back of his hand.

A fresh set of screams came from

inside. I stood like a statue as he bent at the waist, holding me firm by the shoulders.

I knew what was coming. "No, Dad," I shouted.

He knelt and patted my shoulders as glass crunched under his knee.

I could smell his alcoholic, metallic breath as he leaned in.

"No, Dad," I said, whimpering.

"Look after your sister, keep yourselves safe," he said. "I have to go get Mummy."

He was gone before I could grab him.

I thought of running after him, chasing him along the side of the coach. Tish had calmed. She was heavy, but I had her tight. She played her fingers through my hair.

Any other time I would have snapped at her to stop, despite knowing she'd still carry on, squealing and laughing. Everything a game.

I said nothing, just backed away with glass scraping under my trainers.

As the gun shots came, I ran.

37

I couldn't see, but still I ran. Swerving to avoid a short wall as it loomed out of the darkness, I kept running until my feet found grass where I slowed and turned to make sure I could still see the white of the coach.

Looking up, the half-moon seemed brighter than I'd ever seen, but still it was such an effort to make out shapes in the darkness.

I'd expected to see people from the coach crowded around; people calling to gather everyone up and making sure we were safe, counting our heads like they did in the playground.

I couldn't see anyone. I was alone. Now I had to be the adult.

Crouching, Tish's weight seeming to grow in my arms; I leaned back against the stone, hoping it would stop my body from shaking. Her fingers were still moving gently in my hair and I listened to her slow breath, the rhythm of her suck as she comforted herself.

With my free hand I wiped my face, the drip from my eyes was so cold I was scared it would freeze.

I stared at the coach, tucking Tish in closer. Her hand stopped moving, her breathing slowed.

Nothing was moving, but everything was. The breeze in the trees, the bushes swaying. There were no lights coming from inside the coach. No one moving around, that I could tell anyway.

It was good news, wasn't it? Dad would be out soon with his arm over Mum's shoulder. I was ready for her to be hurt, knowing it to be the reason why she hadn't climbed out straight away; the reason she'd stayed behind. It wouldn't have been her choice.

It was nothing to do with what happened yesterday, my little, barely noticeable crime. Not even a crime really; taking a few crisps from the table when I was supposed to be brushing my teeth. No, not that. Couldn't be. And it definitely wasn't the reason Dad had left us to find her. He hadn't chosen Mummy over us. Had he?

IN THE END

He'd gone to get her and if she didn't come, he'd be back out on his own. He would come out of the coach and call our names. He'd open his arms and I'd run toward him, where he'd scoop us both up and take us somewhere safe. Nanny's, maybe? It was a boring place. No comics. Nanny didn't like to have them around. Didn't like to be reminded of Grandad. Why wouldn't you want to be reminded?

At least it was safe and a long way away, which looked like the best place to be right now.

I think it had been maybe ten minutes or more. Each moment since I'd crouched I thought I would get up, but couldn't, backing out at the last second; each moment expecting sirens and blue lights bright in the distance.

I was freezing, Tish was getting closer and closer. She was cold too, but stayed asleep. Thankfully.

Nothing had changed, no movement. I knew I had to do something. People could die from being out in the cold. Everyone knew.

I stood, took several steps toward the coach and there he was, a dark figure about Dad's height and with his wide, thick chest. I was sure it was his big puffy coat, the one Mum hated because she said it made him look like a teenager.

He was walking a little funny and was by himself. Mummy was probably doing her make up or something or didn't want to come out in the cold. An image came into my head. We were all back on the coach. I sat behind Dad as he drove us away.

After every step he seemed to stumble. I'd seen those movements before, normally when he'd been out with his friends at night.

I was nearly at the coach when I first smelt something horrible. I turned to Tish and leaned in closer.

No, it wasn't her and it definitely wasn't me. It must have been Dad who'd pooped himself.

"Dad," I said, trying to take the whine out of my voice, like he always told me.

IN THE END

He didn't speak, but for the first time he seemed to notice I was there, turning in my direction and speeding up. He was still quite slow.

I stopped walking, hearing a sound behind me. I turned; there were lights on the road. I'd seen no other cars since we'd left the house.

I kept staring forward then stepped to the side, realising I was in the middle of the road, right where I was told all the time to avoid. 'Remember the Green Cross Code,' my parents would say each time I left the house.

The smell was getting nearer and so were the lights. I had to turn away; they were on full.

I turned back to Dad, still squinting, the engine getting louder; they must have been going so fast.

As I turned, I let my breath out; it was Dad after all. I could see by his haircut and the blood on the side of the face. Then I looked behind him, my eyes wide as I thought it was Mum, but I soon saw it was someone else. Someone in a white coat with black, no, reddish mark on their chest and they stumbled as they took the last step before falling to the floor.

"Dad," I said, pointing to her, but he didn't turn, didn't move. He just kept his eyes on me and Tish.

The engine noise was getting so loud I thought they would hit me. Dad looked like he was going in for a hug, but in slow motion. I was in arms reach, his face expressionless like he had bad news.

"It's Mum, isn't it? Just tell me," I kept saying, but he stared back. Tears ran down my face and Tish moved.
The stink was horrid. I had to hold my breath.

"Dad," I said. "What's wrong with your eyes?"

I held my hand out, grabbing his outstretched arm, pushing myself against the coach while pulling him close.

What was wrong with him? Couldn't he see the car was about to run us both over?

Stumbling forward, his skin felt

IN THE END

weird. He was cold and he smelt like meat when you unpacked it out of the supermarket bags, stinking like it had been out far too long.

As the headlights grew brighter than I thought they ever could, I felt his teeth bite down into my hand.

38

With the pain still building, Dad's mouth ripped away, but it wasn't Dad anymore. I knew as the car smashed into his side, sending him, arms loose, flying like a crash test dummy across the road.

I grabbed Tish tight, giving a shake. She groaned as if she was struggling to wake. I coughed as the air filled with smoke, tyres squealing against the road. The car had stopped just beyond the edge of the coach. A constant pound of a muffled drum beat rumbled towards me.

Fixed to the spot, I didn't want to move. The smoke gagging in the back of my throat and my hand pulsing with pain, blood dripping from what looked like a part missing between my thumb and finger. I had to look away, my head swimming as I'd watched the black blood stream down to the road.

As I looked up I saw the passenger door open; whoever was in the driver's seat leaned across. I couldn't see who

IN THE END

it was, but they must have recognised me. Still, I didn't move from the spot, even when I saw someone, something, stumble down the stairs of the coach and tripping over the thing still struggling to get to their feet, one of its legs bent in the wrong place.

The bright white of the reversing light blinked on and the car sped backwards. The man who'd climbed from the coach was on his feet. It was the soldier, the gun no longer in his hand as he walked towards us in the headlights of the car stopping at my side.

I couldn't recognise the man in the car. He wasn't one of my friend's parents, not someone from school. I'd never seen him at the house, either.

A stranger. A teenager, too; a thin moustache over his lips which made him look younger, not older. He wore a tracksuit and heavy, thumping music pounded from the open door. He nodded towards the opening, then looked at my hand. Looked at Tish and nodded again, like he might have changed his mind, but changed it back again.

He turned to the soldier for just a second. I turned, too.

He was getting close. We looked at each other again. His eyebrows raised. Still he hadn't spoken.

My mum's words ran through my head.

"Never get in a car with a stranger, unless it's a policeman."

I thought of asking him what his job was, but the words wouldn't come. The man still stared, raising his eyebrows. It was time to choose.

I looked down at Tish. I'd be okay on my own, but it wasn't just about me anymore. I had my sister to look after and I took a step towards the car, could feel the warmth rolling out and saw my Dad's blood streaked up the white paint of the car bonnet.

He spoke for the first time, his voice low. I stopped moving.

"I've got sweets if you want one," he said, and a laugh came deep from his belly.

I turned and ran and carried on, even when I felt my breath had run out. Not stopping for walls or bushes or hedges or trees. Diving in and out. I'd been away from light for so long I could see quite well.

After what seemed like a long time and with the sky finally beginning to brighten, I had to stop in a copse of trees. It was that smell again, but maybe not so bad. I looked down at Tish and she smiled back.

While rifling through my pack I took notice of my hand for the first time. Running had taken all my concentration to stop us banging into things I could only see at the last moment.

It had stopped bleeding, crusted over, but hurt like it looked it should. It wasn't the worst pain in the world, which was still being kicked in the gonads. I thought of what I could use as a nappy, maybe three pairs of my pants tied at the side might work. I'd brought enough.

I thought of my mum's reaction to what I'd collected up. Maybe I was right this time. I smiled as I opened the pack. Mum had put nappies and Tish's things in my bag.

Laying out one of my T-shirts on the ground, I changed her; not a big deal, but I used the strong-smelling stuff on my hands three times as I let her run around.

We shared a can of beans once I won the struggle to get the ring pull thing up. They tasted all right once you'd got used to the cold. We drank water and I listened to Tish laughing as she picked up leaves and let them drop to the ground. I couldn't help but smile. She was enjoying the great adventure.

Climbing the height of the stone wall, I kept twisting back to make sure Tish hadn't run off or was about to pick up dog poop. She'd done it before, but I wasn't in charge then. I couldn't let it happen now.

The wall didn't feel too stable, but I needed somewhere high up. Whilst I'd run, I'd decided we should head home. We'd collect Rusty, somehow finding a way to get into the house. I'd get Mum's address book and we'd head to Nanny's. She'd know what to do.

A gunshot rang off somewhere

IN THE END

in the distance. I looked around, but I couldn't see anything moving, even though by now the sun had made the sky blue.

Tish laughed as the sharp noise came again. Closer this time. Maybe?

I wasn't laughing.

Since I'd eaten I'd started to feel funny inside, like I needed to lay down under my covers.

The covers in my room. My room at home.

There was only one problem. I had no idea where home was.

39

The road looked the same as every other where we lived. Still, I stayed high on the wall, looking in all directions, hoping there would be somewhere I recognised. I looked for my house first, of course. A cottage with a thatched roof, but the same could be said for most of the houses for miles.

The fresh breeze helped to settle my stomach as I tried squinting, staring into the horizon, searching out anything that could be a building. I thought to look for my school. It would be easy to follow the road home from there. It would take less than half an hour walking.

The problem was it was only a little bigger than my house; two small buildings instead of one. Every year they only just got enough kids to fill the amount of space needed to keep it from closing. I knew soon I would have to go to a bigger school, the comprehensive closer to town. We'd have to drive, a long journey twice a day.

IN THE END

Before today, of course. Before last night. Before what happened to Mum and Dad.

Me and Tish would have to live with Nanny.

I turned, almost falling, a stone loose under my right foot. Tish wasn't there.

How long had it been since I last saw her?

Jumping from the wall I ran in a circle, twisting left and right, craning to see around the trees, not wanting to charge off in one direction in case she'd gone the other way.

"Tish," I called. "Tish," I said again, then waited. All I could hear were the rustle of the branches above my head. No little footsteps. No little laughs. No cooing at her latest fascination.

"Tish. Where are you?" I was shouting at the top of my voice as I widened the circle, my head darting all over the place. I looked at the ground. Looked for her footprints, but the mud was cold and hard. I wasn't leaving size four prints, so how would her little feet be marking out her path when she weighed about the same as my bag?

"Tish," I called again.

How could I have been so silly? How could I have let Mum and Dad down so quickly?

With my head turning to the right, I didn't see the branch coming out from the ground. I tripped, stumbling forward. My knees scraping as I hit down hard.

Tears came and I turned, planting myself on my bum. My head was hurting like I'd been playing on the Xbox for too long. My stomach tightened, my jaw falling loose.

I knew this feeling and turned to the side. The beans came up, so did the water and last night's dinner, lasagne and those crisps which had nothing to do with Mum staying on the bus.

Feeling better almost straight away, the world swaying only a little as I stood, the crack of a twig caused me to twist.

There she was, running, her hands out wide, her face lit up like she'd been the one searching.

IN THE END

"Where've you been?" I said. "Don't do that again," I added as I bent down, pulling her close.

She screwed up her nose at my breath, the stink reflecting back. It smelt like I'd eaten what goes down the toilet. My head swam.

Holding her tight, I took the few steps to where I'd left the bag at the base of the wall. I just about made it before my legs gave way.

Leaning heavy against the cold stone, I wrapped her in my coat as she sat on my lap, taking her cold hands in mine. I took a quick look around to make sure it was safe, then turned to look over my left shoulder and watched the sun peering over the stone wall.

Taking a deep breath, I knew I had little choice but to sleep. At least just for a moment. Even the memory of something we learnt in school last year couldn't keep my eyes open. At least I knew when I woke I had a way of finding home.

***

"Tish," I said, the cold air a shock as a sharp breath pulled in. I could feel she wasn't lain in my arms like she had as I'd fallen asleep only moments ago.

The morning was still bright as my eyes blinked open, relief coming as I saw her in front of me, bent over, picking at the grass. Her pink trousers were dark, soaked through, her nappy sagging between her legs. I must have been out for longer than I'd thought, but it had done me good. The headache had gone and my stomach felt like it had relaxed; felt normal again. Empty, but normal.

Smiling, I kept my eyes on Tish. She was picking blades of grass and throwing them in the air. I turned and saw the bag was missing from my side. It was a few paces away, flat, the contents strewn across the wet ground. I spotted an open nappy, the tapes pulled apart. I think she might have tried to change herself.

I couldn't have been out long. It was still morning. I remembered the last thing I saw and turned to my right; we'd done it in science last year. We did an experiment over a whole week, plotting the position of the sun throughout the day.

I looked up, but it wasn't there, either. I turned left to where I'd seen it before, but it wasn't where it should be. As I concentrated, I saw the sun coming over the stone wall. But it couldn't be right. It was lower than it was when I'd closed my eyes.

The only way it could happen like this was if I'd slept through the whole day and today was tomorrow.

Standing, I expected to feel weak, but the opposite was true. I was full of energy, even though I'd not eaten for two days.

Walking over to Tish, I changed her bum whilst I tried to hold back my guilt for the pink, sore skin. Luckily, Mum had packed some of the white cream.

Hugging her harder than I should have, I could feel she was freezing cold. At least she hadn't gone hungry. The empty packets of the dried fruit scattered around the clothes told me all

I needed to know. Still, I opened the last of the beans and we filled up.

I was hungrier than I'd been for a long time and eager to get on with the trip home, confident we should walk to where the sun was coming up, sure I could remember seeing the sun setting from my bedroom window before.

We set off through the trees, coming out the other side. I climbed over the wall after lowering Tish first, repeating over the opposite side.

We walked across fields, the view blocked by large trees everywhere with Tish happy to toddle along beside me, enjoying her fresh nappy and dry clothes. Soon I heard a sound I recognised and a wide smile bunched my cheeks.

A helicopter. Cool, and it was getting close. I grabbed Tish, pulling her in tight and ran towards the sound.

40

Running, I heard a sound I'd copied so many times in the playground. The chug, chug rattle of machine gun fire added to the beat of rotor blades cutting through the air.

Pulling from the trees I saw the dark-green Merlin; the real-life version of what I'd flown so many times around my room. The helicopter was hovering close to the ground, maybe as high as a church steeple. The side door was open and I just about saw the gunner gripping tight as he trained the long gun at the ground.

I knew without having to think that he was shooting at more of those things, the hosts of whatever terrible disease had taken over the dead bodies.

Still, I couldn't help but smile. This was a rescue mission and I wondered what the helicopter would be like inside. Tish gave a giggle and I turned down to see her smiling back, but as I squeezed her tight, she wriggled for freedom. The chatter of the machine gun fell silent.

"We'll get to Nanny's really quickly now," I said, giving her a playful shake.

Looking back up, my gaze caught on a long stack of smoke rising high in the distance. I chanced a look left and right, seeing columns of grey smoke each way I turned.

These were new, not something I'd seen when I'd spent so long staring at the horizon to search for home. I clutched Tish closer as I remembered what had happened.

Picking up the pace, I ran towards the helicopter and I shouted for help. Tish joined in with her own made up words.

The helicopter moved from its hover, spinning around, hurrying to the right and stopping mid-air. It twisted as if searching below, then without warning, it moved left and the door gunner let out a long blast.

When the gun silenced, I shouted as loud as I could to call for help, but it hurried away, flying higher and becoming a dot in the sky.

IN THE END

"It's okay, Tish, they'll be back or someone else will come," I said.

Her giggle pushed back the tears, then her expression fell, her eyes opened wide. The loud clap of the bird scarer was common enough and we soon both relaxed.

I walked again, putting Tish down and realised I'd forgotten to follow the sun.

We ended up walking slowly. I was following Tish as she ambled through the open fields, heading towards a big clump of trees. It was the biggest wood I'd seen while we'd been walking.

Another shot broke through the air and I didn't give it a second thought, until five, six or seven went off, one after the other. I hurried a little closer to Tish. There were people hunting and I didn't want her running into their path.

Tish was still following an imaginary line, swerving left and right, with no sense in her direction. I didn't have the heart to grab her up and restrict her from playing.

We'd walked like this for ten

minutes and my wound itched, but it took my mind from the two shots which seemed to have been the last for some time.

Her path straightened and she headed a direct course. Her head lifted high. After a few moments she stopped and her little arm raised, her head turning my way.

"Russ," she said; her name for our dog.

Following her outstretched finger, I shook my head. The dog was black, not a gingery brown. It was the same breed, a Labrador, and she was running off, heading fast towards it.

The dog was standing with his head down, leaning over like it was eating dinner.

"No, Tish," I said, running to catch her, not wanting her to see the dog covered in blood, its face buried in the side of a dead deer or something else as disgusting.

I caught her, but only after shortening the distance between us and the animal. It was still bent over, but now I could tell from the length of the body lying on the ground that it was a man, not a deer. The dog's body blocked the view of the face as its black head bobbed up and down.

"No," came a call, a woman's voice.

My gaze startled up, pulling Tish tight as she flinched.

"Stay where you are."

The woman was far along the edge of the forest, had blonde hair and, apart from the dark marks on her face, it was about all I could tell. She was panting as she bent over and held her palms out toward us. It was obvious she didn't want us any closer, but Tish wasn't having any of it and wriggled free, kicking out her legs.

I couldn't hold on, her coat slipping against mine and she was on her feet, running to the dog.

I chased, soon seeing something else, a mound and knew it was one of them; the same smell. I tripped, stumbling over my own feet, launching my hand out to grab her leg, but I missed.

41

LOGAN

Warmth lapped at my cheek and foul breath brushed my face as I woke. Somewhere close, a high-pitched voice of a child screamed a name I didn't recognise. Another distant call came, high and frantic.

The hellhound.

My eyes shot open to a slobbering dog, blood and sinew dripping from its jowls. I startled up, falling back as fire raged across my chest.

Pushing away the hound, I realised it must be the same creature which saved my life, but it bore no resemblance to the crazed animal which fought the abomination intent on my neck. Blinking away my disbelief, wiping my wet face against the back of my hand, I saw a toddler. Dressed in pink, she swerved around the body of the rotting creature, not even glancing as

IN THE END

she ran towards me. Chasing after her was a boy, a few years older, scrambling to his feet, recovering from a fall.

What the hell was going on with the world?

I tried to stand again, but sank back, the pain in my ribs more than I could manage right now. As the girl arrived, she petted the dog's head and he turned her way, closing his eyes as if in a heavenly place.

"Oh, my god."

I recognised Cassie's voice. She was walking around the pair, not hiding her surprise at my breath.

"I thought," she said, looking between me and the dog enjoying the girl's rough strokes. "I thought it turned on you," she said, falling to her knees as she helped me to bend at the waist.

As she wrapped her arms around my chest and squeezed, stars burst across my vision.

"So did I," I said, my voice strained.

She pulled back and stood, her expression falling.

"It's not safe here," she said, and

offered a hand.

With her help, I stood, uneasy at first.

"No, it's not," I replied and for the first time took in the small boy stood at the girl's back. His hands were on her shoulder as he towered above her. "Who are these two?"

Cassie turned away, shaking her head and looked at the pair, considering them as if she'd not noticed them either.

"Where are your parents?" she said, looking back the way they'd come.

The boy stood in silence while I watched him concentrate to keep tears at bay.

"It's okay," I said. "There's a group of us. If you've got anyone else with you, they can come too."

He barely moved his head as it shook. He was hedging his bets.

"You should come with us," I said, then turned to the dog still being patted by the little girl. "And you, too." I tapped the dog on the head. "It's not safe here."

"The zombies," the boy said, with no emotion in his voice.

IN THE END

I paused for a moment, then nodded. Still, he looked unsure but I couldn't wait for a decision. We were all in danger and so were our friends. I hoped they were together, weren't scattered. Weren't alone.

I followed the boy's gaze down to the gun and bent, nearly screaming as pain lit across my chest, but broken ribs were okay. Doctors couldn't do anything but take away the pain.

Letting the empty magazine slip to the ground, I fished the full one and slid the loaded gun into my pocket.

The boy's gaze followed me all the while.

Cassie stepped toward the boy, kneeling at his feet, placing her hands on his upper arms.

"I have a sister, too. She's just a little older than you. I know what it means to want to look after her. To keep her safe. If you come with us," she said, turning her head to the toddler, "we can help look after you both."

Cassie waited, watching the boy's eyes as he looked up at me, then down to the pocket where the gun bulged before turning back to Cassie.

The uncertainty hung clear in his stare until a rustle in the bushes at our backs turned each of our heads in the same direction. Spinning back around, I saw his nod was more obvious than any other movement he'd made so far.

I walked, heading the way we'd been running. Cassie held back. I heard the dog's paws padding beside me and turned; the girl was following the dog. The boy set off after. He was slow at first, but his speed built with Cassie behind. Her head, like mine, scoured along the tree line.

Our pace was measured, but movement in the bushes, or the sounds in my head, wouldn't let me keep it that way for long.

I turned to Cassie and she understood. So did the boy and he went to pick up the girl, but Cassie moved her hands towards her, leaning down, hovering as she waited for his permission. He nodded and she took her in her arms. The pace picked up, the dog

IN THE END

still trotting at my side.

As we ran, the trees left our side as we came to the edge of the forest. Scouring the horizon, I spotted a figure running, then two. They were at the height of a hill a little way off in the distance, one in front of the other. Whoever it was, they were being chased.

I ran faster, looking back to Cassie who'd slowed to urge the boy to stay back.

Ignoring the pain, I ran. It was Naomi.

I watched as she stumbled, disappearing over the brow of a hill as she fell. What chased her had been a middle-aged man with balding hair and fat collecting around his middle, tattered clothes barely left to cover. It pounced after her like an Olympic gymnast. The dog stayed at my side and, trying my best to ignore the pull of the pain, I gave it everything. Taking the gun from my pocket I was minutes away, praying she could hold off long enough for me to do what I could.

I wasn't too late as I arrived over

the hill.

Her hands around its throat, it's mouth snapping forward; deja vu, but from a different perspective.

I let a shot ring off into the air, hoping it would distract the crazed monster enough for Naomi to get the upper hand. It didn't flinch. Its humanity gone.

The shot rang off and her grip gave way. The beast lurched forward and bit down on the side of her face.

42

Without command, the dog jumped at the beast and, grabbing a patch of exposed skin, he bit deep into its haunches. Still, whatever this thing was, it didn't budge as the hound shook its head with its mouth clamped down hard.

I pushed the gun square to the creature's temple. It only went limp as I blew what was left of its brains out the other side in an explosion of colour.

Rolling the body off, a clump of Naomi's loose flesh fell from his mouth and hit her with a wet slap against her face. She tried to scream, but had no breath, her arms frantic, blood pumping in spurts from the fist-size hole in her face.

Dropping to my knees I pulled off my coat, ripped open my shirt, the buttons flying as the cold bit into my skin. I tore the sleeves off, one by one, tying each length around her face. The white cotton went red as quick as I could pad out the wound with the remains.

"Where's Zoe?" I asked, my head darting to each of the trees, the only features on the gentle flow of hills, twitching from where we'd come, despite knowing there was nowhere to hide but the tree line and the place where we'd all been running from.

"Where is she?" I said, before looking at my hands, thick with Naomi's blood.

She'd settled down, her fight slowing as her skin greyed. She wouldn't answer. She was already going the same way as Chloe.

"Ellie," Cassie screamed, arriving at my side. She hadn't forgotten the last time we'd seen Naomi had been with Ellie fighting to get free from her arms.

"Andrew," I added to the call, then shook my head. "We need to move her," I said, not looking back. I picked Naomi up in my arms and, cradling her like a baby, I pushed the makeshift bandages against my chest. Her lack of weight scared me.

Cassie continued to call at the top of her voice, the tiny kid still in her arms. The boy said something as he picked up my coat and offered it out, high in his hands.

I bent, wincing with pain, but I couldn't complain. I wasn't near death.

The kid put my coat over Naomi while he still talked, his voice too quiet to understand. All I could manage was to walk, stumbling every few steps as I tried to go faster.

We were heading down into a short valley, my eyes fixed on the brow, hoping for what we would see the other side.

"Ellie," Cassie screamed. Her call ripped through the air as she ran past, the dog staying by my side. The little girl was crying, her face bunching.

The boy was talking, but I still hadn't heard what he'd said.

"A house," came Cassie's cry as she stood on the brow of the hill, not turning our way before disappearing over the edge.

I was soon behind her and saw the little cottage. The boy had stopped talking. I'd seen his face light up at

Cassie's words, but it fell as he'd caught sight of the squat building on its own nestled at the side of the road.

To its front was a sparse rocky garden, with a long fence at the back surrounding a wide stretch of grass. Inside the fence was a large wooden shed, or it could have been a barn, but who really cared?

The road was sparsely lined with trees and as I followed it into the distance I thought I saw more buildings. Cassie continued running down the hill, still calling for her sister.

"Andrew," I shouted. The boy said something again and I stopped, turning toward him. He was taking in the view, squinting off into the distance.

"What is it?" I said in a hurry.

"I think we should try to be quiet," he said, and I watched him turn.

"We need to find our friends," I said, shaking my head.

"But we don't want to find them," he replied, his hand outstretched, pointing back to the woods.

I turned and saw only trees, but as

IN THE END

my gaze settled I spotted movement. The more I stared the more movement I could see. It wasn't the trees moving, but those things.

I carried on staring, hoping to see if they were running, chasing after or ambling along as if out for a stroll. I couldn't believe the world had gone so far that I was glad when I could tell they were the undead, but only the slow ones.

The boy was right, they were heading in our direction. I turned, picking up the pace toward the cottage.

Cassie stood in the road as we arrived. She was facing outward from the cottage, but she'd stopped calling to the surroundings. Instead, she gently shook, rocking the girl from side to side. She must have seen them too.

The dog ran ahead. It seemed to know the plan, his nose twitching as he moved around the building.

My arms ached as I let Naomi down gently to the short strip of grass in front of the house. She didn't respond and I knew there was nothing I could do until

I got her inside. Even then, I doubted I could help.

My hands were tacky as I let go, my chest running with sticky blood.

The dog was back at my side, looking up at me as if giving the all clear. I ran to the door and tried the handle. It was locked. I shoved my shoulder hard against it, but it held firm.

The boy spoke again in a quiet voice. This time I listened.

"We need that," he said. Again, he was right.

Looking back, Cassie was still staring out the same while blood had pooled in the grass around Naomi's head.

I headed around the building, the dog and the boy following as I picked up a discarded stone from the rock garden.

The bigger windows needed to stay too, but I found a small high pane around the side I could reach with my hand outstretched. It wasn't much bigger than a large dinner plate. The pain would be unbearable, but with a squeeze I was sure I could get inside.

IN THE END

Making sure the boy and the dog were out of the way, I threw the hand-sized rock and watched as it bounced off the double glass and fell to the floor at my feet. I glanced to the front of the house and saw Cassie sobbing as she rocked the toddler back and forth.

The boy handed me the rock and I threw again. This time, the first pane gave, then, standing on the tips of my toes, the second pane was gone, with the remains of glass soon following.

I turned and the boy had disappeared, but before I could spin back I saw him walking toward me with my gun in his hand. My eyes went wide as he held the pistol with such confidence, the barrel pointed down towards the ground. He must have grabbed it from my jacket pocket.

"Um," I said. "Hand it over."

He looked up, his face lit with hurt.

"But what if those things are inside?"

A thought stumbled across my mind. Was he offering to go inside? There was no way I could let that happen.

"I'm going in," I said, holding out my hand.

"Not with your injuries," he replied. "You'll pass out before you reach the other side."

Again, he was right, but I couldn't ask him to do this.

I didn't have to; he was already at the wall, waiting for me to boost him up.

As his feet disappeared through the window, I heard glass breaking from inside and the dog barked as if he was next to be helped up.

I couldn't stifle a chuckle as I ran around the front, wrapping my sticky arms around myself from the cold. I waited with my ear at the door, listening to the silence, broken only by Cassie's comforting, low-pitched calls.

I couldn't look at Naomi. I had to turn away from Cassie's red eyes. Instead, I concentrated on the dog's long face, the pink of its mouth as it panted, watching it sat at my heels; its wagging tail stopping only when from behind the door came a muffled, high-pitched scream.

43

A dark shape arrived behind the thin rectangles of leaded glass. Fingers rattled the handle and scrabbled across the locks. The dog barked and the figure stopped. The top latch had clicked off but he had no success with the solid mortice. The figure wasn't moving.

I kicked myself for not getting his name.

"Kid, find the long key," I shouted.

The figure moved, jolting forward at my voice.

"Oh my god," came Cassie's call.

I span around and saw five of the slow creatures ambling over the hill, spotting another group, double in number, rising over the crest before I turned.

Cassie stepped back, almost tripping over Naomi's motionless form.

"Find the long key," I shouted again, trying to think how we could get everyone else through the small window.

"Got it," came the call from inside,

but something was wrong. The sound was much quieter.

The lock rattled and the boy pulled open the door. A girl stood further into the darkness. They must have swapped places when she realised the boy with the gun was with us. Still, she screamed as she saw my bloodied appearance; her eyes wide open, hands at her mouth.

"Ellie," I heard Cassie gasp as I picked up Naomi. The call came again, but this time she screamed with excitement.

With my hands sliding with her sticky blood, the putrid stench caught in the wind as I followed behind Cassie's forward charge and slammed the door behind me with my foot.

Placing Naomi's limp body on the couch in the first room to the left, the boy had his arms around his sister, nodding to the gun high on a wall unit shelf.

Cassie knelt to the floor, fussing over her sister, pulling up her clothes and examining every exposed patch of skin for injury before hugging her through heavy, joyful sobs, despite Ellie's annoyed insistence she'd not been near any of the creatures.

The dog had disappeared, racing room to room, his nose switching from high in the air to hovering just above the carpet.

"Cassie," I shouted, sharp and clear. "Pressure," I said, pointing my hands to Naomi's face.

After a double take in my direction, she took in the room as if for the first time. Cassie dragged her sister over by the arm, not letting her out of touching distance as she pressed her hands hard onto the wound.

I shot out of the room, heading straight to the kitchen, ignoring the other closed doors. I rifled through the cupboards and drawers searching for a first aid kit or anything else I could use, but only finding clean dishcloths. The cupboards were bare, cleared in a hurry.

I scrambled up the stairs to find the bedrooms rifled and disorganised. The people who had lived here had been lucky. They'd had warning, were given at least a few moments to collect up treasured things before their evacuation.

I found the bathroom with ease, but the medicine cabinet above the sink stood empty.

I ran down the stairs, passing the dog on the way and was kneeling to Naomi's side when a great thump hit the front door.

We all looked at each other in disbelief, even though we knew those things had followed us. Still, we gave a collective jump as a dark shape thudded against the living room window, its shadow looming across the room.

I looked to Cassie, holding out the cloths.

"Can you?" I said.

She nodded and I raced up the stairs, the dog joining my side at the window of the front bedroom.

Swiping the net curtains to the side, I saw nothing unusual until I opened the window, the stench rising as the seal creaked.

I peered down into the cold air and watched the group of fifteen gathered around the front door, their number spreading out either side to surround the building.

Watching in awe, I made myself calm, taking deep breaths through my mouth. Staring out to the hills, I tried to picture what normality had been. With the stench and the low rumbling moan, all I could think of was the others still out there. There was little we could do in here, but I had an idea.

Listening to Cassie's voice still high and hearing her gratitude at the realisation her sister was safe, I found a child's bedroom and, after a short search, located bold markers in a drawer.

Back in the front bedroom, I shoved aside the bed covers and, with dried blood flaking to the white surface, I scrawled my missing friend's names in big, bold letters.

"What happened to the others?" I heard Cassie say, her voice rising up the stairs.

I could barely hear the reply, just making out they'd separated. Ellie hadn't seen what had happened to Naomi, Zoe or Andrew. The sound of each name came like an electric shock. The pilot, as she called him, had been with her when they walked into another group of those creatures.

He'd distracted them, drawing them towards him, making them follow as he ran in the opposite direction from her. They'd both seen the house and, as he ran, he pointed her towards it.

I had the sheet off the bed and out one side of the window.

Tying off the end, I tried to throw the corner across and catch it from the other opening. On my fourth try I'd grabbed it in my fingertips and tried to tie it down.

"But how did you get in?" Cassie said.

My fingers stopped working the knot, my breath held in the long pause.

I moved my hands from the sheet, not noticing if it stayed in place. I stepped to the landing, watching the dog's ears twitch up.

"The back door was open." Ellie's voice was clear.

IN THE END

I was already moving when Cassie spoke again.

"Did you close it behind you?"

I didn't hear the answer before I'd jumped down the first few steps.

44

Launching myself down the stairs, the stench grew worse. Pain radiated around my chest as I patted my trousers in vain, knowing full-well the gun would stare back from the high wall unit in the front room.

Three openings came into view as I raced. The door to the kitchen stood open, the room already explored. The other two white doors straight ahead hung closed, but it was only one of them I wanted to open.

On the last step, I hesitated. Should I turn away and get the gun or charge towards one of doors unarmed, hoping I'd made the right choice and the invasion hadn't already begun?

Knowing I'd delayed too much already, I raced to the first, feeling the lightweight hardboard almost buckle as I used it stop my momentum. My heart sank as I realised it wouldn't last long if it had to be our final barrier.

I stepped back, not taking a breath

IN THE END

for fear of the foul air, not knowing what I could do if they were already on the other side. Fragrant air wafted out as I pushed the door open. A toilet glared at me from against the wall while a dark figure drifted past the frosted glass.

I felt the cold draft before I pushed the second door open, before I saw the dead body turn the corner as it swung. The dark wood of the back door was wide toward me, the chill, pungent air striking my bare chest.

Again, I hesitated for what seemed like an age, staring at the mud-caked trainers so close to crossing the threshold.

My gaze rose up the white tracksuit bottoms, following the line of dark holes strafing the legs. Each was ringed in deep scarlet, the wounds tracking up the white body and across the creased, matching tracksuit top, through her left breast before ending at the shoulder. The circles of red widened as the bullet holes rose, their course only just missing her young head.

My gaze hovered for far too long,

watching as she stepped forward in slow motion, at least in my head. With eyes clouded white like her hair, her features were grey and sunken, but her lips were bright red with a gloss sheen, like she'd paused for a moment around the corner to add an extra coat.

This was someone's daughter. I looked to her hands, which were much like mine, caked in red, flaking blood, but at least what covered me was not my own. The thought filled me with such guilt;. if it was, then Naomi would be okay. If only it worked like that.

She was a wife, according to the ruby ring on her long slender finger, the nails with a perfect manicure, the covering the same vibrant red as her lips.

The dog broke my spell, barking as another creature appeared the other side of the door frame. I barely saw the Asian guy, only noticing the stub of sharp bone where his right arm should have been.

At last I'd taken the final steps and pushed against the door, heaving the wood as it caught on something solid. Looking down, I saw the woman's trainer, the toes jammed between the door and the frame. I could feel her weight pushing back, building as more joined the stack.

The boy arrived with the gun in his hand, offering it butt first, his eyes wide as he saw my struggle. I couldn't take the weapon without losing my ground, which I was only just holding.

Shaking my head, I felt my anger building inside as I cursed my poor decisions. Why hadn't I checked the back door? Why didn't I go for the gun first?

The corridor grew lighter and I looked up, saw dark shapes shuffling across the windows in the front door. These things knew of our struggle and were heading around the back.

I took a look at the pistol still offered out and made a frightening connection.

The monsters were communicating.

We were going to need bigger guns.

45

With each deep, incessant bark, the glass squares in the door rattled against their lead edging. Pushing hard with my shoulders and hands flat against its surface, I winced as the hinges complained, creaking against the wall.

Stalemate, although I guessed the creatures on the other side could keep it up for longer. My gaze fell to the trainer stuck in the door's path, its mud-covered fabric wedged to the wall. There was only one way the door was going.

I turned my head around the small anteroom to shelves hung along the short walls, then down to where a stout chest freezer sat.

Despite the madness of the effort, I couldn't help but think of the food inside. So much had happened in the last few hours, but in reality it had been barely two days since the start; since we lost those things impossible to live without. Electricity. The internet. Both would be no use right now as a heave from the other side brought back my focus.

I gave a shove in reply, my gaze back on the shelves, roving for weapons. The iron might do, but the rest were useless, the electric mixer nothing but a great doorstop in this new world.

Turning back to the boy, the gun still held by the barrel, he was trying his best to pull the dog back as he growled between each bellow.

The dog needed a name, but he never had a collar to give us a clue. The boy held the dog back, the mutt not pulling out of his hands. The boy turned the gun and pointed it at the wedged shoe.

"No," I shouted. "No. Too dangerous." I paused, pushing a little harder and realised there may never be a good time for introductions.

"Kid, what's your name?" I said, straining against a renewed effort.

The kid looked up as if I'd told him Santa Claus wasn't real, his face distant, eyebrows raising. Maybe he'd forgotten what he was called.

"Jack," he eventually said in a quiet voice.

"Jack. I like that."

The kid looked past me as another shove added to the pile, another low moan of air rolling out the putrid stench.

"My name's Logan," I said, pausing. "I'd shake your hand if I could," and tried to squeeze out a smile.

The kid wasn't impressed, his face deadpan. "Go see if Cassie..." I paused again. "Go see if the woman in the other room can lend a hand," and gave the door another heave.

Before he ran the short distance, he placed the gun carefully in the opening of the kitchen beside me, then was back in just a few speeding heartbeats. He shook his head.

I understood, picturing Cassie's arms drenched in Naomi's blood. I wanted to say she might have to come anyway. Instead, I decided to try something else to test how these things would react.

Pulling a deep breath and trying to let my muscles relax, I spoke again.

IN THE END

"Jack, take the gun and get ready to run to the front room. If I don't follow, just shut this door," I said, nodding toward the thin interior barrier. "Get the woman to pull the furniture across and stay there. You understand?" I watched as he stared back, looking like he was about to ask a question, about to ask me what I was up to.

I didn't have time. "Pick up the gun," I said, and he did what he was told. "And take the dog too, right?" I said, raising my brows. "We have to give him a name."

The kid looked at the dog, turning his head to the side and the tiniest of smiles appeared.

I took a final deep pull of air whilst trying to hold back my gag reflex and turned my head down to the floor, planting my foot back a few inches and letting my hold relax.

The door gave as I expected, slapping against my foot.

The kid jumped, looking to my side as I fought to stop the movement and keep my hold. The woman's dead foot was loose and free to move. It didn't. My test had failed and I'd lost valuable leverage, the weight so much stronger than before and my foot was slipping, the soles of my trainers squealing as they slid against the tiles.

The hallway darkened with my feet sliding, a hand peeling around the edge. It was the woman's; I could tell from the red of her nails, the fingers dowsed in dried blood.

I tried to push back, but I was already giving all I had. Something fluttered to the floor and I followed it down. A finger nail. False. For show; the remaining pink nail rough underneath, the edge jagged and bitten down to the skin.

My gaze shot back to the front door as the glass rattled with the boom of a fist against the wood.

"Help," came the call. It was Andrew's panicked voice, I had no doubt.

The toddler wailed high, Jack turning, looking between his sister and the front door.

"Let him in, Jack. He's our friend," I

said, a new calmness in my voice. "Our friend," I added in a whisper, the words relaxing as a weight lifted.

Jack turned with his face bunched in a question.

I confirmed in a nod and felt the pressure ease at my back. The weight was literally lifting. I felt a sudden relief that everything would be okay, but the feeling was only short-lived.

The events of the day flashed before my eyes. I looked down at my blood-soaked chest, remembering Naomi laid on the couch, Zoe lost out in the wilderness.

Jack was halfway to the door and I gave a heave, taking back some distance I'd lost and the realisation came; it was getting lighter because they were going after Andrew.

"Hurry," I shouted, but Jack couldn't speed any more. He was there, his hands tangling at the locks, getting twisted like in a dream. It was already bad, a nightmare, but worse still. There was no possibility I would wake up.

The light from the front room

dimmed. There were more of them coming around the edge. No time left.

The door sprung open and there was Andrew, red-faced, eyes wide, with terror running through him. But he was in one piece.

A smile bloomed on my face and mirrored by his, but both dropped as I saw a hand come around the door, grabbing the hood of Andrew's coat and yanking him back.

He pulled himself free, falling to the floor. He was inside.

Euphoria spread over me.

"Shut the door," I screamed. More hands raked at the edges.

The temperature fell and my heart sank with it as I saw in the distance Lane and Zoe running towards us with one of those beasts racing close behind as Jack slammed the door at his back.

46

Andrew hadn't caught what I'd seen. He was too busy scrabbling from the floor and racing to my side at the back door. Pushing. Heaving. Kicking at the woman's foot. Peeling fingers from their hold until the latch clicked into place.

With the back door secure, pain ripped across my chest, the cracked ribs only a part of my state. My muscles took a breath for the first time in what seemed like hours, but I couldn't relax, I couldn't take time and rushed past Jack, grabbing the pistol from his hand. The front door was back open in one swift swing, surprising the creatures from where they'd drifted.

Bang. Bang. The gun sang. Two shots and one either side were down.

A black shadow raced past my side and I caught sight of the dog, choosing his new name in an instant. He was racing towards the pair I'd stepped out of safety to rescue, or at least give a chance of life as it was meant to be.

Bang. Bang. Another two down and Andrew was out with the iron upturned in his hand, water spilling across his path.

Thump, went the corner of the metal across a grey face. Down went the creature and with another solid pound it stopped dead. Again.

Bang. I sent a shot across his front, forcing another sprawling to the ground. Thump went the iron and I shot after. We'd taken six or seven out, three sprawled to the floor, but more were coming from each side of the building.

I heard Shadow's muffled growl and knew without looking he'd latched on. I turned and saw Zoe and Lane were close, running towards the open door.

The creature was down, Shadow gripping tight to his leg. He'd forced it to the ground and now it's full attention was on the dog.

I ran after, not wanting to chance a shot. Andrew called me away, the thump of the metal resounding again. As I grew closer, Shadow winced, squealing; a clawed hand dug deep in his chest.

IN THE END

"Shadow," I said, calling his new name and smiled as he released, running in my direction.

Bang went a shot, and then another. The body did what nature had once meant it should.

I turned and ran alongside the dog, taking two more shots before slamming the door.

My back slid down the wood. Batteries flat. Energy expired.

There was much back-slapping and hugs all around. After checking below the fur on Shadow's side, with relief finding his skin intact, I climbed to my feet by the time it had all turned to tears.

Naomi was still alive but following the same story as Chloe had already written. I couldn't take part; I was zapped. Emotions drained. I had to get her blood from my chest and I took the steps one by one, slow and steady, leaving the sobbing behind.

It was Zoe's heartfelt cry I had to

shut out. I couldn't hear more pain; there was no more room inside my head.

Water came from the tap, the tank in the loft not yet empty. I washed as best I could, sparing as much as I was able.

Drying myself, I went from room to room, hearing downstairs had calmed. There were three bedrooms. Three people had lived here. Parents and a child. The dad had been, could still be, my size and I was warm again, at least across my body.

Sitting on the edge of the bed in the largest room, I listened to the slow steps while I counted each of the ten remaining rounds.

Cassie appeared at the door, her hands bloodied and buried in a rag. She looked like me; exhausted with it all.

"There's water left in the tank," I said, my voice monotone.

She nodded and drifted away.

I still sat in the same place, my gaze not having moved from the door since she'd left.

She was back, her coat off, shirt

IN THE END

sleeves rolled up, but still I could see the bloodied ends. Without speaking, she sat right beside me, my body tipping towards her as the mattress took her weight.

We leaned in and she turned. I followed, our eyes catching. Our lips headed together. They were so warm. Fresh. Her arms, too, as they pulled around my body.

Mine found hers and, as if recharged, we delved into each other's mouths like nothing else mattered.

She pulled my hands to her back when a powerful thud shook the building. Glass falling to the ground.

Screams called upward and I pulled away; both our mouths in a thin smile. I reached for the gun and, one after the other, we ran down the stairs.

47

Gasps sang through the air as seven sets of eyes stared at the small side pane of the front room window. Shadow shouted a warning, snapping off a bark as I arrived.

The outer layer had cracked, a head-sized section missing; the glass lost between the panes.

With no obvious cause, I turned to the staring faces, my gaze shooting back as a head climbed from below the window line.

Something, once someone, rose unsteady above the sill. He'd been an older man, his hair blond and straw-like, his skin leathery and weathered. He wore a thick checked shirt with a line running across his forehead where a hat had recently been. Just below the line was an indentation, a break in the skin, but no blood poured out. There was no heart pumping.

Heads turned as I'd arrived, then to Cassie as she followed just after. I couldn't help but steal a glance as her slender hands delved, pushing away her shirt tails. With my cheeks heating, I checked their expressions. I was sure they hadn't noticed.

Zoe's eyes were red and wet with tears as she knelt beside the sofa, her hands wrapping Naomi's pale fingers.

For the first time, I noticed the Christmas tree in the corner and was transported to my parents' house only the week before. It was Christmas morning, the first time I woke there in ten years, the tree resplendent with brightly-coloured parcels bulging from underneath. Here it would be Christmas till this was all over. Decorations around the South West would be up until someone sorted this shit out.

No one spoke as Cassie led the children away and, together with Lane and Andrew, we manoeuvred the wall-length dresser across the window.

With cupboards scoured for anything of use and Zoe still holding her hand, we moved Naomi and the sofa, pushing it across the cupboard to stop it from toppling if the worst should happen.

The room was nearly pitch black with the curtains drawn, just the light from the hallway seeping in. Somehow, we got Naomi up the stairs, carrying her between four of us. Her body hardly responded as we turned her around the corners, landing her in the front bedroom where I pulled in the sheet from outside and sealed the windows up tight.

Zoe lay beside her, stroking her hand. There was nothing left to do but keep watch. I had to stay close.

"You can leave now," Zoe said, as I leaned against the door frame. She kept her gaze on Naomi, didn't turn my way. "You can leave," she repeated. "I know why you're waiting."

I kept quiet and held my ground, a deep sadness gripping my insides. Zoe was one of my best friends and there was nothing I could do to stop her pain.

"Go away," she shouted, tears falling.

Shadow thudded upstairs, his nose in the air and his bright brown eyes

IN THE END

between me and the bed. I slipped away and he took my place.

Cassie was in the kid's room, tidying up the mess, some of which I'd made in my search for the pens. The two young girls were asleep in the bed; it had been a boy's room, the Spiderman bed cover one of many tells. A Superman sleeping bag was rolled out on the floor.

"Where's Jack?" I said.

She turned my way, a smile rising and for the first time I saw a dimple just below each of her high cheek bones.

"Lane's looking at his hand downstairs. The girls are whacked," she said.

I felt a yawn fill my face.

"We all are," I replied, matching her expression, then turned away. Sleep was a long way off for me. I knew I would have to break Zoe's heart when the time came.

I peered out of each of the windows, looking down through the cold air.

Out the back, three or four of those things were roaming around, each looking like they had no care in the world.

From the front, Zoe opened her eyes as I arrived and I patted Shadow, still in the same place.

Zoe closed her eyes as I went to the window, not watching as I looked down at the devastation and the bodies lain across the road. The farmer who'd smashed the window was ambling around the front, stumbling as he came to each of the truly dead.

I pulled the curtains closed and left Shadow on duty.

Already I'd learned to hate the calm. It was time waiting for the next crisis to strike, waiting for the next event to tear our world further apart.

Every little noise in this foreign house spiked my interest. I drew the gun in my mind ten times a minute, pointing it towards the dark.

I found Lane and Andrew in the kitchen, with Jack sitting on the edge of the worktop by the sink. Jack's hand was in Lane's, who was leaning in to inspect a semi-circular wound between his thumb and forefinger.

IN THE END

"He's been bitten," Andrew said, Lane's first aid kit open in his hand. It was one of the few things we'd been able to keep, the rest of our hoard lost, scattered around the campfire when we were overrun; a mistake we would not repeat.

"Bitten by what?" I asked, fearing the answer. "When?" I said, as Andrew and Lane only replied with a raise of their eyebrows.

"Two days ago," Andrew said.

"He thinks," Lane added.

My gaze fixed on his and then on Andrew's before turning down to Jack, the only one in the room who seemed to be oblivious.

He'd been bitten two days ago. Why wasn't he dead?

"How are you feeling, little man?" I asked.

"Fine," he said, his voice quiet.

I looked up to Lane. He replied with a nod.

"You must be tired," I said, but he shook his head.

"He thinks he slept all day

yesterday, after he was bitten," said Andrew.

I ruffled the kid's hair and Andrew followed me to the dining room, where someone had put everything which might be of use on the table. There were a few cans of beans and a small stack of nappies, but not much else other than a collection of half-full spirit bottles. Very little food.

"There's a village down the road," I said, but Andrew dismissed my statement.

"We need to watch the kid," Andrew said, his voice quiet as he leaned in.

"He seems fine," I replied.

"You want to take the chance?"

"Maybe it's not a death sentence. Being bitten, I mean."

Andrew kept quiet and Lane appeared at the door.

"He seems okay. More than okay," he said, his voice quiet as we listened to light footsteps on the stairs.

"With the others…" Andrew said, but his face turned to the floor as he stopped talking.

I patted Andrew's upper arm.

"They wouldn't stop bleeding. Chloe anyway," I said, Andrew filling the pause I'd left.

"And Naomi," he said, looking to the ceiling. "The others didn't last long enough."

Lane's voice was quiet as the footsteps headed over our heads.

"I had a look at Naomi and you're right, it looks like there's a clotting issue. I'm no doctor. We're trained in first aid for combat trauma, but there's more going on than just the bite. It's not the same for the kid. It's healing really well. I didn't need to bandage it."

Lane was looking between us both. I glared at Andrew.

"You sure you want to take a chance?" he said, this time in Lane's direction.

Lane was about to reply when Shadow's volley of barked calls stopped the words from coming.

48

The pistol led the way up the stairs, myself, Lane and Andrew chasing Shadow's sharp homing calls as best we could.

I knew what I'd see as I crested; knew Zoe would be dead, or dying, bleeding out. Naomi was no longer her friend or her lover, whoever she'd been. Instead, the door sat closed with Shadow in the hall, barking towards the handle.

He followed behind as I pushed in. Zoe lifted her head, glaring back from the bed, still tucked in her embrace, the side of her face red with Naomi's blood. She scowled at our intrusion with an expression I'd never seen her wear. Lane and Andrew had turned before arriving.

"For your own protection," I said, pushing the gun back in my waistband. "And ours, too," I added.

"You never liked her," Zoe's voice barely said as she lay her head back down.

I bit my lip and stifled a reply,

knowing nothing I could say would make a difference as I turned away, leaving the room, pushing the door as wide as it would go.

Cassie was in the hall with the others and followed as I ushered them into the main bedroom, pushing the door closed at our backs.

"I'm going to the village we saw on the way in."

The three stared back, each face turning thoughtful. I could guess what they were thinking, Andrew especially, his gaze following toward the room next door.

I pulled the gun from my waistband and offered it in the centre. They each swapped glances.

"We need food, water, heat, if we can."

They couldn't disagree with any part of what I'd said.

"You can't go without a weapon," Andrew said, his eyes wide at the suggestion.

"I can't leave you without protection," I replied. "At least I can run. It's quiet at the moment," I said, nodding out of the back windows. "There might be somewhere better for us to stay tonight."

There was silence as Andrew walked over to the window, pulling across the net curtains and staring outside.

"Your ribs?" Cassie replied, squinting down at my chest.

I shook my head; the empty feeling in my stomach was worse.

"I'll come with you," Andrew replied.

I looked down at his side as he turned back.

"You're worse than me. Someone's got to look after the kids." I held the gun out to Lane and he took it, pushing it into the pocket of his jacket.

"I'll come with you," Cassie said.

My heart jumped.

"No," I replied, without taking the time to consider the words. "The kids?"

A deep furrow arrived on her brow.

"I'm sure these two can take care of them. They've got the gun."

I didn't reply, just stared in her eyes, trying not to get lost.

IN THE END

"Why don't you want me along?"

"It's not that," I said, looking to Lane and then to Andrew for support.

Both had turned away, finding somewhere else to focus.

"You need more hands to carry what we find," she replied, her voice impassioned.

"It's not safe," I said, trying not to turn away.

"But you're the big hero, right?" she replied, pushing her hands to her hips.

"I don't want you in danger's way."

Her eyes flared wide as the words came.

"Because?" she said. "Say it."

I looked up and somehow Lane and Andrew had slipped from the room.

"Because I'm a woman?"

"No," I said. "Yes. But not because you're not strong or brave enough."

I didn't see her shoulders relax. She tilted her head to the side; raised her eyebrows, telling me to say what I meant.

"Then what?" she replied, not able to wait any longer in the silence.

"Because I don't want to see you hurt. I like you," I said, raising my voice. I stopped talking and she took a step backwards, turning, but not before a smile raised on her lips.

"A lot," I added.

"Then I'll be good company," she said, and headed out of the door.

Was she swinging her butt just a little as she left?

I took a deep breath and let the air slowly come out. I was nervous twice over. The run would be dangerous, but I was hopeful there would be food and water on the other side. Now I was nervous Cassie was coming along, but they were different nerves, more a feeling in my stomach. A feeling I hadn't felt since my wife had left my life.

Zoe's slow pained sobs pushed away my daydream. I took slow careful steps, standing at the doorframe, peering through. I didn't know her pain, didn't know what it was like to watch someone you love die.

At least Naomi had a chance; some hope. The boy had survived and so she

IN THE END

might, too.

I drew a deep breath. I couldn't dwell; I had a job to do. I had to keep busy. It was time to get on with living.

Downstairs, rucksacks were piled by the front door. Cassie stood with her smile gone. In her hands, she offered a large duffel coat with the fur around the hood.

I pulled it on.

She was ready, her coat over her shoulders and buttons done up to her chin, the hood pulled high.

Andrew appeared from an understairs cupboard I hadn't noticed before, a crowbar and a long screwdriver in hand.

I wanted the crowbar; it would make a more effective weapon. I handed it to Cassie and took the screwdriver.

Andrew returned with a short, stubby torch which I pushed in my pocket.

I hugged no one goodbye. It wasn't the end. We wouldn't let it be.

"We're only going down the road," I said as we left, Shadow barking as

Andrew held him back, the locks turning as we ran past the farmer.

    I glanced back, ignoring the pain as we raced along the road towards the village in the distance. Even then I knew we would not see them all again.

49

Soon we slowed from a fearful pace, letting the white vapour from our mouths settle. Other than the farmer limping from the cottage, we'd seen no more of the creatures as we added to the distance from our haven.

Relaxing the screwdriver from my grip, I watched the village grow in the distance. To continue to call it a village was a big step; I could see four houses.

Each sat squat and close to the ground, much like where we'd just come from, but otherwise individual. A small post office sat nestled in the line as the road wound out of view. No corner shop yet, or one of those local supermarkets, but I hoped there would still be plenty of road to see when we got in close.

Cassie looked to the sky and along the horizon.

I followed, looking up and remembering the helicopters, bracing myself to run and hide as soon as we heard the first signs of their spinning rotors.

Cassie's gaze fixed on a valley, cutting between the shallow hills to the left.

"Might be a river," she said, pointing in its direction. "If all else fails."

I nodded, chancing another look back, pleased to be putting distance between us and the farmer.

Soon, the first of the cottages were on our right. Outside, lights hung around the edge of the low roof, their lamps drab and unlit, not unusual in the bright daylight. The curtains were drawn. The gate closed. No newspapers stuck half-out from the letter box. No candlelight came through the thin rounded panes of glass running up and down the door.

There were no sounds as I leaned in. The round, brass handle stung my hand with its cold, refusing to turn.

"We should..." Cassie said in a whisper, stopping as I held my palm high.

I'd heard something and she leaned in beside me, following the question in my expression. Her face drew in close and I could smell her perfume, not the kind which came from the bottle, but just as evocative.

Together we listened and I turned, concentrating through the mottled glass, but whatever was on the other side was obscured in darkness.

I turned again, Cassie looking to the door as our eyes met. Another sound brought my attention back. There was definitely someone moving around in there.

I chanced a look at Cassie, our faces so close. She drew back a pace, turning to look along the building.

"Hello," I said in a whisper.

Cassie shook her head.

"We should try the other end of the village first," she said, her voice even quieter.

"Hello," I repeated, a little louder this time.

Cassie's hand touched the top of mine.

"We should..." she said but stopped as we heard a series of what sounded like footfalls.

My mouth opened to a smile, eyebrows flashing in her direction. I turned to the door and something hit the wood hard from the other side. A small pane of glass burst open, glancing shards across the side of my face.

A gaunt, grey hand launched out in a foul-smelling cloud and grabbed my coat, the force pounding against my ribs. I doubled forward, hitting my head and was face to face with sunken eyes, squashed against the semicircle of textured glass.

50

A thin, yellowing sleeve covered the arm. Cassie's iron bar crashed down across it with a great puff of effort, but still the grip held.

I looked down and saw the skin tight around the bones. I tried pulling back, pushing away from the door, but no matter how much I tried it wouldn't let up. My left hand grabbed around the wrist but let go, the skin so cold; unreal, like a life-size doll.

A two-handed swing from over Cassie's head cracked against the forearm, snapping it down the middle. The grip sprung wide like the release of a bear trap, but the arm stayed out, waving from the window, leaving the last half of the limb swinging from side to side.

Cassie pulled me back from the door with such force I nearly fell to the ground before I made any distance.

Stumbling, I somehow kept on my feet as she pulled me along. I stared back, the drooping hand waving to the constant bang of its head butting hard from the other side.

Regaining my composure, we ran in the centre of the road, keeping an even distance between each of the buildings.

Looking back, the farmer was nowhere. We then turned to watch the village open out and end. There was no supermarket, corner shop or pub, just the post office, looking no bigger than the size of a phone box.

Cassie slowed first and I matched her pace. Her hands reached into her pocket and she pulled out a cloth, beckoning me closer with her other hand.

I followed her request and stooped a little. The cloth came away with a light dapple of blood, but I felt little pain as she gently dabbed the wound.

"We need to be careful," she said. "You need to be careful."

A wide smile filled my face and she handed me the cloth.

"The Post Office is our best bet. Do you think?" I said, pushing the cloth to my pocket.

There were ten houses, each painted white, but all so different and similar at the same time. A thought came to mind and I turned around on the spot, taking in each of the houses for the second time.

"No cars," Cassie said, before I had a chance to voice my findings.

"Evacuated themselves?"

She shrugged.

"We should find a map in the post office. We can walk to the next place, maybe find a car or at least somewhere with food."

Nodding her reply, we walked but took our time to peer in each of the houses, stepping no closer than we needed too, not leaving the road.

Most were wrapped up tight, windows closed, curtains drawn, the occasional low-key Christmas decoration. All bar one.

A house, again much like the others, sat in the middle between two similar properties, with the Post Office next to the row of three. The curtains weren't closed and upstairs a window hung wide.

We shared a glance at the sight, stopping in the road, both unsure of what to do next. The front garden was immaculate and lined with evergreen bushes tapering in perfect cones. The patience required meant someone had time on their hands.

Sharing the raise of eyebrows, we took our first slow steps towards the house. Staring forward, we waited for the smallest of signs, telling us we should turn away.

Cassie was right; we needed to be so careful.

It wasn't any sight from the house which made us stop, or footsteps from the farmer, or any of his new friends. It was the sound of a large engine in the background, the noise already building as we waited; a truck, or something larger. Too noisy for a coach, the engine thrashed too hard for an official.

I turned to Cassie and she turned to me. My head filled with a vision of the helicopter and its devastation. A vision of those big jeeps they had in

IN THE END

Afghanistan, but painted green, the machine gun mounted high and trained at every angle; the soldier's eyes scanning for everything which moved. Shooting first, asking questions later.

Her head must have filled with similar thoughts. I didn't need to do anything but tip mine across the road and she grabbed my hand, sending a shot of electricity up to my chest.

We ran, covering the distance in no time at all, between the two houses and jumping a short wall. The sound of the engine was almost upon us as we fell to the grass behind a wide chimney stack jutting out high from the side of the house.

51

Our hands released as we fell to the ground, both of us scrabbling to turn and get sight of what was coming.

Peering low around the wide exterior chimney breast, I moved back, raising up on my knees so I could make out the road over the side of the squat front-garden wall. The spaces between the houses were wide, giving a view of the road, which meant whoever was coming would have a great view of us.

I jerked my head around, spotting a half-rotten wooden trellis collapsed against the neighbouring house. In-between the diamonds formed by thin diagonal strips of wood, old, long-dried vines ran in all directions. It was perfect. With the engine building to a great fuss, I stood, grabbing the trellis, yanking hard to free it from the brittle bounds.

With it released, I swung the wood out, leaning it against the brick stack and settled back in my place as my heart pounded against my efforts to calm my breath.

Most of the dead and dried vegetation had fallen, taking with it the great barrier it would have been. The foliage spread across the path, but it was too late; a pickup truck and a Land Rover Defender had rocked to a halt right in front of us.

Cassie went low, shuffling under me.

I crept in closer, my front against her warmth. She shifted. I pulled away, whispering an apology for getting so close.

She shook her head, dismissing my worry.

Like two meerkats I raised higher above her and watched through the great gaps in the wooden slats as each of the four doors of the bright red pickup swung open.

With the engines left running, four men jumped from the cab. Still taking in the sight, two more jumped from the Defender behind, each somewhere between eighteen and thirty, only one older by ten years, but he dressed the same age as the others. They wore a thin covering of facial hair, not unlike my own, but with tracksuits zipped up to the neck. In each of their hands they held a weapon of sorts; baseball bats, crowbars, long lengths of iron.

The driver of the pickup came around the front. In his hand he swung a long knife, the end curved and much wider than the handle.

I felt Cassie lean back towards me, her head making a slow turn as if to check I was watching. Both of us shook but forced ourselves not to dart into hiding as six pairs of eyes scoured the view, both knowing it was easier to see movement, so did our best to stay still.

They hadn't seen us yet. Their looks fixing on another target; the first house in the row of three on the opposite side.

In unison, each member of the group drifted, apart from two, one hanging each at the front and the back of their little convoy. The others headed to the door of the house they'd paid the most interest to.

We didn't hear the knocker go, only

IN THE END

the smash of the glass repeated, once, twice and then some more, over and over. The strikes soon hit wood and I felt the warmth of Cassie's body rattle, start and repeat until the wood gave way and the group disappeared inside.

With just the pair left, we stood our best chance to do something; do anything but wait to be found. We didn't know much, but knew it would be just as bad, if not worse, than if we were found by the soldiers.

Despite all I'd seen in these last few days, death wasn't the worst I feared for Cassie.

We did nothing but listen to the chaos ensuing, the racket pouring from the little cottage. Glass broke. The front windows smashed. Cupboards banged. Bags flew out of the door and the newly-made openings, the loot collected by one of the remaining pair in turn; the only time they'd take their stares from the road.

We knew what they were looking for, but it wasn't the same things as us.

The racket continued for a few

moments more until the sentry at the front raised on his toes. He was a tall man with no hair, his blue and white tracksuit stained a murky brown across the front.

We watching as his eyebrows pointed towards the sky, the baseball bat slapping as it swung into his cupped left hand.

We followed his look and then his slow smiling walk, the bat slapping back and forth, but we couldn't quite see what he walked towards because our angle was obscured by the house to the left.

The racket continued as he walked out of sight, the hard slap of wood echoing as it hit over and over against something we could only guess.

He was back in view, carrying a self-satisfied grin, wiping the end of the wood against his trousers. He looked up, stopping dead in front of us.

I felt Cassie's body stiffen; her right hand sought my leg. I grabbed her cold hand and squeezed.

Something had caught his attention. We'd heard the noise too, a distinct

IN THE END

sound coming from inside the house we were leaning against.

The guy's smile had gone and he turned in our direction, his eyes squinting, settling on the trellis and gave a great, elongated call.

"Boss."

52

The machete-wielding driver came out first, his expression fixed with a question to our guy with no hair. His attention soon followed in the direction the baseball bat motioned.

Neither had seen us, despite his stare in our direction. At one point I was sure he'd made eye contact, but it was clear their interest lay in the house. They were welcome to the surprise on the other side of the door.

The noise came again before they'd all come out of the first house, throwing bags and high-value goods into the back of the pickup. Each followed in the footsteps of their leader, their weapons at the ready, whistles and calls of excitement running through the air.

This time they knocked with a gentle wrap of knuckles at the front door as each walked into the house's shadow and out of sight.

This was our chance and we had no choice but to take it. Cold air plumed

IN THE END

around me once more as I pulled away from Cassie, with my hand still on the top of hers.

I led her, both of us bending over, running down the side of the garden whilst trying to keep our footsteps light. The fence stood six-foot-tall at our side and ran a long way out.

The search for safety ended too quick, the garden devoid of anywhere to hide with grass rolling out to the fence at the back. The only feature was a moss-covered wooden bench nestled to the side of the fence line, half way along.

Still we ran, Cassie behind me as I pulled her along with my hand at my back, not daring to slow or look around at the repeated smack at the front door.

I dragged her past me, pointing at the bench and motioning my instruction.

Her raised eyebrows confirmed she knew my plan but matched my fears; the bench looked as if it would collapse as we climbed.

Still there was no choice and we were upon it. I slowed. She didn't, instead leaping into the air with her foot on the arm as the wood complained.

It was too late; her hands were on the fence, legs carrying over as she disappeared the other side to a soft landing.

Not being able to match her momentum and commitment to the move, my feet slid across the moss as I climbed on the seat, resting a foot on the arm, feeling it sag under my weight.

Grabbing my hands onto the top of the fence, I looked back and saw net curtains in the windows lift. Landing on the other side, I held Cassie back, my eyes wide as I chanced a whisper.

"There's someone alive inside," I said and, as if to confirm, we heard the definitive sound of the front door swinging wide, rattling as it hit the wall behind, followed by a woman's shrill scream.

Cassie's eyes grew wide, matching my concern. We'd both thought the noise was from someone long-dead roaming around where the previous inhabitants of the body had lived. One of those creatures wouldn't care to lift the curtain to see what was going on in their garden.

We held there for longer than we should, both of us deep in thought, shaking our heads.

What if it was a family, or a group of decent people like us? What if it had been us, our friends inside?

The racket from before started up again; this time there was shouting, an argument, and we ran. There was nothing we could do, but we didn't race away, instead without either of us guiding, we ran back towards the houses, diagonally along the new garden and were soon in front of the neighbouring house.

I held Cassie back and peered around, inching forward at a snail's pace. They'd left no-one out the front.

I did a quick scan, seeing only the farmer dead again in the middle of the road, only knowing who it had been from the clothes; the head caved to a pulpy mess.

Grabbing Cassie's upper arm, I ran

across the front garden, leaping the small fence no taller than my knee. We ran across the road, turning only when across the opposite front garden and leaned against the wall as we looked back the way our friends were, whilst pulling deep breaths to regain control.

Cassie saw it first, nudging my arm with her elbow. I don't know whether we recognised it from before.

It didn't matter; it had seen us and veered from the bend in the road, heading in our direction.

The creature was slow and we should just have run away; should have just taken care of ourselves, but someone needed our help, even though we were in no place to give it.

Cassie was first to head into the garden, jogging around the house and slowing as we came around the second corner. She stopped, retreating to the safety of the brick. The two sentries were walking back to their posts.

Shouts were going on in the background but aimed elsewhere. I ran back the way we'd come and saw the creature still heading in the direction it would have last seen us; the direction I'd just shown my face again.

Back around the house I saw Cassie looking out. She stepped back and met my eye.

"They've seen it. The skinhead's heading its way," she said, her breath still coming fast.

I looked around, only just managing to pull back as the guy turned in our direction, his round head tilted at an angle. He wasn't as thick as his looks. He'd realised the direction the creature was taking and had altered his own course around the house to cut it off.

Our one chance was if the creature had locked onto the new threat, or promise of food, or whatever the motive of those animals could be.

I motioned for Cassie to follow back the way we'd come, but rounding the corner our shoulders sank as we saw the creature on us, having ignored the thug who was about to score himself three for the price of one.

53

The metal claw dug through the creature's bright-white shirt as Cassie drove home a high swinging blow, its features unchanging as it staggered back against her push to free the bar from its flesh.

I turned away, screwdriver out with the shaft pointing down from my fist. I was ready as I ever would be to defend us against the other animal about to appear from around the corner.

It wasn't the first time I'd wished I'd taken time to find a bigger weapon. Cassie's shoulders knocked at my back and I turned, watching the end of her swing, pulling the prongs from beneath its skin. My gaze caught the back door and its brass handle, all of a sudden fixed on why neither of us had tried it.

Cold in my grip, I held the handle hard like my life depended on what happened in the next few seconds and as it pivoted, the door swung open.

I stood in disbelief for longer than

IN THE END

a moment. My breath fell away and I eventually turned, still without saying a word.

My hand leapt forward to Cassie at my back, just in time to pull her out of the arch of a sweeping clawed attack. I yanked so hard she tripped backwards over the concrete step, the air rushing out of her lungs as I struggled to lessen her fall.

Still, I dragged her further in, only letting go to leap back to the door; pushing it closed with my shoulder and pulling back a split second before it could slam.

We still had a chance. The creature was on the other side, his hands batting useless against the glass.

I dropped to the floor with my back at the door, leaning hard in case it gained sentience and pushed the handle.

Cassie had the right idea and scurried up against the kitchen counter, staying low. Together we listened to each other's breath and the excited thud, thud, thud of beech against once-human flesh; listened to the satisfying crack of bone against concrete, our eyes fixed hard on each other.

I broke away for a moment, seeking out the lock only to find it empty. No key in the door.

The thing was down, at rest again. This time as it should be. Permanently.

The one who'd done the deed was not. He stood on the opposite side of the thin wooden door and all he needed to do was push the handle.

My gaze darted around the room. We were in a modern, open plan kitchen, a breakfast bar at my side, tall stools not so far away. Across all but one wall were dark granite-doored cupboards. I couldn't see any more detail and was too low to catch if there was anything of use on the counter tops. A long knife or a cleaver sitting in a knife block would be my preference; still I'd have to get in quick. Get in quietly, like the SAS, minus the years of training and the balls of steel.

I heard footsteps, feet scuffing on the concrete behind. Cassie's wide eyes told me she saw shadows moving closer.

IN THE END

There was no time to form a plan, to figure out the best course of action.

Slowly moving from my butt to my knees, I watched Cassie roll from where she'd settled; watched her walk on all fours, scrabbling with me at her back to the carpeted hallway.

The hall was bright and I continued to follow, continued to take her lead as she rose to her feet, jogging across the short gap to the stairs before carefully lowering to each step as she rose.

With my first step from the ground floor I heard a smash of glass and leapt up higher, pushing her on. She'd heard the sound too, the twinkling of the glass to the tiled floor from what we knew was the business end of the baseball bat raking around the rectangle of glass.

We were up the stairs and in the front bedroom, the floor creaking wild with each step as we took in the straight-edged double bed in the centre. A wardrobe ran across the far wall and a door tucked in the opposite corner.

A call came from outside, but we couldn't get the detail. The skinhead replied. He was in the house, his bat dragging along the worktops and knocking over whatever had been in its path, according to the constant shatter.

"Give us a hand. We've hit the jackpot."

54

Hoping it was the promise of the plush interior, the high-end kitchen, the mirrored chest of drawers, the flat-screen TVs we'd seen in each room and not the promise of our bodies for sport which gave rise to his excitement.

Motioning to Cassie, I stepped slow and cautious across the thick-piled carpet, heading towards the door I hoped held a secret escape hatch to a hidden basement.

Pulling the door open as fast as I dared dashed my hopes that the owners were paranoid, obsessed with their safety. At least they kept their hinges well oiled.

Inside stood a dark, narrow walk-in wardrobe with rows of shoes shelved on one wall from floor to ceiling. On the opposite side, clothes hung down from a pole, the floor piled with plastic boxes; everything neat, spick and span.

Stepping with care, we walked along the centre, bathing us in total darkness as I pulled the door closed. By touch we felt our way to the far end, pausing with each lull in the commotion below.

Our breath held as another voice joined in the laughter but resumed as the chaos increased in volume. The floor creaked as we arrived at the end and Cassie crouched as, wordless, I took an armful of clothes from the rail and scattered them across the floor. With a second armful, I sat pulling the clothes on top of our heads and trying my best to cover us both before moving only to pull the screwdriver back into my fist.

Cassie shuffled closer beside me as we heard the footsteps on the stairs directly below. Her breath stopped, if only for a moment, as their voices grew louder, their excitement cutting clean through the walls.

I tried to visualise the pair. One we knew; one we'd seen too much of already, his bald head fixed in my mind, probably forever. The other I could only guess, but it was the weapon my mind fixated on.

Now they'd reached the top of

stairs, the gently warping boards underneath confirming. Their voices soon moved to our side; they were in the main bedroom and right next to us.

I concentrated on their words, seeking their intention. Were they really such a threat? We'd only seen the skinhead defend himself.

The two voices were distinct, the skinhead's much lower. Still, the second had morphed into the sentry who'd stood at the back of the pack, a short guy with an iron bar in his hand. I knew it was wishful thinking.

Howls of animal excitement bounded through the walls, Cassie jumping as a window smashed and some feral chant rang out. A distant joyous call came back.

I reached across with my left hand and, finding Cassie's, I squeezed, wordless to reassure her they were looters only out for the prize; they weren't hunting us.

I didn't reassure myself. She squeezed back. I had no idea if I'd helped, but I stopped worrying as they started to talk.

"You hear where we're going next?" came the skinhead's voice, edged with concentration as I felt myself shaking, the first signs of my body thawing; warm for the first time in days.

"Yeah," came the slightly higher-pitched reply. "It's bullshit, right? Some hospital in St Buryan?"

"It's true," the skinhead said. "Some do-gooder set it up like a field hospital. Takes in those who can't look after themselves. The ones who didn't get out. Once we've done the houses down the road, that is."

I turned to Cassie, felt her hot breath on my face. Her hand moved, her arm curling around my mine, squeezing tight.

"I don't get it," came the other voice. "Pass the screwdriver." There was a long pause. "Fuck's sake."

"Careful," said the skinhead. "You damage it and I ain't protecting you."

"Shut up," came the reply. "Go on then, tell me the secret. Why the fuck are we going to a fucking hospital?

IN THE END

Someone ill?"

"Gordy's got the shits," he said, and they broke out in laughter. "Nah, seriously. They got supplies, right? Medicine, food and petrol. Stuff that's worth a thousand times what it used to be, at least while all this shit's going on."

I felt Cassie's arm squeeze tighter. There was silence in the other room and I worried somehow they might have felt it too.

"But won't there be lots of people there?" the short guy replied.

"Yes, you twat. The weak and the sick and those stupid enough to hang back and look after them. There'll be no one protecting them, except maybe a few old men. It'll be a walk in the park and we'll be king of the castle." The pair broke into a high laugh. "You look constipated."

"Fuck off," the other voice replied. "What I don't get is why we're getting all the TVs and stuff? There's no fucking juice."

"You twat. It ain't gonna be like this forever. We live in one of the richest countries in the world and you think they'll let this stop us? You're more of a mug than I thought. Give it a couple more weeks, maybe a month, this will all be over and we'll have a stock pile of TVs to sell when the internet's back on."

There was a pause and I pictured the short guy's expression changing, realisation lighting up his face.

I hoped he was right.

His reply was laughter and we went back to listening to the sound of their effort.

"Shove it on the bed," the skinhead soon said. "Then we'll have a look in that cupboard. I reckon there's sweet shit hiding away."

55

"What I don't get…" the short guy said, but was interrupted.

"What *do* you fucking get?" said the skinhead, as the volume of his laughter tailed off.

Cramps pulled at my calves, but I feared a stretch would make too much noise. Instead, I tried my best to relax and to keep concentrating on their words.

"Fuck off. Seriously though, what I don't get is how after only two days of this shit, there's already a field hospital." His voice got quieter.

A rush of excitement spiked up through my stomach as I realised they'd forgotten to check our hiding place.

"Only two days," the skinhead said, a vein of sarcasm running through his tone. I couldn't make out the rest of what he was saying.

I tried to stand and felt Cassie's warm hand reach for mine. Ignoring her pleading grip, I raised to my feet, although tentative at first as I searched out their decaying voices and any report from the floorboards under my feet.

The sound of their footfalls had been so obvious and I knew the same would be for where I stood. Still, I had to take the risk; just had to hear what was being said, despite each of their words becoming less distinct.

The hospital they spoke of sounded exactly the place we needed for Naomi. She was in no condition to travel, but maybe we could convince someone to come to her; a house call, if we ever got out of this cupboard.

I crept to the door, clutching the screwdriver in my fist, the voices getting louder than the difference a few steps should have made.

"Look. There's an evacuation on New Year's Eve. No one explains a thing and then it stops before it gets going, leaving behind whoever wasn't around to get the first call."

There was a long pause. I had no idea why. According to the floor boards and their changing volumes, they were back in the bedroom and moving around.

"Then, this morning, we saw those army helicopters buzzing around with their massive machine guns shooting at the ground. We must have hid three or four times. Right?"

Another pause.

"They seem to have stopped, too. Haven't seen any for a few hours. Right? But in all that time, someone's set up a field hospital and stocked it with supplies and found people willing to help. That's what I don't get."

The voice changed for the first time in a while.

"You think it's bollocks?" the skinhead said, his tone showing the first sign of a serious edge.

The short guy spoke again, finding a new confidence.

"I've got no fucking idea. I'm just saying it don't seem right, that's all."

The skinhead huffed a reply, his voice all of a sudden loud as if on the other side of the door.

I tried to calm my breath, fearing he was so close he could hear the pounding of my chest.

"I tell you what don't seem right. When a place like this gets done out like a New York apartment and is abandoned for ten months of the year because their London pad has better internet access and the local shop sells beard oil, leaving people like me, honest and hardworking, priced out of the market."

"Honest?" came the short guy's reply, and I heard what sounded like a pained call.

"Anyway, for once you might be right, but wrong somehow. I reckon there's more going on," said the skinhead.

"Huh?" said the short guy, their voices getting quieter.

I crept up closer to the door, but still I couldn't quite make out the words anymore. I looked back to Cassie, but even though we'd been in here for an age, my night vision needed at least something to work with. I was blind.

Swapping the screwdriver to my left hand, I found the handle with my right. Slowing my breath, I tried again to

IN THE END

listen.

    A hurrying call came from out on the road. I could only make out the tone.

    "It was four or five days ago, I think. It wasn't even mentioned on the news," came the skinhead's voice, suddenly clear. "Shit. The cupboard."

    I'd missed the interesting part of what was said, only the last few words coming through, clear as day. The floorboards under the carpet creaked, vibrating with a speed leaving me no time to decide; leaving me no time to hold the handle firm or to lean against the door or move my meagre weapon to my strongest hand before the light poured in and forced my eyes into a squint.

    I wasn't surprised to see the short guy standing there. Wasn't surprised to see him pull up to a stop, his right hand still on the handle as he swung it open, his left empty.

    He looked up from the floor and our eyes locked, our faces sharing the same shocked expression.

56

My right fist swung quicker than he could step clear. My flesh connected clean to his nose, crunching the cartilage with a sound I'd remember for a long time.

He stumbled backward, tripping over his feet, but I passed him by. It wasn't him I feared the most; the skinhead was who I had to deal with. He was the one I knew would run and raise the alarm, changing the odds to somewhere we would never have a hope to handle.

Surging past the short guy, I helped him stay down on the floor with a push of my hand to his shoulder. As I heard the ruffle of movement at my back, I kept my gaze fixed forward.

The skinhead had only just turned. Hugged between his arms was the TV once hung from the wall. My biggest fear was if he leapt forward; using the sixty diagonal inches as a weapon, it would be just as effective as the baseball bat lying

IN THE END

on the bed.

Instead, he stood dumbfounded, dropping the TV as I barrelled toward him, pointing my right shoulder square on his centre, adrenaline pushing the pain out of my head.

The edge of the TV smashed across his black-booted feet. He reeled back, arms still wide, presenting an open target for my shoulder as it barged into his chest and sent us both to the floor.

The air bellowed out of his lungs, his head slapping back against the carpet, the TV sandwiched between us as I fell on top of him, stars sparking across my vision from the new-found pain in my chest.

I closed my eyes but soon opened to find his closed, too; long enough for me to hover the screwdriver over his left eye before it opened.

I thought the skin around his eyes would break as they sprung wide, his pupils darting between the point of the screwdriver and my face as it hovered just above his.

My concern turned to Cassie, but

I couldn't move my attention away, knowing he'd have me on my side if I flinched even the slightest bit. But there was no sound of a struggle. I had to know.

"You okay?" came her hurried voice, before I had a chance to give my question.

I lurched the screwdriver down to his neck, pushing just enough so he knew I was serious. I looked back to see Cassie with her foot on the short guy's neck, the crowbar in a double-handed hold poised above her head. We'd got them and all without making a noise, but now we had to do something with our advantage.

My first thoughts were to tie them up and shut them in the cupboard, but we already knew they were getting impatient outside and would quickly find them, then come hunting for us.

My second thought was for a more permanent solution, but I couldn't stomach an intentional act; I couldn't take someone's life in cold blood.

"What now?" said Cassie, her voice

matching my worry.

"I don't know," I said. "Either way, we're fucked."

"We have to kill them," Cassie said.

The short guy whimpered, but the skinhead's face seemed to harden at the words.

"I can't," I replied. "And nor can you."

"Then what?" she said, her voice calm.

I sensed her gratitude for my words. We all had enough to worry about; already had enough to regret when we closed our eyes.

"We'll shove them in the cupboard, barricade the door. They'll be found soon enough," I said. "And we'll be gone."

"But they're going to the house?" Cassie said, a new tension in her voice.

"You going to be a good boy? Leave us alone?" I said, turning downward. I didn't believe him for one moment as he replied with a nod.

Still holding the screwdriver tight to his neck, I let myself slide from the TV and down to the floor. Keeping an even pressure, I got to my knees, trying to not reel from the pain in my chest.

"Push it off," I said, motioning to the TV.

He slid it to his right, holding his head as still as he could.

"Put your hands in your pockets," I said, and he pushed his hands into his skinny jeans. Leaving a thin red mark, I pulled the screwdriver back whilst keeping it poised, hovering and ready to strike.

A muffled gunshot shook the building. I couldn't stop myself from turning around to the window, my gaze meeting Cassie's at its side.

I watched her eyebrows rise with alarm, but too late I realised my mistake.

The screwdriver snatched from my hand, pain searing in the side of my chest.

57

As my head swung back, I watched the screwdriver twist in his hand. He'd hit me with the handle and relief rained down; I wasn't about to feel the delayed effect of a puncture to my chest.

There was still a chance, despite the pain, which was strong enough to force the breath from my lungs and to hamper my fists as they balled. I swung out my left arm, moving to block a second blow.

His grip was poor and the tool went spiralling under the bed as my arm swung wide against his.

Smashing my right fist against his cheek, he reacted with only the slightest flinch, barely showing the pain searing up through my fist had been of any worth.

A second blow and his hand was up at my head, clubbing my temple again and again with a speed I had no hope to match.

With each strike I felt the weight of my fist lighten, the edge of my vision blacking to form a circle like a Photoshop filter. The blows kept coming and so did mine, albeit slower.

He angled me side on while I fought to find a soft spot on his skull. His aim went wide, catching the back of my head.

My legs gave way and I rolled to the side with blackness falling all around, but I still felt the floor rise to jar against my back.

My eyes were open, but I hadn't missed time. He was rising to his feet, his face bloodier than I remembered inflicting. His features screwed up with rage; anger pouring in my direction but, rather than coming straight at me, he turned.

I followed his gaze to the short guy on his back. Him and Cassie were each holding the crowbar with both their hands, each trying to turn in the opposite direction and twist away out of the other's grip.

The skinhead had moved, twisted around and was launching himself away at pace. He was going for the baseball bat laying on the bed.

    My gaze dropped to the floor and I saw the screwdriver nestled in the thick pile of the carpet underneath. I rolled, barrelling my way with my arms tucked up in vain, but still with every rotation, every twist, the darkness closed in around my dizzying vision.

    Stopping only as I hit his feet, I reached out but before I could make contact under the bed, a size ten boot smashed my legs together just below the knee.

    My hands reeled back and I rolled away; a vision of Cassie still locked in battle cycled past my view.

    Hitting the wall, I once again stopped and saw the skinhead holding the handle of the bat in both hands, raised high above his head, one foot in front of the other in my direction.

    I tried to scrabble to my feet but the new pain in my knee just left me lying. Time was up.

    He was close enough and the swing of the bat committed. Instead of lunging forward, trying to get as close to him as

I could, I pushed up tight to the wall.

The bat swung, catching just the edge of my coat. I grabbed for the rounded end as he pulled it back, as he tried to raise it high.

Instead, he inadvertently helped me to my feet, but not for long. My left knee collapsed and I fell.

Pushing off the wall with my good leg, my arms grabbing around his waist, I propelled myself forward and him back, sending the bat square to his face as he dropped. He lay still for a moment, his eyes fluttering open and closed. I knew it would be just for a moment and saw the screwdriver glinting under the bed.

With one last thrust and using all my energy, knowing if this didn't work I would be spent and would leave me wide open for him to do his worst, my finger connected with the screwdriver handle.

The tip of my index finger touched the wooden end, edging it slowly closer. I looked back and saw him rolling at my side.

With my fingers clutched tight, I lunged the screwdriver down, only

IN THE END

able to aim at his last known direction. Before the driver connected, I saw the bat raised above my head and the screwdriver fell from my grip.

The bat swung down, hitting my shoulder with little force. Blood sprayed from his neck and I saw the crowbar embedded deep as he fell forward, showering me in his warmth.

His full, dead weight landed on my chest, leaving only my head uncovered to see Cassie behind him. Her eyes were wide and not able to hide the shock of what she'd inflicted.

Powerless to help, I watched as the short guy picked up a glass perfume bottle from the mirrored dresser and smashed it against her head, sending her sprawling, bloodied to the floor.

His eyes fixed in awe as he looked around the room, staring at his pal who couldn't be saved. At the crowbar as he pulled it from the neck dripping with blood. At me as he drew the crowbar high. At Cassie as he swung it down towards my face.

58

MACKENZIE

The first sign was the multi-coloured spotlights going dark, leaving the inside of The White Rock lit only with the emergency lights as they sparked to life over the double doors.

The music fell away as the spots stopped spinning, just the rumbling groans of confusion left behind as the last cold beer drained down my neck. I had no idea of the time, but we hadn't sung together so there must have been a long while to go before the telly chimed twelve times over.

The second sign was the long walk home. Mobiles and the landline were dead, no taxis responding and the car park emptied all too quickly.

Leaving with my best buddy and no other choice, we walked, tripping over our feet in the pitch black. Out in the middle of nowhere where we lived, the

IN THE END

darkness didn't mean a thing. Halfway to home the road lit with a constant stream of coaches, each in a hurry and none stopping to tell us the news. Before long they were gone.

Helicopters replaced their noise, the sky filling with blinking lights high above our heads. Between us, we gave up racking our brains through the possibilities. I didn't take too much note until we reached my house and found the place double locked, Mum and Dad not answering to the hammering. The car gone.

With nothing else we could do and no one to ask for help, we walked the next mile to Mike's house in a drink-fuelled haze with the flocks of helicopters coming and going over our heads.

His house was the same, but it's how he'd left it, his girlfriend having already stormed out on Christmas Eve; something to do with spending too much time with his mates.

The power was off there too and after ten minutes of rifling in drawers he'd never been in, we lit candles and started on the beer warming in the fridge.

I awoke still in my coat, coughing to clear acrid smoke from my lungs.

It was morning, I first thought, as I opened my eyes to the brightness in the room.

Realisation took only a moment. Fire had taken control of the other half of the room, the half where Mike had slouched as we both fell asleep. I couldn't see, but knew he wouldn't still be there. He couldn't sit in the centre of the flames.

Coughing up my lungs, I fell to all fours and tried to remember the layout; tried twice to navigate in the bright smoke which blocked each way I turned.

Somehow, I found my way to the door; found my way through the kitchen by the change of flooring. I found my way out to the front of the house in the freezing cold, with the early morning light just coming over the horizon.

I watched the house burning for no longer than a few seconds before I screamed and called out for help,

IN THE END

banging on the four neighbour's doors, but all in vain.

His house was engulfed as I returned; Mike was nowhere to be seen and the horrible truth sank in. He still sat in the corner where I'd left him to die. My only thoughts had been to save myself. Why the hell hadn't the fire brigade come?

I fell to the ground in the middle of the road and there I lay, tears streaming as the fire warmed my face and the cold bit into my back.

After not too long, I headed back to the first house, to where people had lived who I didn't know. I smashed my elbow through the glass in the front door; had the place open in no time at all.

Inside was decked out for Christmas. Long lines of decorations ran along the hall ceiling, tinsel wrapped around the phone just inside the door. I batted the stuffed Father Christmas to the floor and pulled up the receiver, pushing the three digits even though I hadn't registered the tone I needed to hear.

I let the phone drop as no one answered and stared out at the flames as the roof caved in on Mike's house. He'd lived there for five years. He'd bought the place with the girlfriend, but would have to sell; not anymore. It was someone else's problem.

It was warm in the house and I wandered around, trying to think of what I should do next. We lived in the middle of nowhere, all the cars gone. I would have to walk to find out what the hell this was all about.

The rest of the house was decorated the same. Not one corner had escaped the cheap, plastic-coated decorations. The tree sat in the corner of the front room; the presents gone from underneath; the lights washed out. Unlit, the switch not working.

I sat in a great armchair and dust flew up. I could smell the owners and stood. A shadow passed the window. There was someone in the road; someone had heard my calls and ambled down the street in awe of the fire.

IN THE END

Rushing out of the front door, I saw a young, twenty-something brunette, my eyebrows rising; things were looking up. Her clothes were a little ragged, jeans had some dark mark across the front and her top was ripped open, a white bra exposed. I could see her full cups. Things really were looking up.

She hadn't noticed me yet. Her eyes stared at the fire as her feet rose slow, one after the other, heading towards where my friend had died.

"You okay?" I said from the doorway and she turned to meet me.

Above her eyes shined a great bruise; blood had dried as it had rolled down from the injury. Her gaze latched onto mine. She was pale and seemed a little dazed. It was clear she'd been in a car accident and I looked down the road for the car but saw nothing.

Running inside, I pulled a coat from the hook and rushed back over, offering out the warmth. She couldn't take her eyes off me. Things were looking up, but first I needed to get her to the hospital.

59

Her hand reached out, batting the coat to the side. I took a step nearer, raising the best smile my banging head could manage but I drew back as I caught more than just the acrid smoke still burning inside my nostrils.

Turning on the spot, I searched again as I tried to figure out how I would get her to the hospital when I couldn't even get myself a ride.

I stepped around her, attempting again to push the coat to her shoulders, but she twisted and followed my turn in stiff, unnatural movements. I started to think maybe the head wound had done substantial damage.

Reaching her hands out, the smell of the acrid smoke intensified as she grabbed hold of the arm of my jacket. With a tremendous grip, she wouldn't let go, her mouth opening and closing, leaning to pull me closer.

I backed away, protecting my hand as she drew it to her mouth. She was

IN THE END

in serious trouble, her brain damaged. I hoped the doctors could do something about it.

I pulled my arm clear and stepped back, over and again as she reached out, unrelenting. The neighbour's coat fell from her shoulders.

The roar of an engine broke the cycle. Finally, someone was coming who could help the injured woman to safety.

Stepping backwards, I carried on around in a circle, with her continuing to follow in the middle of the road as I kept an eye on the building rumble.

I expected to see one of those coaches from the night before, or a fire engine, an ambulance, police maybe; hope holding out they weren't a thing of the past.

I hadn't expected the Land Rover Defender rocking on its squealing tyres as it barely made the corner. I hadn't expected to see someone in the driver's seat I recognised more as he grew closer. Although still hopeful, the shine of his bald head and the snarling grin couldn't have been anyone else.

It was Damien Edwards. We'd gone to school together; we were at the same school, at least. He was a loner. He was someone who hung at the periphery of our large group, but no one would have called him a friend. He was troubled. Conflicted. One moment full of confidence, talking for hours about nothing at all, the next bullying some kid; whoever he'd picked out at random to break the boredom.

I'd rarely been his target, but I'd watched many others in his crosshairs. He'd done all the maturing he ever would long before he joined halfway through secondary school. He was the kid who'd pulled the legs from a spider, then ate the rest just to show you he could. When we laughed, he'd tell us to go fuck ourselves, punching out in a random direction. He'd been a skinhead ever since he'd joined; we had no idea if his hair could grow or if he shaved every day.

He'd left school at sixteen like the rest of us and got a job, but was fired more times than I could count.

IN THE END

He didn't play nice with others. Each time I saw him, usually for an awkward conversation in the pub, he'd have another tattoo to show off. Now he drove down the road in a car which couldn't be his, wearing a broad smile as he saw me fending of the mentally damaged young woman who needed help.

"Mackenzie. Fucking knew you'd get left behind. Did they miss you because you're so fucking short?" he said as he pulled up.

When I didn't reply, he turned to Mike's house as more of the roof caved to the ground. "He toast?" he asked, eyeing up the burning house.

I didn't know what to say, distracted by the ever-increasing ferocity of the woman lurching towards me.

"She fighting you off?" he said, eyeing her up and down.

I looked back and he must have seen my harried expression; he jumped from the driver's seat as he pushed the door wide.

Forcing the woman away again, I noticed the triangle of the long knife gripped tight in his right leather-gloved hand.

"You don't get it?" he said, laughing as he spoke.

I shook my head. I didn't have a clue what he was talking about.

"You think she's fit, right?"

I stepped back, not responding. The woman swapped her attention to Damien and let me step back without following. I watched as he offered out his left hand.

The woman snapped her teeth together before lurching forward and biting down with a snap as she just missed the thick leather. Damien grabbed her by the hair before she could rise for another strike and her eyes rolled to see what had her in a hold.

"She's not there anymore," he said, twisting her face toward me.

I shook my head. What I saw was a woman in trouble. I tried to protest, but the words wouldn't come.

"Still don't get it, do you?"

When I didn't reply, he thrust her head forward. Her bloodshot eyes snapped wide, latching onto mine. I

IN THE END

jumped back and she lurched again, her hands grabbing my arms. I stumbled backwards to the ground and she came after me, her body and the wicked stench falling.

I tried to scrabble back, pushing hard with my legs, but they couldn't move against her weight.

Her head punched forward. She had my arms pinned to my side. Her breath stank like rotting shit, the stench forced out with her every effort. I looked deep into her eyes, hoping to see I'd been right, but there was something missing; everything missing. Only decay left.

In my peripheral vision I saw Damien's boot arrive by my head and he leant down.

"You get it now?" he asked; his breath didn't smell too much better. His hand reached out to her hair, pulling her head up.

She didn't complain; her mouth continued to snap open and closed.

"Choose. I haven't got all day."

I turned to see the sun glinting off his knife as he knocked her right grip from my arm and pushed the handle of the blade into my hand, letting go of her hair.

Her head snapped forward and without both my hands to keep her at bay, I watched her wide mouth fill my view.

60

Teeth snapped, grazing my nose and her head pulled back, saliva dripping cold to my cheeks as she dived for a second try.

Despite knowing she was trying to take off my face, every muscle in my body felt tight and wouldn't release. My mind couldn't let me muster the will to take her life, my hand frozen around the handle of the knife.

She lurched forward again, her perfect white teeth snapping together. I knew there was something wrong, something alien; absent, but I couldn't put my finger on what it was.

I did the only thing possible in the moment. Closing my eyes, I gave up.

Feeling her weight collapse over me, the air forced from my lungs and my eyes shot open. I rolled her to the side, turning away as her blood, cool as ice, splattered across my face.

Panting for breath, I looked up and saw Damien standing over me, a wide, yellow-toothed grin beaming down, blood dripping from a paring knife in his right hand.

"I saved your life, you pussy, now you owe me," he said, and snatched the knife from my hand. "Welcome to the new world, baby," and jumped back in the Land Rover, leaving me lying, panting on the floor.

With his door slamming closed I stood staring at the body, her brown hair still perfect with just a thin line of blood running slowly from the wound at her temple.

"Get in," Damien shouted, but I didn't move. I was still transfixed on the dead woman at my feet. He repeated, his tone sharper. This time it wasn't a request.

It was time to choose again and I took the cowardly way out, climbing into the passenger seat, knowing I'd failed the test. I couldn't protect myself and knew the only way I was going to survive was to surround myself with those who could do what needed to be done.

We didn't speak. The hierarchy had

IN THE END

been established. Instead, I watched out of the window, stared along the empty roads; the parked cars all gone, too. The streets empty of life; only farm animals out in the fields.

We drove for about ten miles, not seeing a soul while the fires on the horizon grew in number. When eventually we saw people in their cars, they were queuing. I could see some sort of checkpoint way off into the distance, but I couldn't even muster the courage to tell Damien to stop the car and let me out as he turned the wheel away, following his instinct to keep from anything official.

His only reaction was when we came across a small group of what seemed to be people he knew. I was barely introduced to the four when their intent became clear; they were breaking into a small group of houses, helping themselves to everything of value.

Damien was happy to go along and so was I, apparently. I did what I was told, stayed at the back of the two cars while Damien was posted at the front and we watched, waited; me with an iron bar I'd been handed, Damien with a baseball bat.

I didn't know my role until I spotted someone coming up the road, their walk so much like the woman who'd been killed whilst on top of me, as were the five others following behind.

My muscles froze, giving the same reaction as before. A tension gripped my chest and my limbs locked up. I could barely muster the words to call Damien, my voice high and feminine when I eventually did.

I watched on, managing only to move well back while Damien called for the others. They exploded out, bombarding each of the things my head couldn't give a name. They barely had time to fight back under the unflinching onslaught. All I could do was lose whatever I had left in my stomach on the side of the road as one by one they passed me, looking down their noses, my eyes to the ground.

And so it went on for the next two days. I'd watch as they'd go around

IN THE END

the houses, smashing down the doors, pulling out everything which once had a value. Most times I would just have to stand there; every so often I would call and have Damien take care of those we happened upon. I tried once more to build myself up, to take control, but my body wouldn't let me, even though it had become obvious those things weren't recognisable as human. I was barely of use, no more than a lookout and it was how I was treated.

In the evening, before darkness took over, we'd head back to a warehouse on a tiny industrial estate. All the buildings were abandoned, like everywhere else. There we'd pile up what we'd found; cash, electronics and food. They'd start a fire; burning pallets soaked in petrol for warmth and we were each handed our share of the spoils.

I was given the smallest share, barely a portion, but I didn't complain. I knew there was no one to come along and help if they kicked my ass and left me for dead.

The next morning, I woke up

determined to change my situation. Fixed on getting past my fear, I was intent on getting respect.

We started the day like the previous. It was a small group of houses, but we didn't get any visitors. With each downward look from the others, my resolve increased. I wanted to be treated as an equal and the only way was to ditch whatever was stopping me from killing these creatures.

The second set of houses proved more promising. Not long after we'd arrived I saw one of those creatures heading towards Damien's end; a farmer it looked like from how he'd dressed.

Damien dealt with it. I followed up behind as I saw another, but my chance had gone. He'd despatched him before I got near.

I followed him to the garden and spotted the inside of the house, a glitzy, modern style full of loot. My mum would have gone mad; she hated anything but the traditional.

Damien seemed pleased when I pointed it out and let me break in,

IN THE END

allowing me to tag along to gut the place and letting me talk now we were alone.

About to finish and being called back to the road, I opened a cupboard door and there stood one of the creatures. It launched an attack, knocking me to the ground, rushing past me and going for Damien.

I hadn't frozen. I knew this was my chance, but another launched out, blindsiding me.

Shaking off the blow, I saw her on Damien. She was easy to deal with and I pushed her to the side. It was my turn to save him, to get even.

Snatching the crowbar from the nasty wound in Damien's neck, he fell on top of the creature who'd attacked me. This was the moment I would prove my worth.

61

LOGAN

"Noooo," I screamed, with the short guy's gaze intent on mine, the word coming slow as adrenaline pushed my senses to the limit for what I knew could be the last time.

I watched his eyes change shape, saw them widen; a light blinking on behind. The crowbar still swung but veered off to the side and I felt the pressure on my chest as it crashed down on the slumped, shiny smooth head of the man already dead.

In his eyes I saw the confusion, saw his battle; saw Cassie rise high, my screwdriver in her hand and watched as he noticed her, but not until it was too late, the tip of the driver plunging past his eye, buckling his legs. His arms fell moments after, the crowbar clattering to the floor alongside his body.

I tried scrabbling up, tried pushing

IN THE END

the dead weight from my chest. It had only been moments, but the smell already caught in my lungs; flesh putrefying.

Cassie stood, her mouth agape and breath panting hard, blood rolling down the side of her face. She turned, saw my struggle and helped me pull the body by the arm.

I saw the moment she caught the fetid smell; her nose turned up, expression hardened. The body was off and I knelt to the bed, wiping my face of blood on the once-pristine covers. Turning as I climbed to my feet, I saw the end of the crowbar diving deep through the skinhead's eye socket as Cassie let go.

A second booming gunshot rattled the house; a shotgun, I was sure, as we caught each other's glances before running to the window.

From our new vantage point, we watched the older of the looters staggering backwards along the path from the cottage we'd last seen his group attacking. Behind him, he left a trail of blood, his face fixed through the open door.

A flash of light lit up the inside of the neighbour's cottage, followed by a third boom which came louder than we'd yet heard. The guy's body shook, but he hadn't been the target.

"Look," Cassie said, and I turned, following her bloodied, outstretched finger in the direction their cars had first arrived.

Blinking away the drying blood, I rubbed my eyes, hoping when I opened them the first vision would have gone. As my view cleared, I saw twenty or more of what appeared to be old-age pensioners in gowns, jumpers and tweed jackets, each walking with a new lease of life; their posture hung over and their pace slow, but still they looked too pronounced, too put together for the age they'd been before they'd died.

"Where the hell are they all coming from?" I asked, not expecting an answer.

"We weren't the only ones left behind," Cassie said, as another gunshot rattled the glass. As our heads turned

IN THE END

the length of the window, we caught sight of the old guy I'd seen lifting the net curtain as we'd jumped from his garden, his hands rushing to reload a long shotgun.

Continuing the turn with speed, we twisted our heads in the same direction. We were both desperate to look past the buildings blocking our view, trying our best to reach out to know if our friends were okay. Could they hear the shots? Would they be ready if we couldn't protect them?

"We need to...," I was saying when I turned, but Cassie was already moving, already grabbing the baseball bat from the floor. Already at the door.

I followed, holding my chest and limping on my knee, only stopping to pull the crowbar from the skinhead's eye whilst trying not to listen as it sucked out from the deep wound.

"Get to the cars," I shouted, as I followed down the stairs, rushing as fast as I could to get to where she waited at the backdoor smashed to the side, weaving around the obstacle course of

TVs, consoles, DVD players and plastic boxes overflowing with designer shoes.

Out of the door, Cassie looked left and right. Our eyes met only for a moment, hers dropping to my knee as I leaned heavy against the wall. She paused, offered me the baseball bat and I shook my head; I didn't need a walking stick.

Around the corner of the building I waited at her shoulder; I was about to edge my way out when another gunshot ripped through the air, followed by a searing howl of pain.

My search for the sources of both noises interrupted as Cassie was off, running fast between the houses and not looking back. She was out and across the tarmac and crouched down by the side of the pickup, its rear overflowing with boxes and gadgets and all before I had cleared the gap.

I waited at the front of the house, seeing the procession of the elderly impossibly close, almost at the rear of the Land Rover.

Cassie's gaze was darting

IN THE END

everywhere, but she couldn't see another man backing away from the door of the looter's cottage. He dressed the same as the others with a long kitchen knife high in his right hand, the left held up empty. She couldn't see the body lying out on the path leading away from the house; it was the man we'd watched emerge, trailing blood.

I watched her flinch as another shot raced from the house; watched as the guy dropped the knife, collapsing to the floor and hoped the neighbour with the gun knew we weren't part of the looter's gang.

I watched the car knock her back as a shot slammed against the front of the pickup, exploding the front left tyre.

Cassie turned, saw me standing between the buildings. She held her palm out for me to stay put, but I looked away as I saw one of the tracksuits appear. He was running hard from the back of the vigilante's cottage toward the Land Rover and its rumbling engine.

The group of dead elderly inmates of a forgotten nursing home all twisted in his direction in a uniform turn. Somehow, his speed had caught their collective attention and they ignored Cassie altogether as they changed their course, veering towards the passenger door.

He didn't make it. A flash came from the doorway and the gun lowered for the reload as the shot slammed against his tracksuit, his wails of pain confirming it wasn't a clean kill.

Still the creatures headed in his direction, his vocal agony seeming to urge them on.

I ran, or tried, hobbling and almost collapsing on my knee each time I put down weight.

Cassie had seen my move and made her own, leaping towards the Land Rover. The creatures saw her run and the group split down the middle, half changing their course.

Still, she made it to the door and pulled it wide. She was in, despite the wrinkled hands scrabbling and bones crunching as she slammed the heavy door hard. Grinding the gears, she

IN THE END

kangarooed around the pickup.

    I changed my course and headed for the passenger door. I was going to make it, but as I turned to the cottage I saw the old man in the doorway, his face wet with tears and both barrels of the shotgun pointed in my direction.

62

With the Land Rover bucking, Cassie struggled at the controls as I came around the passenger door with no shots fired and my limbs still attached.

We were making slow progress, even once I'd sat in the passenger seat, still only just drawing alongside the cottage. I couldn't help but tempt fate and, turning to stare at the door, I hoped he'd not just cleared a jam; hoped he wasn't reloading a shell and wouldn't be repointing both barrels before pulling the trigger.

He stood still with his expression set harsh, the shotgun pointed to the ground and an old woman leaning on his shoulder. Her hand moved, hugging his waist. Her gaze fixed on mine, a kind smile on her creased face. We were out of their view in a moment.

"Swap over," I said, and Cassie stared back, her face set in a terrified expression as she let go of the wheel and lifted her feet.

IN THE END

Our heads rocked forward as the engine stalled. Fists hammered at the windows, the daylight dulling as torsos crowded, their flesh weak against the glass.

Checking my door, I made sure it was locked, Cassie matching as she questioned with just her expression.

"Climb over," I said, and watched as she rose from her seat, awkwardly curling her left leg across the centre console.

Right soon followed left, then came her body. For a moment she hovered above me, but her hands gave way and she collapsed to my lap.

My senses lit and not just with the pain as I felt her warmth through our clothes. Her hands were on my thighs, flat, drawing me in.

Clenching my teeth, I hoped time would not move on but the soft hammering of the windows reminded of our situation; reminded us we had to get going and had to move, had to get away from those things and from anyone who wouldn't care for what we'd just shared.

Pushing her high against my pain, she hovered above me with her hands on the door and I slid as I issued a tirade of foul language before slapping down into the driver's seat.

The car was surrounded with the elderly creatures, wrinkled skin, thin hair and the smell already radiating as if the windows were wide open.

I turned the key and the engine sprung to life, the car leaping forward just before it died. Glancing at Cassie, she looked through each of the windows as she backed away, moving as close as she could to the centre.

I pulled the car out of gear and turned the key again, letting the engine roar. The creatures reacted as we moved, the front four disappearing below the bonnet, the bull bars pushing them down; the suspension and hefty tyres hiding most of the sensation of their bones crushing as we drove.

Twisting to watch the crowd follow, Cassie called out before I could round the corner.

"Stop," she said, slamming her hand

on the dashboard. "You're leading them to the cottage."

I hit the brakes hard, having to lock my arms to stop myself from hitting the windscreen.

She was right. In the mirror I watched the group of fifteen or more barely stumble as they crossed over their fallen.

"Turn around," she said, and my gaze caught her. Her eyes were wide and serious.

I gunned the engine, turning the wheel full lock to the right before coming to a rest and staring at the pack, their stares locked in our direction.

Cassie had taken a wide paper map from the dashboard.

"They've marked where they've been," she said, turning the paper so I could look from the windscreen and to the black crosses scoring out several clusters of houses radiating out in a circle.

Looking forward, but only for a moment, my gaze returned to the paper and I found a wider concentration of buildings with a large cross pinpointing a darker area. I nodded in its direction and she let the map drop.

"Let's lead them away," I said.

Letting the speed build, I took out a cluster of three and split the group as their heads snapped forward, denting the bonnet one after the other.

Watching in the mirror, I slowed as each turned and started to follow.

Cassie twisted in her seat and nodded, picking up the map and concentrating on the marking I'd pointed out.

"It's the hospital they were talking about," she said, not looking up from the page. "That's where we need to be."

"What about the others?" I replied, using all my willpower not to speed away, taking us as far from those things as I could.

"What have we achieved?" she asked. "Did you hear what those two were saying?"

"About the hospital?"

"And everything else."

I shook my head. I'd heard so

IN THE END

much, most of it I didn't understand.

"I hope they can help Naomi," I replied, nodding.

"We can try," she said, and reeled off the directions. "It's about ten miles, but take it slow," she said, peering between the map and back through the rear window.

I drove as she instructed, keeping those things in sight for a good five minutes before we were confident they weren't going to turn back.

Still, I didn't speed. I was mindful of what could be around each corner, expecting someone to jump out at any moment and curse my dreams again.

It took longer than I'd wanted for the roads to widen to anything more than a narrow two-lane.

After twenty minutes of tentative driving, we were within two finger widths of our destination, on the map at least. Ahead sat a large car, a Mondeo, resting with its nose in the hedge, another the other side, narrowing the way. The gap looked just wide enough for us to fit.

With no-one around, no sign of

life, we agreed without words it must have been one of the first checkpoints. Neither of us questioned for long as the engine note changed, spluttering and giving me cause to interrogate the dashboard.

I watched the petrol light which must have been bright orange since I'd taken the controls. The engine soon died and I dipped the clutch, hoping to get every inch of forward movement.

Rolling to a stop long before I wanted, I was out in the cold.

Cassie stood on the door sill, peering up high over the hedgerow on one side and the dry-stone wall on the other, watching as I limped around the car and opened the back door to find the inside empty.

Taking the map, baseball bat and the tyre iron I found tucked under a panel at the rear, we left the safety of the car and walked along the road.

"Ten minutes," Cassie said, her expression bunching as she looked down at my limp.

I was glad she couldn't see the pain

IN THE END

in my chest or she might have insisted she go for help alone.

Ahead, the two cars grew in our view. The sound of an animal moving within the hedge turned us inward. I looked behind and saw the long road stretching away, knowing how perfect this place would be for an ambush; an ideal location for looters to take us at will.

We walked on, boosted by the utter silence until a twig snapped in the hedge-line at our backs. With my hand tight around the cold iron, there was nothing there as I turned.

It took a few moments as we walked again to notice the tall pillars of undergrowth which hadn't been there before; to notice the two tall towers with cold barrels open in our direction.

Only when the deep voice made me jump did I realise the camouflage had worked so well.

"Drop the weapons."

63

    I was sure we'd be dead before my iron clattered to the ground. As the ringing echo of the metal died, the beech of the bat hitting the tarmac with less of a fuss, we still stood upright as my heart felt like it would burst from my chest. I looked down the barrel of the gun as I tried to make out where the dense covering of leaves ended and the person began.

    After more than a few moments of frustration and nothing else, other than our joints starting to seize, I wondered if I'd dreamt the whole situation up; if in the terror of the moment I'd missed an issued command.

    It wasn't until I heard the rumble of a large engine in the distance and saw grey exhaust smokepluming high in the air, I knew sure enough a truck would appear around the corner and was taken back to the moment we'd seen the first helicopter.

    Could it have been only this

IN THE END

morning?

    With the rush of elation still fresh, the certainty we'd been saved switched off in an instant as the machine gun had rained down, doing more than breaking our hearts. I wouldn't let myself be tricked this time and pushed away the hope our nightmare would be ending.

    Sure enough, only moments later, an olive-drab truck with a heavy fabric rear cover rocked on its suspension around a distant corner.

    Rolling into view, it stopped just before it would have to negotiate the gap between the improvised roadblock. The driver stayed put as it ground to a stop and four soldiers in camouflage fatigues bounded from the back, their rifles trained in our direction.

    "Hands on your heads," the lead guy said in a commanding voice.

    Like the others, stripes of dark paint ran down his face, his body covered in armour and thin, yellow-tinted glasses ran across his eyes.

    When I raised my hands and Cassie did the same, they seemed to relax like they were testing we understood language.

I looked in her direction, raising my eyebrows, hoping she understood the sentiment. They hadn't killed us yet.

They still hadn't ten minutes later. It was only after patting us down and starting to walk to the truck at their command, did they stand back and raise their guns, screaming for me to explain how I'd hurt my leg.

The explanation seemed only to elicit more questions as one of the four stepped away, his gaze fixed on me as he mumbled something into the boom microphone swinging down from his helmet.

Despite my insistence it was by the size ten boot of a looter, they cuffed my hands tight behind my back with the plastic ties before I went any further.

Hoisting me up the back of the truck whilst paying constant attention to my leg, they sat me on the hard metal bench running along the centre. A soldier sitting opposite, his hand on his holstered sidearm.

IN THE END

With Cassie sitting the other end, the heavy fabric folded down to cover our view, light coming only from the dim red torches hanging overhead.

I felt the truck reversing a long way before we turned. They wouldn't talk; were silent to my questions, but I soon went quiet myself, reeling from the realisation we weren't riddled with holes and our throats hadn't been cut.

It was only when we jolted to a stop, the cover lifted and I saw the white letters against the blue sign, I realised we'd arrived where we'd been aiming for all along. St Buryan Hospital.

Squinting to the view, I watched soldiers standing guard around the two-storey building. As I was lowered, I caught more guards at each of the two entrances; groups of four walking around the perimeter, peering out along the road with binoculars, others helping to finish raising giant sheet-metal fences.

Guided side by side, we were escorted by the four soldiers through a set of doors, disinfectant clawing at our nostrils as our slow, uneven footsteps echoed in the long hallway.

We didn't travel far, stopping as commanded at two doors side by side. On each door loomed a handwritten paper sign. MALE. FEMALE.

Ushered to the respective doors, I reared back as they opened from inside. Feeling the pressure of a hand at my back, I glanced to Cassie to see her already looking in my direction with wide eyes and raised eyebrows.

I tried my best to reassure her with a thin smile, but I couldn't do the same for myself. Turning back, I saw a man in a white coat stood just inside with a wide grin on his face, beckoning me in with a wave of his hand.

I stepped across the threshold.

The soldiers didn't follow.

64

"We need your help," I said, almost breathless, the bright white room opening out with each step.

His wide, toothy smile remained fixed, but his beckoning halted as I caught sight of two soldiers standing behind the door. In their hands were yellow Taser stun guns held at forty-five degrees, their arms folded at their fronts. Although they'd drawn me in, they weren't the first thing I'd seen.

I turned back to the dentist chair in the centre of the room, my attention following down the side of the arm to the two sets of clamps hanging down, each fixed with four bold, oversized screws. On the other side stood a tall stainless-steel table with dull metal instruments resting on a green paper cloth.

It was only then I noticed the nurse in dark blue scrubs holding a stainless-steel kidney bowl. Inside rested a long syringe filled with a red liquid.

I felt the ties snipped at my back

and my hands swung free around to my front.

White coat guy ushered me towards the chair as the door closed and locked at my back.

"Please take a seat," he said, the smile still there.

"We need your help, please," I replied, shaking my head. I squinted in the first artificial light I'd seen for over two days.

He took a step forward. I didn't need to step back to know at least one of the soldiers mirrored his movement, at the same time exposing the Taser's prongs.

"What is this all about?"

The white coat's sympathetic smile widened.

"We have to be sure. Please, take a seat, sir," he said, and took another step toward me.

"Is it about my leg?"

His smile widened even further, shaking his head to the two at my back.

"Do you know what's happening outside?" he asked.

IN THE END

I raised my eyebrows, not voicing my reply.

"Yes, of course you do. Then you'll understand why we can't take any chances. We have to check you out. If you prefer, you can just take your clothes off here. Once we're sure, you can be on your way."

"We came here to get help."

The white coat raised his eyebrows, at least pretending to be interested.

"It's our friend, Naomi. She's been bitten," I said, and watched as he turned to the nurse; her eyebrows raised. They shared a look of interest.

"How long ago was this?" he replied.

I had to think for a moment; so much had happened.

"This morning," I said, trying not to remember the details.

"How many hours?" the nurse added, her voice impatient.

I no longer had any reference of time. I'd never been one to wear a watch and my phone had died long ago.

"A couple of hours, maybe three."

Their faces sank and I swapped

my attention between them, but still he spoke as if going through the motions.

"Did you stop the bleeding?"

I gave a fast nod.

"After how long?" he replied.

I shook my head again and tried to remember. She was bitten out in the hills and we'd dragged her into the cottage as quickly as we could. She was still bleeding when we got her inside, but was she when I had to defend the building? When Andrew and Zoe made it back?

"Half an hour, maybe," I replied, hopeful.

His face fell further and he shook his head.

"There's nothing we can do for her, I'm afraid."

I felt the breath fall from my lungs.

"There must be something?"

"We can make her more comfortable, or..." he said, and turned to the nurse, "we can stop the worst from happening."

My eyes widened and the nurse took over.

IN THE END

"We can stop her from turning," she said, her expression jaded, but maybe there was a hint of compassion behind.

A radio squawked somewhere in the room; an urgent voice calling though, but using words I couldn't quite catch.

"Now, sir, we need to get on. We have more to deal with than you can imagine," the white coat said.

I turned, hearing movement at my back. The right of the two soldiers had stepped forward again and held the Taser out.

"Easy way, or the other?" the soldier said, tilting his head.

I unzipped my jacket. As I pulled off each item of clothing, I felt the gaze of the white coat and the nurse peering over every inch of my skin.

The white coat stepped forward as I pulled down my jeans. The soldier stepped right to my back as the white coat peered down to examine my knee.

Nodding to the nurse and the soldiers, he stood and looked me in the eye.

"Everything, sir," he replied.

I drew a deep breath and turned to the nurse.

"It's cold in here," I said, and pulled down my boxer shorts.

The radio crackled again as I drew on my clothes, only just in time to be hurried back through the door and shoved to the side of the corridor by a blur of soldiers carrying one of their colleagues, horizontal, between them.

His hands and legs were bound as they rushed him into the room. I just about saw a blooded gauze pushed against his hand with blue gloves.

The door closed and the guard who'd stood there as I'd arrived turned his fallen expression away from the door and looked at me, his face pale.

"Do you know him?" I said.

The soldier didn't respond, his face staring at mine like he was looking to share his pain.

He gave a shallow nod as I held my expression fixed.

"I've got someone like that," I

IN THE END

replied. "She can't be helped, but it's not always a death sentence."

His eyes narrowed, longing for the rest of my words.

"We know someone who didn't die."

He looked to my side and straightened up, coming to a salute.

"Really?" came a female voice, and I turned to see a woman, her hair silver white, green eyes fixed intent on mine.

Cassie walked by her side from the direction of the other door whilst straightening her clothes with her face full of alarm.

"Where are they?" the woman asked, stepping into my personal space.

I could feel electricity crackle off her words, my blood rushing with panic as if I'd just made a big mistake.

65

"Can you help us or not?" I asked, stepping back.

Her feet stayed put as she leaned forward, her unblinking eyes fixed with an intensity which made me want to turn and run the other way.

I didn't run. I didn't turn away; instead, I took a step forward and spoke again. "I need to speak to someone in charge, or we're leaving."

"You are," the woman said, the wrinkles on her facing relaxing. Her stare dissipated as she took a step back, her hand pushing out and lips curling in a forced smile.

"I'm Doctor Lytham. I apologise for our introduction. I'm sure you can understand we're still finding our feet here."

I squinted towards her, but Cassie seemed to shake her head.

"What is this place? Why weren't you evacuated?" I said.

A panicked scream raced across my

nerves. Cassie's gaze caught mine as we twisted to the room I'd just left.

The soldier standing at the door hadn't reacted. He was left unmoved as the sound died. Only then did he raise his eyebrows, asking the doctor a question without words.

Turning back, her face hadn't changed, her arm sweeping out to guide us down the white corridor. Her head gave the smallest of shakes, dismissing the guard's unvoiced question.

She turned and walked down the corridor, her heels clicking along the hard floor.

"What are they doing to him?" I asked, my voice more urgent. Cassie was already following. I hurried behind, despite my instinct to get clear of this place; I would not leave her with this woman who reminded me so much of Cruella De Vil.

Every few steps, the antiseptic smell built, the taste coating my tongue as we passed door after door, each with a porthole window painted white.

We rounded a corner to find it much

the same, with two guards stood either side, their backs to us. As we passed to the click of her heels, I turned back to see neither of the soldiers would meet my gaze.

"Did you work at the hospital before?" I asked, as I hurried to catch up.

She turned, smiling high with her cheeks, her head shaking.

"There wasn't a great call for my specialism in this corner of Cornwall."

"What specialism is that?" I asked, walking fast to stay alongside.

"Let's call it tropical diseases," she said, giving me the least reassuring smile.

"Is it or not?" I said.

Looking across Cassie I saw her worried expression, then turned to the doctor, whose forced smile was back again. Her eyebrows raised.

"I'm seconded to Public Health England. We're trying to understand the outbreak."

"And find an antidote, a cure?" I said, my voice rising with excitement.

IN THE END

"Is it a tropical disease?" Cassie butted in from my side.

"Yes," she said in my direction and turned to Cassie, repeating the same.

"Have you found a cure?" I asked. "Please, if you have, we need your help."

Approaching a double door on the right, she stopped, pushing both open and holding them wide.

A few steps inside, a clear plastic sheet with a zipper in the middle separated us from two figures in white plastic suits covering them entirely. Around their waists were white belts, a holster each side. In the left holster sat the yellow of a Taser, in the right the black of a pistol.

Beyond the guards, a long hospital ward stretched out, with ten beds on either side. In each bed lay a patient with reddening bandages on either their arms, legs or faces. At least two protective white suits busied around every one of them, changing bandages, drawing blood or pushing buttons on a bedside display which looked much like those on an A&E ward.

Watching in silence, we listened to the buzz of activity, which was broken only by the sudden shrill of an alarm.

We were drawn to the raise of a white-gloved hand. The suit stood at the middle right-hand bed. The two guards stepped from their post, each drawing their Tasers. A suit hurried from the other side of the room, holding a red liquid-filled syringe.

"Now for your answers," Doctor Lytham said, letting the doors swing closed. "We have promising lines of evaluation, but we haven't found a cure."

After following a few steps down the corridor, she opened another door and ushered us into an office. White packing crates lined the walls. Many were closed, but most were open, their contents spread across the two sturdy wooden desks in the centre of the room.

"We've isolated the disease to a new species of the Ophiocordyceps genus," she said, as she offered the two empty seats on the nearest side of the desk.

We sat as she took one of the two empty seats the other side.

"I don't know if that means anything to either of you?" she said, her cheeks bunched in expectation.

"Zombie ants," I said.

She raised her eyebrows and slowly nodded.

"Ophiocordyceps Unilateralis," she replied. "Could we use you?" she asked, tilting her head to the side.

Cassie turned like I'd been keeping something from her, like we'd known each other for years and she was only now finding out I had some hidden depth. It was getting harder to remember we'd known each other for less than a day.

"No," I replied, shaking my head. "I watch a lot of documentaries."

The doctor's shoulders deflated.

"We're calling it Ophiocordyceps Sapien, for obvious reasons."

Cassie looked at me with a tiny shrug.

"Because it infects humans," I replied, then turned back to the doctor. "But how? Have the papers not been warning of this ever since David

Attenborough filmed it?"

Her mouth raised into a smile.

"Even a stopped clock is right twice a day," she said, her lips flattening.

"We don't know how it started," she said, and I turned my head to the side. "We're examining as many victims as we can, but the fungus is so virulent our best chances are with those newly infected."

"What have you found? Are you close?" I said, feeling my heart pounding in my chest.

"All we know so far is if we can stop the bleeding, we can extend the time till the fungus takes control."

"You can keep them alive longer? How much longer?"

She shrugged. "We don't know yet."

"But you can't stop it altogether?"

"Not yet. We need more data. We need to know when anything unusual happens. Like if someone doesn't die from a bite," she said, raising her eyebrows, letting the silence hang as she watched me turn to Cassie's blank face. "That's why I'm so very interested in what you said."

"You're trying to help?" Cassie replied, turning between me and Doctor Lytham.

There was a knock at the door and it swung wide before anyone could raise an objection. Standing in the doorway was the white-coated man who'd examined me as we'd arrived. Across his white coat was a diagonal splash of what looked like blood.

"Major, that's a negative on B29," he said, panting.

I looked to the man and saw the khaki shirt underneath, turned to the doctor and saw the same under hers.

She spoke, her gaze locking to Cassie. "What else would we be doing?"

Scraping back my chair, I stood. "Trying to clean up the mess you made?"

66

Dismissing the white coat with a flick of her fingers, the door closed and we were alone again.

The major, or doctor, whichever was the truth, hadn't reacted to my accusation and now I was concerned about what she might do.

When she finally spoke, her voice was calm, her crow's feet deepening as the forced smile came back. Her upturned mouth made me want to jump across the table and take her by the shoulders, shaking her until she told me what she knew; told me the government fucked up playing God and it had all gone wrong. Told me she was part of the problem and not the solution.

"I'm not sure what conclusion you've just jumped to, but just because I'm an army doctor doesn't mean there is anything more sinister going on," she said, her cheeks bunching high.

Despite the constant smile, her stern expression did nothing to reassure me. "The military is best equipped to deal with the situation and that is all."

I stared back, trying to keep my expression as neutral as I could, forcing myself not to glance at Cassie, already knowing the concern on display.

"We've heard things," I said, the words helping to stop from launching a tirade. Even though we'd only caught part of a conversation, everything the two thugs had said back in the bedroom had made sense. How could all what was going on outside just appear with no warning? How could this place be transformed in just two days?

Someone must have known before. The woman sitting across from me had to know so much she wasn't saying.

Her cheeks bunched higher still.

"I'm not interested in what you've heard or what you think you might know. We're here to get people to safety. We're here to stop the spread. Who are you to get in our way?"

"And what a good job you've done," I said, turning towards Cassie. "How many more were left behind like us? Do you even know?" I added, turning back toward her.

"We can't do the impossible," she replied, shaking her head as she squinted in my direction. "Indications show eighty percent of the population was successfully removed from the quarantine zone."

"What about the others? What about us? When do we go?" I replied.

She didn't reply straight away. Instead she looked me in the eye, unwavering.

"What would you do in my position now the infection has taken hold?"

I didn't reply. I knew my answer would be the same has hers.

She nodded. "You can't leave until we know what we're dealing with. We can't let what's left of the twenty percent out until we have a cure."

She was right. I let out a breath; despite the questions coursing through my head, how we'd got to where we were now didn't matter. We'd seen first-hand what was going on outside these walls, what was happening to everyday people. With no need for much of an imagination, I could take a good guess at how quickly this could be the end.

What could I do? I wasn't an all-action hero and we weren't in a Hollywood movie, whose script had been audience-tested to get the right level of peril before everything turned out fine in the end.

So many had died and I knew what we'd seen was only a tiny part. Too much had already been lost for a happy ending.

For the second time since this had started, I thought of my parents. I thought of my life before the New Year had turned. Everything was different now. I didn't know if they were alive or, if they were, then how much longer they would be able to stay that way.

I turned to Cassie and wanted to smile, wanted to take her somewhere quiet and enjoy the one good thing to come out of this whole mess. There were people who needed help and, even if the boy wasn't part of the cure, we had to find out. What else could I do? Despite my unwillingness to trust this woman, what option did I have?

"Okay," I said, nodding, watching as her smile relaxed and her brow bore down to what I could guess was its normal, stern position.

"So, tell me you've been wasting my time. Tell me you've not seen someone who has survived a bite. Tell me you haven't witnessed what could be our first clue in bringing this nightmare to an end before it takes out the rest of the country."

Still, I couldn't just blurt out the words she wanted to hear; something was telling me it wasn't right to just hand over Jack.

I couldn't help but turn to Cassie; couldn't help but look deep into her eyes as she stared straight back like she was trying to reach into my mind and tell me something. Trying to urge me to go one way or the other.

67

"Jack," I said, knowing as the name came out I could no longer take it back.

Staring at Cassie, I watched the intensity of her expression melt to a smile.

"His name is Jack," I said, warming with her reassurance. "But he's only ten, or thereabouts." I turned back to the doctor and watched her hands slide through the mess of paper spread across the desk.

"When was he bitten?" she said, as she seemed to find what she was looking for.

I looked to Cassie, turning away as she nodded.

"Two days ago, when this all started, but we only met him this morning."

She looked up from a page of paper she had in front of her as she found a pencil.

"How can you be sure?"

"There's a wound on his hand. Looks

like a bite. Plus, it's what he told us."

She continued to stare in my direction before turning down and scribbling.

"Did he say if he had any ill effects?"

I shrugged.

"He said he slept an entire day, but he didn't mention anything else."

The pencil ran across the page.

"And there's no chance he could be lying?"

"He's a good kid. What would be the reason?"

Looking down at the page, she made more notes, before striking through part of what she'd written.

"Where is he?" she said, her pencil hovering.

I looked to Cassie and saw a flash of what I thought was concern in her eyes.

"What are you going to do to him?"

Her smile came back and I stiffened upright in the seat until she let the facade drop.

"Blood samples, that's all. We're not the monsters," she replied. "There's a simple test. If he continues to suffer no symptoms and we find the Cordyceps fungus in his blood stream, we'll know he's creating the precious antibodies we need."

"Then what?" I said, my voice more stern than I'd intended. I looked to Cassie and her eyebrows raised, urging me on.

"More tests, but it's hard to say until we see the blood work," she replied, her own posture stiffening. "Where is he?"

"We were holding out with our friends in a house about ten miles away. They're waiting for us to come back with supplies."

"Where exactly?" she said, the pencil still hovering.

"I couldn't tell you," I replied, shaking my head and watched as she leaned forward, tilting her head to the side.

Her eyes squinted, but still locked on to mine.

"It's the truth. Ever since this started we've been on the move."

As she shook her head, I felt rage building in my chest.

"Look here," I said, moving to stand. "What with watching our friends die, scavenging for food, hiding from those creatures, being shot at from the skies, attacked by looters and kidnapped by the military, I didn't have a chance to consult the map I didn't even have."

Cassie's hand reached across from her chair and I felt myself calm with her warmth. I sat and watched the doctor take a deep breath, the wrinkles on her forehead flattened out for a moment as a scowl flashed across her face.

"But we can take you there," I said.

Her head angled up and her shoulders relaxed as her hand went below the table. From her pocket she pulled a radio handset, her long wrinkled fingers tapping across the numbered buttons before she held it up to her mouth.

A quiet male voice came from the speaker. "Captain Bains, Ma'am."

"Captain, when is the next patrol due back?" she replied, her gaze not

IN THE END

leaving mine.

"Sixteen hundred, Ma'am."

The doctor shook her head. "Have you got another squad available for a retrieval?" she asked, her eyes still fixed. "About ten miles?"

I nodded.

"Ten miles out. Collecting a group of?" she said, raising her left eyebrow.

"Seven," I said, and she repeated the number down the line, adding two passengers would accompany the patrol as she watched Cassie's nod.

"We'll need three vehicles, plus at least six on security," the voice came back.

"Can you spare them?"

There was a pause for a moment before the reply.

"Yes, Ma'am, they can be ready in ten minutes."

She killed the call without signing off and placed the radio on the table.

"Okay," she nodded. "We'll get everyone together and take it from there."

Moments later, there was a knock

at the door and we were introduced to Sergeant McCole, a tall, but stocky man, made wider with the full body armour and camouflage kit he wore. With weathered skin and jet-black, short hair, his thick, unkempt eyebrows added to his unwelcoming expression.

"Have either of you had any military training?" were his first words as he led us down the corridor, leaving the doctor in her office.

Shaking my head, I voiced the answer, looking at Cassie as she did the same.

"No."

"You'll do well to remember that. We're the professionals and you do as we say," he said, without looking to us as he walked at speed down the long corridor, not checking to make sure we kept up, whilst pushing on a camouflaged green and brown helmet.

I nodded at his back.

He let the double doors go as he stepped through. I caught them before they swung back, holding one side open for Cassie and getting my first view of

IN THE END

the three khaki-coloured Land Rover Defenders, their engines running.

Soldiers sat in the driver's seats of each. In the front and rear vehicles, another stood behind with his upper body out of the roof in the rear compartment, a rifle resting at chest height.

Beyond the vehicles, I saw great progress had been made erecting the fence. Each metal panel stood more than twice the height of the vehicles and slanted outwards a few degrees, with razor wire spiralling across the top edge. Concrete blocks and great water containers sat on angled legs to hold it firm, each delivered by a khaki-green forklift truck buzzing around the site as soldiers manoeuvred the panels into place. Only the space for two panels remained and a third was being installed by five soldiers in just their green t-shirts, their armour nowhere to be seen.

Still without turning, Sergeant McCole motioned us to the back of the centre vehicle. He didn't look to see if we'd understood. His gesture distracted as he talked in the microphone built in to his helmet.

I couldn't hear what was being said until he turned and caught my eye.

"With all due respect..." The words stopped and his eyes turned to a squint. "Yes, Ma'am," he replied, and barked in our direction, "what are you waiting for?"

Nearly running, we climbed up and into the musty rear of the middle vehicle, settling on the hard bench seats and turning to stare out of the windscreen. We watched as the pace of activity increased. An excitement in the soldier's movement grew obvious as more joined the fencing crew.

The passenger door opened and McCole climbed in. His hand pulled up the handset in the cab, but before he had a chance to speak, gunfire lit up the silence and all heads turned to the left, our view blocked by the green canvas.

"Use the rear entrance," he said, not quite shouting. "Don't stop for anything. That's an order."

68

"What's going on?" I said, as we watched with intent through the windscreen, the convoy running in the opposite direction to rushing troops laden with weapons and green ammunition tins.

McCole didn't reply but turned in his seat, scowling. Still distracted, he pulled a map from the pocket of his combat trousers.

Knowing I wouldn't get an answer, I turned back to Cassie sitting opposite and reached across the gap between the two bench seats. She didn't pull back as I took her hands. A warm smile appeared across my lips, mirrored by hers. She was as pleased as I was we were going back to collect our friends, her family and finally taking the first steps to get out of this nightmare.

Surrounded by Britain's finest, armed to the teeth and expert in how to deal with these creatures, we were safer than we'd been for days.

A growl rumbled from my belly as I looked into her eyes across the gap. She rubbed her stomach and smiled. We hadn't eaten since this morning, but soon we could worry about those everyday things again. Soon we would have all the food we'd need and could eat together in safety.

Turning back through the windscreen, I watched the rear of the lead vehicle as it guided us around the perimeter fence. To the occasional drill of gunfire, smoke stacks slid in and out of view, their colour a rainbow of greys depending on how close they were to burning themselves out.

I watched as fields of green stretched out on the horizon. Watched as a car park, empty of all but a few cars went past, then, finally, the first buildings of the village came into view.

Around we continued in our wide circle until the direction changed with a sharp turn, pushing me back against the cold metal, our speed not slowing as sentries, then the fence, flashed out of sight.

IN THE END

McCole picked up the radio handset clipped to the dashboard.

"Take a wide circle down the Boskennal Lane and come out at the head of Land's End Lane. Go cross country if you need to," he said, releasing the button.

"Sir, that's the main entrance?" the questioning voice came back.

"That's an order, Private Curtis," McCole said, his tone not inviting a reply. He got none.

Cassie and I continued to watch out of the window as we followed down the deserted streets. St Buryan wasn't a large village by any stretch of the imagination but still it felt so eerie to see no people, no traffic each way we turned. The only signs of life we saw were from the past; windows smashed, drying pools of blood, walls peppered with bullet holes. Cars smashed, their metal crumpled around trees and buildings.

Still, we carried on around the streets, turning right and right again, slowing only to bounce up the curb. The

Defenders took the green fields with ease, all to the occasional background of gunfire.

I watched as McCole picked his rifle from its stand in the footwell and inspected the chamber, then did the same with his side arm.

We turned right again, back onto the road and before long the front Land Rover's brake lights lit and stayed on, our vehicle slamming to a halt a few metres from its back. The radio came alive with the same voice from the last call.

"I count fifty Cords all heading to the FOB, sir, along Land's End Lane."

I let go of Cassie's hand and together we leaned toward the windscreen.

"How far out?" McCole replied.

"Half a click," the voice said, as he released the button.

"A second wave," McCole said, but not down the radio which he hooked back to the dash.

He spoke again, but this time it must have been using the radio on his headset.

I watched him tense, turning to scowl in our direction.

"Back up," he said, his voice betraying no emotion.

One by one, the convoy turned, the rear vehicle taking the lead as we made our way out of the village in the opposite direction, finding a second roadblock whose sentries I couldn't see, despite being sure they were watching us.

The gunfire receded each moment, leaving the drone of the Land Rover's engine only broken by the occasional pop of a distant explosion.

It was another ten minutes before I could be sure we were on the reverse of the route Cassie and I had taken to get to the hospital in our stolen Land Rover.

With my eyes trained and constant on the back of the lead vehicle, I guided us through each turn, gaining confidence as the roads unfolded as I'd expected.

About halfway to our destination and along the road which would take us all the way, the brake lights of the lead vehicle shone as it reached a scattering of houses staggered either side of the road.

A voice I hadn't yet heard came over the radio.

"Sergeant, we have a Cord in the centre of the road. About a hundred yards forward."

"Cord?" I said, not knowing if I'd heard correctly.

McCole ignored my words, instead speaking into the dashboard radio. "Just follow protocol, soldier. You've done this before."

"Cords?" I asked again, this time turning back, watching as Cassie shook her head.

"Sir, it's not giving a classic reaction," he said.

I could hear the worry in his voice.

"What do you mean?" McCole said into the radio.

"He appears to be feeding on a body," the uncertain voice replied.

"Feeding?" McCole replied.

"And he's staring right at me."

"Move forward and engage, soldier," McCole said, not hiding his annoyance.

IN THE END

"We should turn around," I said, leaning forward to get his attention, but he shook his head and opened his door.

Climbing out he stretched the spiralled cable of the radio as he tried to peer around the lead Land Rover.

I stood, pushing aside the Perspex covers of the roof hatch and stared forward, ignoring McCole's shouts for me to sit back down.

Looking past the gunner in the lead vehicle, I could see something bent over a body in the road. Just as the voice had described, he was staring in our direction. In that moment, the understanding hit me. They'd named the creatures after the fungus; Cord, short for Cordyceps. As I congratulated myself, the radio came alive, the lead Land Rover slowly rolling forward.

"He's charging."

"Bullshit, soldier," McCole shouted down the radio, but the words were so loud they would have heard from the other vehicle.

McCole let the radio go, leaving his rifle on the seat as he walked out to the side to get a better view.

I looked up to see the creature heading our way, his speed building as his mouth snapped open and closed. I turned back to McCole, who stood for a moment unmoving before he looked up to meet my gaze.

"You seen these before?" he asked, the colour running from his face.

I nodded, barely able to breathe as the bubble I'd imagined around us popped. They hadn't seen the worst of the worst; hadn't seen the creatures who gained such extraordinary speed when they took over their host.

"Sir?" the voice said over the radio.

"We need to get away," I shouted, as we both turned back ahead to see the creature had already covered half the distance.

McCole's reply went unheard as the air lit up with a bone-chilling scream, followed by a chorus of searing replies.

69

Fixed in place with my legs locked at the knees, I stared at the solider standing in the lead vehicle as he unleashed the full force of his rifle.

McCole scrambled back through his open door. The first barrage had missed, only seeming to spur the creature on.

The second volley exploded against its shoulder in a haze of flesh pluming backwards out of what had remained of a ragged blue t-shirt. The creature didn't slow. Instead, it leapt into the air, the rifle's aim following, shot after shot missing repeatedly as the creature landed on the floor, its legs bending cat-like before bounding back high.

Round after round rained toward the creature as the soldier leaned backward, trying to find the angle which would stop the advance.

He was too late, as was McCole, who had his rifle from the cab aimed at the indistinct shape looming large as it raced through the air.

The target was now larger, the soldier clutched in the creature's grip as it rose, soaring higher until it seemed to stop in mid-air.

Still, I stayed locked in position as McCole fired with no discrimination and halted the hellish, pained screams.

"McCole," I shouted, and this time he paid attention. He turned away from the bloodied mess slapping hard on the tarmac, the intertwined bodies of the two lives gone.

His gaze followed my out-stretched arm, soon seeing the movement in the distance on both sides of the road moments before the barrage of hellish calls ripped through the air from the hunched-over figures, whose number we had no chance of counting.

"We need to go," I shouted, but the words were not required, the vehicle at the back already kangarooing in the opposite direction; the hedge clawing at the metal, gears crunching against each other.

With McCole back in his seat, we began our turn, the door slamming shut

IN THE END

halfway through.

    McCole screamed for me to get back down, but I couldn't drop, despite Cassie's calls. All my body would do was let me turn and watch on as the Land Rover now behind us sped backwards, bouncing over the bodies of the pair riddled with holes.

    Our distance built; we could go so much quicker forward. I shouted for McCole but we didn't slow.

    I shouted again and the engine quietened as we idled, but the new convoy leader raced out of sight around a corner.

    I watched as the lonely Defender reversed, knowing the driver's gaze would have been on us and not able to see the closing gap ahead, not able to hear the chatter of feet against the tarmac.

    I could. I saw as they caught up, saw the wheel turn as the driver looked around at the pair of unearthly creatures already on the bonnet. I heard and saw the crack of the glass, felt the four by four swing to the side, crashing hard into the wall buried deep in the bush.

I watched as the wheels slipped and slid, smoke pouring from the tyres as his foot held fast, his only chance to break down the wall.

I knew McCole would have turned in his seat, watching with me as the engine noise died; the wheels stopping their squeal, leaving only the smoke.

No one said a word. Each of us peered forward.

Something flew from the smoke, its arms and legs flailing, but came to a stop as he hit the floor head first, the helmet flying from the smoke a moment after.

We watched as the smoke slowly cleared, alarm niggling in the back of my head. It was time to move and save ourselves; there was no hope for our man and all we were doing was lessening the odds of our own survival.

No one voiced those words until the smoke cleared; until a creature pounced onto the soldier's body and ripped apart clothes, rending flesh in great sprays of blood. It could only mean one thing; he was still alive but wouldn't be for long.

I shouted to McCole for a gun, my words spraying across the top of the Land Rover.

He did as I asked, cocking the pistol and passing it up, butt first.

I didn't note what I had in my hand, but it already felt so familiar. Drama from the last few days flashed through my head. I'd been through so much already. How much more would I need to take?

A warm hand hugged at my thigh with a gentle, reassuring motion and I looked down to see Cassie peering up.

Her face was as wet as mine, eyes wide with terror, but still she had taken the time to connect. I would not let her down.

I turned back to see the smoke had cleared and pushed out the gun. I never fired, instead using all my energy to scream the command as loud as I could.

"MOVE!"

70

We surged forward and I took my cue, dropping into the rear compartment, watching wide-eyed out of the dusty rear windows as the pack of monsters continued to gain.

It wasn't long until the distance between us stopped shrinking and eventually we had the upper hand. I let my breath even out, let myself feel the ache as I loosened the grip on the handgun.

Still, the creatures continued their onward chase, but they were no match for the horses under the bonnet.

A warm touch found my arm and I turned to the dim light and saw Cassie's wide smile. I couldn't help but dive into her open arms.

Clinging together for what seemed like an age, I felt the short bristles on my cheek warming against her soft skin. For a moment I forgot the drone of the engine, my heart racing for a whole other reason, only pulling apart as two deep voices swore from the front.

Sitting back on the hard bench, my left hand holding her right, we turned to the windscreen and saw the wreckage of the Land Rover which had raced off, its nose folded around the stub of a tree, leaving the trunk and the sprawling bare branches blocking the road.

Together we repeated their expletives, before twisting back around to stare through the rear windows and into the distance, hoping once we'd left their sight and turning many a corner, the creatures would have slowed and dispersed to worry someone less fortunate.

I turned as we slowed, looking to the driver and McCole, waiting for their plan, but they were just repeating our gestures to each other.

"Can we push it out of the way?" I said.

The driver and McCole swapped looks, each nodding as the Land Rover continued to slow.

Cassie and I made room while McCole scrabbled into the back and stood up through the roof to aim his rifle the way we'd just come.

I scrambled into the front seat, watching the steam rise from the crashed Land Rover as we came level, fingers of wood scratched and snapped, protesting at our advance.

As the front grill bit down hard into the protruding branches, the glass in the headlights smashing, I looked across and saw the other driver's head lolling forward and slumped over the deflated white airbag.

At first I wasn't sure if he was dead but as his head moved, fear spiked he'd come alive again. As our Land Rover continued to make slow progress, I pulled open the door and jumped to the road, ignoring Cassie's worried calls.

With the gun in my right hand pointed through the window, I gripped the door handle and pulled.

His face turned and I knew I had to make my choice. His jaw hung slack and wide; with no blood he looked like he'd been punched in the face.

I pushed the gun into my jacket

pocket, grateful he didn't lunge as I gripped him around the waist and helped him to the ground.

    The scrape and crunch of wood had stopped, but the engine's roar had not. The mass of branches were too much for the Rover without a running start. The rear doors opened and Cassie jumped to my side, pausing as she stared down at the soldier, weighing the decision I'd made only moments earlier.

    Eventually taking my place, she helped remove his helmet as he squinted through the pain. I ran around to the back of the crashed Land Rover and pulled open the back doors, reeling as I found the space filled only with two camouflage rucksacks. The passenger and his long rifle were gone.

    Pulling the heavy bags by the shoulder straps, I stood back beside the soldier as Cassie knelt. With his helmet on the road, I watched him peer around, trying to make sense of what had just happened.

    By the time our Land Rover had given up my plan and backed up, its metal scraping and wood snapping as it withdrew, the chaotic sound was overshadowed as McCole cried out and the report of his rifle rattled an assault.

Everyone's attention was drawn to the three creatures behind us who continued their chase.

My reaction was instant and matched Cassie's, grabbing under the guy's arms and dragging the soldier over the sheared end of the tree trunk.

McCole's rifle stopped and another took over.

I glanced back to see that by the time the driver's shots were done, McCole was out on the road, kneeling down to reload. The driver ran around his back, performing a well-practiced role.

We were soon over the long trunk, dragging the soldier despite his fight for us to stop. Doing as he begged, he climbed to his feet with his sidearm out and popped off bullets into the frenzy.

We ran, not able to watch, not able to hope the two creatures still running wouldn't last long enough to leap into the air and make their deadly attack.

Still, I twisted around as we raced forward, looking back as a pained scream lit up the air. A curtain of doom fell around with its grating call, knowing when I turned to face forward a monster from our nightmares would block our way.

I was right and stopped dead in my tracks. Standing on the road was a woman who'd died in her mid-forties. Her face was still bright with colour, cheeks rouged and lips, I guessed, were the same underneath the blood and sinew dripping from her mouth as it ran down her sweet, daisy-covered white dress, its outlines still visible underneath the dark-scarlet apron.

Sweeping Cassie behind my back, I fired before the gun came level, my hand waving wild with each recoil. Bullet after bullet veered wide until the click of the empty chamber echoed in the sudden quiet.

I watched the creature's skirt billow as she crouched, not pausing as her legs flung her high in our direction.

71

I couldn't step back. I couldn't move. It was all I could do to make myself the biggest target possible, covering Cassie as much as I was able whilst hoping she would make the right choice and run.

High in the air, the creature started its fall. My gaze locked onto its white, unblinking circles, barely hearing the racket of gunfire at my back.

Instead, I watched the monster jerk with a spasmodic movement, whilst feeling the full force of its cold weight as I crumpled to the tarmac.

Surprise forced my eyes wide, rushing through me as Cassie's head bared down close to mine. Behind her, clouds built in the sky until McCole's pained face blocked out the view.

"Can you get up? We need to go," her voice said, with an echo I was sure only I heard.

IN THE END

Standing was easier than I'd expected, the heavy weight gone from my chest leaving only the thick crimson stain running down my face and across my front. I spat to the road and a great wad of clots landed, but I knew it wasn't my own as I tried my best to keep my empty stomach from overflowing.

Stepping over the body of the woman who once was, I didn't need Cassie's help to keep myself steady, but took the offer so she'd be close.

McCole ran by our side, his rifle slung over his shoulder beside another heavy-packed rucksack, his face thick with the same frown. In his left hand he held his pistol, his right tucked under his left armpit, but I could still see the growing ring of darkness radiating out and across his camouflaged jacket.

Urged on by them both and the not-so-distant screams reverberating in the air, I cleared my mind of all but keeping one foot in front of the other.

McCole went first, his pistol pointed out as we scraped through a gap in the hedge-line, grateful for the wide-open field the other side.

We ran, then jogged, soon slowing to a walk as the adrenaline cleared and the weight of the packs and our empty stomachs returned.

With a quick change of direction towards a small copse of trees, we settled at the base of a wide oak and slumped to the ground as the memories of the last few moments bore down.

The distant screams hadn't repeated since we'd had grass under our feet and I lifted my head while McCole gave a cough, turning to Cassie as we both remembered his hand.

"Show me," Cassie said, as we pried off our rucksacks.

McCole squirmed on his butt and he gingerly pulled his hand from under his armpit, but as the blood cascaded he pushed it back under and bit his teeth together hard; he'd lost his pinkie finger.

"QuikClot gauze in the med kit," he said, his mouth barely moving.

The words of the doctor came back in my head: stop the bleeding quick and he'd have a chance.

IN THE END

Both Cassie and I turned, upending the bags. Mirroring our motions, we rifled through the Aladdin's caves, pushing aside heavy camo bags, bottles of water, warm clothes and ration packs.

We found the dark-green first aid kits at the same time, unzipping the waterproof bags in chorus, pulling the long strips of plastic-wrapped material with QuikClot Combat Gauze written in bold red letters.

Cassie was first to get hers open and I dropped mine as McCole shouted.

"Just one."

I turned and took a hold of his pale wrist, blood running down the stump of his little finger.

Cassie didn't pause, didn't squirm or turn her nose up at her task. Instead, she scanned the instructions, pushing the gauze down hard and wrapping as his hand went limp; his eyes closing as he passed out.

Blood reddened the gauze as she wrapped but slowed as each layer added. Sticking the end down, she stood, raising the drooping arm as high as she could.

I uncurled the fingers of his left hand from the pistol and rested it on the floor beside him as I drew a deep breath, trying to ignore the coppery taste in my mouth. I turned around in all directions, breath slowing with every angle when I saw we were still alone.

I repacked Cassie's bags, knowing we would have to move at any moment; would have to decide about McCole if any of the scenarios running through my head played out.

Still turning, I watched the hedge-lines, pausing each moment I caught the wind in a tree. I cleaned my face with an antiseptic cloth, disgusted by the red colour returned with each wipe.

Using as little water as I could, I rinsed out my mouth and took a great gulp, forcing myself to stop before it had all gone.

Cassie took the water as I offered and we shared half a Mars Bar which tasted like it was made of pure energy. The glow of sugar rushing through my body came quick and I took my turn to hold McCole's hand high.

IN THE END

"What now?" Cassie asked, as she scanned the horizon, her face full of dread. We both knew these quiet moments were so far apart, but when they happened they always meant something worse would come when we least expected it.

"Nothing's changed," McCole said, sucking air through his teeth as he pulled his hand from mine. "We get the boy back to the FOB. The hospital," he corrected himself, remembering his audience.

I nodded and turned to Cassie, shouldering the pack as she did the same.

"But how?" Cassie replied before I had a chance.

"We get the Land Rover back," he replied, picking up the rifle as he struggled to his feet.

I followed his look towards the road and a column of white smoke rising.

Together we watched as a great explosion tore outward through the hedge, forcing us back as a great plume of black smoke billowed to the air.

72

"There goes the PE-4," McCole said, stepping around his blood soaking into the grass.

Walking toward the new gap in the hedge, I turned to Cassie as we caught up, my confusion visible as McCole replied without my need to ask.

"Explosives," he said, taking a hard swallow. The colour from his skin all but drained, despite the tan. "Prepare for anything."

I raised my brow in Cassie's direction.

McCole winced as he shuffled his shoulders, trying to re-balance his pack.

"Are you sure you don't want painkillers?" Cassie asked.

"You don't want me on morphine. I need to stay alert," he replied, letting his shoulders relax.

"Have you really not seen those things before?" I said, knowing from his reaction back when it all kicked off, but a sprig of hope lingered it was just from the shock.

He shook his head, dashing hope for the second time.

"No," he replied. "What the hell are they?"

"I don't know," I said, looking around. "But they're mean motherfuckers," I added, and a shiver ran along my spine. "Third time now. We've always come off worse. They're so much faster. The others are like sheep, gathering in herds, wandering about, only bothering people when they're seen. They're easy to get away from as long as you're not surprised, but those other things, they were still human once but react so much differently. They're like wild animals. Predators."

"Top of the food chain," McCole replied.

I nodded.

"Like two different strains," Cassie added, not taking her gaze from the horizon.

McCole turned away, shaking his head.

"What have you been told?" I asked.

"Me?" he replied, looking back, closing his eyes for longer than a blink. "I'm a soldier, not a boffin. We know as much as you've guessed already. We should have built the fences so much taller," he said, shaking his head.

I raised my eyebrows and turned to Cassie, still looking along the hedge line.

"You must have been told more," I replied. "Why is the army really here?"

McCole turned my way.

"Take this," he said, offering out the rifle.

I paused, looking him in the eye. We both knew he had more to say, but it was clear he wouldn't be telling me any time soon.

I took the long gun and I laid the pistol in his open palm before he handed it to Cassie.

"Aim and pull the trigger all the way. Don't point at anything you don't want to be dead," he said, turning back to check I was listening too.

As we walked, he continued with instructions, handing over two new magazines for the rifle. Watching as I followed his words, he released the old magazine and pushed thirty new rounds in its place.

"Same thing," he finished. "This isn't an action movie. Don't fire from the hip unless it's your last resort."

I nodded, feeling the grave weight of the rifle in my hands. Pushing the stock into my shoulder, with my right eye through the sight, I took in the magnified view as I let the gun travel across the horizon.

"All clear," I said.

"Don't believe it," he replied.

Soon we were within touching distance of the destroyed hedge, the space between our steps getting less and less as we moved around large shards of misshapen metal and smouldering debris once part of the Land Rover.

The space where the Land Rover had been was empty, a crater of steaming tarmac in its place. Beside the wide hole we saw the underside of what had been our transport, the Defender flipped on its side and pushed deep into the hedge. It wasn't going anywhere soon.

Our steps were slow, with McCole taking the lead, covering left with the pistol outstretched.

I followed at his back, almost touching him, my eye against the sight and body turned to the right. I could hear Cassie just behind us, covering the rear.

The ground was uneven as we crossed onto what had been the road, with heat rising as debris crushed under my feet.

"Clear left," were McCole's words; there was nothing in my scope.

"Clear right," I said, but a great animalistic scream obscured the words.

Instinct alone lowered the gun and pulled the trigger as I screamed at the blackened, skinless face shrieking towards me.

73

The hand on my shoulder slowed the barrage of fire, calming my finger on the trigger despite the creature still trying to claw its way up from the floor.

Cassie had seen what I hadn't; she'd seen it would never succeed. She'd seen there was nothing connected below its hips to stand on, its legs blown clean off in the explosion.

"All clear," came Cassie's words, strong and decisive as I pulled in a long breath.

McCole nodded as he peered around my shoulder, pointing his pistol down the road covered with metal and black stony debris.

We walked, my legs jelly on the uneven ground, but we could do nothing but fix forward and watch the bend as it turned so slowly with each footstep. All hopes were on what we'd find, praying to a god I didn't believe in that infected souls wouldn't be gathering around our treasured vehicle.

Several times over, McCole held his gun to the sky and we'd stop to listen, but only hearing his ever-labouring breath, we'd move on, step after step, getting ever closer to the most dangerous part of the journey.

We soon came to the apex of the corner, our view so short, our odds even shorter.

We saw nothing new as we stepped through each degree of the corner. The body of the driver flung across the road was missing, as was the creature which had dragged him from the smoke. Only his upturned helmet remained to mark the spot.

The Land Rover emerging from the hedge-line told us we hadn't made it all up. Relief grew as we saw it all in one piece.

Our pace increased, but soon slowed as McCole's didn't pick up, his pale right hand hanging by his side. We had to get him off his feet.

On the road beyond the Land Rover, the body of the first soldier to die was missing too, but the creature who'd ripped him from the truck was not. It lay, half flattened, its flesh ground into the tarmac by the great tyres as the driver had tried in vain to escape.

The engine still idled as we grew near and I couldn't hold back my speed as I jogged around, holding the rifle at my hip, not looking to McCole to see if he agreed.

All was clear around the vehicle; along the road too. Slinging the rifle over my shoulder and crunching cubes of glass under my shoes, I pulled open the Land Rover door, sending the stench of burning rubber into the air. The Defender pulled from the hedge with ease and I jumped out, leaving it lined up straight on the road after dumping my rucksack and rifle on the passenger seat.

Around the rear, I pulled open the door, with no complaint from the metal. The hardy beast barely had a scrape or dent from its ordeal.

McCole's laboured walk ended as he batted away our attempts to help him into the back. Cassie joined him for fear of his imminent collapse.

Back in the driver's seat, I willed away a sudden flush of safety and tried to ignore the feeling that for once everything was going right. We had the upper hand, but I knew it would only lead to the next calamity; the next catastrophe to change someone's life forever. With so little left to lose, I could guess who it would be but I wasn't willing to let it happen.

I shook away the few seconds of thought, having learned my lesson, and I peered down at the dashboard. The fuel gauge showed the tank nearly full, the engine temperature in the centre where it should be. There were no red lights or amber warning signs telling me the engine would cut out right at the least opportune moment.

Still, I was ready for the worst to happen and I pushed down the clutch, selected first gear and stalled the engine as I tried to pull away.

This was it. This was the time. I looked to the hedge, then to the road ahead, turned a full half-circle to my left and repeated to my right, looking to see

IN THE END

what would be coming as we sat with the engine dead.

Nothing came. Nothing was coming. I dipped the clutch and turned the key. The engine started. With a deep breath and a heavy right foot, we rolled forward, letting the speed needle climb.

McCole coughed in the back while Cassie peered out of the windscreen; we made good time repeating the earlier journey. The only difference was the direction and the clouding sky as it darkened.

We arrived at the outskirts of the hamlet soon enough and saw the pickup truck still in the middle of the road with its front tyre deflated. The only differences were the missing bodies, only the dark patches on the tarmac remaining.

I slowed as we passed the house where the old man had stood, nodding to the top floor window as he nodded back, speeding up as he answered the signed question with a shake of his head.

Adrenaline built but there was nothing I could do to temper my excitement. We'd taken much more time than we'd expected, but we were bringing with us so much more than we could ever have hoped.

To Zoe, Andrew, Lane, Ellie, Jack and Tish, we were not only bringing food and transport to safety; we brought hope.

Hope of a cure.

Hope of some version of a happy ending.

Sadness soon tinged my thoughts. I knew by now Naomi would be gone, or near the end. There was nothing that could be done about her, but we could play our part in saving many more who were not past the same point.

As we came around the corner, a beam of sunlight broke through the cloud as if lighting our way and shining down on someone coming through our cottage's open front door; someone coming to greet us.

But they weren't waving. Their hands were down by their sides, their mouth hanging open with a great rend of flesh missing from their cheek.

IN THE END

Another I didn't recognise stepped from around the corner and I slammed on the brakes, Cassie's mouth opening wide to bellow a heart-rending scream.

They'd been overrun. We'd been denied our happy ending.

74

ZOE

We were here because of Logan. Naomi lay here dying because of him. He hadn't caused the world to end but he'd got us this far. He'd saved our necks, with a little help from Andrew, but it was Logan who'd been strong. He was the one who'd led us to this cottage and had done all he could.

Still, it wasn't enough. It was Logan who couldn't protect Ni, couldn't save her from this fate. He'd tried so very hard but I couldn't forgive his every decision. Many differences could have saved her life, could have meant another outcome. My life for hers, or maybe someone else. He'd tested his own to save me, to save Lane; had reached out from safety to get us in, but why couldn't he have done the same for Naomi? Was it because she had what he wanted?

IN THE END

He'd killed so many of those things. Shot them dead with guns, smashed their faces in with blunt objects, but he grew distracted. He lost his edge.

The new woman could never join our group, wouldn't fit; even if there was a group left. Even if so many weren't dead.

She hadn't been through what we had, she couldn't understand the pain of watching so many friends die. I realise this now as my tears dry. I realise this now as my throat heals from the raw emotion I couldn't keep in; as I keep my dearest warm, even though she doesn't know I'm here.

He said nothing as he manoeuvred her like an object, directing her transfer up to the bedroom. He wanted to stay. He wanted to appease his guilt, but I wouldn't let him spoil my last hours with her. If he had his way, he'd end it now. Would be easiest for all involved, right?

No. Not right. Naomi was a person. My friend. My lover. She would go, but I would be the one to say when; to do what had to be done, but only when she was no longer there. No one would take that away from me. Not him.

He came back, checked so many times. Each time with a pretence, but I knew his game and I wasn't having any of it. He even left the dog to watch. What was the mutt going to do when the time came?

I heard their talk, his not-so-quiet voice. It wouldn't surprise me if those two didn't sneak away and fuck somewhere in a corner. Maybe once they had, he'd be more like the Logan who had been my friend.

But would I stand for it? No. The door is staying closed. Get the fuck out, you black little shit. And you, too. You call yourself a friend?

I woke and it was still light outside, the skin on my face tight. I knew why and didn't care. All I wanted to know was had it happened? Was she still with me?

She was, for now.

Nothing came back as I kissed her

lips, but there was still warmth. Some warmth.

I started at a knock at the door and was about to launch abuse when I saw Andrew with his hand clutching at this side, his expression open, projecting towards me.

My resistance crumbled. I nodded as he pointed to the bed, keeping silent as he sat at the end of the cover, looking over to Naomi with water welling in his eyes.

I nodded and he turned my way.

"I'll watch her if you want to clean up."

"Where is he?" I said. "Logan," I added, as Andrew raised his eyebrows.

"He's gone to see if he can find food, just up the road."

"Alone?"

"Cassie's gone with him."

I couldn't help but scoff, but good old adorable Andrew didn't notice.

I took up his offer, looking back with each step until I was out of the room, with the world still baring down on my shoulders.

The house was quiet as I scrubbed at my face. It was her blood, but I couldn't live with it on me. I wondered if he could?

I stared at my clean skin and saw Naomi behind me in the bath, heard her laughter breaking up her song and leaned heavy against the sink to stop myself crumbling to the floor.

A call went out, voices across the house and she vanished.

Footsteps running, disturbing the dry floorboards. With a deep lungful of air, I straightened up and, opening the door, I saw Andrew standing wide-eyed, peering down the landing. He looked up and spoke.

"The boy's gone."

75

LOGAN

Cassie and I counted five, but every moment we waited in the Land Rover their number added, each wandering in and out of the house like they owned the place.

One thing was for sure; there was no frantic activity. Whatever had happened was hours ago.

"Where now?" McCole asked.

"Nowhere," I said, turning to Cassie as I held her hands between the two compartments. "We have to check inside. They could be hiding somewhere, scared to come out." I kept looking to Cassie, not letting her lose hope.

She nodded, widening her eyes.

McCole didn't complain. With his pale skin and laboured breath, he was in no position.

I drove slowly, the cold wind still blowing through my missing pane. I kept the sealed-up window of the passenger side between me and those things as we rolled past the house to get a better look, hoping to draw out any more lingering to trap our friends.

We counted eight, which took up to follow and snaked around the corners as I kept our pace slow, with Cassie watching out the back.

My gaze fixed ahead, waiting to race off from any launched side-on attack we had no hope of defending against.

Driving as far as we could stomach, Cassie heaved open the back door and, mentored by McCole, spent a full magazine, despatching the tail in our wake.

This time, at speed, we were back outside the house with a tire iron and a small shovel in our hands, not wanting to draw them near with the thunder of guns.

We left McCole with the engine running, his pistol aimed through the back window.

The house was quiet inside but the smell was anything but. It reeked with

IN THE END

the same stink I never wanted to get used to, the forewarning stench which in this new world could mean only one thing.

The hallway was littered with bodies. Cassie peered down close to my shoulder, trying to get as much information as we could to be sure it wasn't one of our friends, her family, laying with their heads bashed in.

We stepped over three bodies, their blood thick and long congealed. We found fresh blood, too, from someone who'd been defending themselves. It was their trail we followed, their handprints up along the walls, heading to the kitchen.

The trail stopped among the scattered contents of the kitchen cabinets littering the floor. The fridge was upended and barred the shallow larder cupboard, which I'd earlier found empty of anything of use.

I paused, looking on at the wooden door and heard something behind the wood, realising why the fridge was in front.

Looking up as movement creaked on the boards above, my finger rushed to my lips as I took my place in front of Cassie. Together we scanned the dining room to find everything as we left it, our meagre supplies still in the centre of the table, untouched; they'd had no time to collect them up before leaving, or before...

I stopped myself from thinking any further.

Movement above again cut my search short. The small bathroom was empty, despite the splash of blood up the door. The living room window was still barred and the light blocked by the great wall unit. Naomi's discarded, blooded bandages were still on the floor and the pieces of the puzzle locked into place. The floorboards creaked directly above.

Each step groaned with my weight, my head upturned as I summited the stairs. Dark patches stained the floral carpet; they weren't there when we left that morning.

The door to the bedroom where

IN THE END

Zoe had been so protective of Naomi was closed. The master bedroom where I'd changed was open. It was the room where Cassie and I had made our connection.

There was no one waiting to attack, the bed almost fresh.

Cassie didn't follow. She was in the kid's bedroom and her tears were easy to hear, but, when I arrived, the room was empty and the covers thrown to the side.

The bathroom door was left wide, the sink stained pink, but otherwise there was no sign. It left only the one door unopened. The one room where we knew danger lurked.

All was not as I'd expected. Naomi was there but it was just her body standing, eyes white and sunken in her sockets. A quick look around the room told me Zoe had not been taken, hadn't suffered the same fate.

I did the deed. Saying goodnight, I caught her body and laid her to rest before covering her with a sheet from the bed.

It felt so wrong leaving the house. Felt like I was abandoning them, like I was leaving my last connection to my friends.

Where had they gone? The question rattled around my head as we rolled along.

Cassie was unable to add anything to my self-questioning, despite my assurances they'd got out alive.

She couldn't take her gaze from the rear door of the Land Rover as we rumbled along the road and out of sight.

76

ZOE

Andrew and Lane left me alone with the two girls. Me, the least maternal person in the world, except after Naomi, of course, but I guess she couldn't be counted anymore.

Andrew and Lane had left by the back door, jumping over the fence after we'd overhauled the room where the other two had slept; where the other two were still unaware I was left in charge with Naomi.

It was Lane who'd seen the door open, who'd smelt the outside world drifting in and slammed it shut to run around the house, counting everyone; upstairs, downstairs, only calling out as the number hadn't added up.

There were two of us missing; the boy and the dog. Nothing gone but a thick coat. The men of the house had puffed up, running after, leaving me to play house.

Did they know what a state I was in? Still, I checked both doors were locked, as I'd been told.

I checked the two kids were still sound asleep. The two sisters, but not of each other and no relation to me. Still they were precious, right? Was anything precious anymore?

I stood at the bedroom window with the curtains open and watched out, staring across the field, up and down the road as far as I could, which wasn't very far at all.

I turned back to watch Naomi stir, my hand grabbing for my chest as I focused, waiting for the sheets to rise and fall, soon turning to the window and looking back through the rain across my vision, even though the clouds were only just building.

All I could do was wait. All I'd been doing was waiting, going along with their plan and look where it had got me. Look at where it had got Naomi.

I turned again and watched her breath pause, picking up my own only

IN THE END

when hers did.

A decision had been made and this time it was my own. When Naomi and I were no longer, I would go it alone. If I lived for an hour, a day or maybe more, it would be on my terms, not on those of another.

Yes, I felt something inside me react. Yes, I could feel the guilt rising in my chest. Logan had done his best, but the best wasn't good enough.

I thought about going now. I thought about leaving the children sound asleep to be found by the two big strong men, or by Logan and his wife to be; if they ever came back. If they could ever make the journey.

I looked out again, across the window and down the road, turning either side to see the empty street rolling out. The plan was set and I wouldn't be turned away.

77

I couldn't leave. I had to wait until I had nothing here left to live for, but it wouldn't take too long. The wardrobe was easy to move, easy to push across the door.

No-one would divert me from my plan. Not even those creatures chasing after Andrew and the boy, racing down the street towards us. Not even the banging at the front door or Lane's colourful calls for me to turn the key.

They were soon in anyway, their noise inside the house told me so. Voices calling my name confirmed, but they didn't need me. What did I have to give, anyway?

A fist hammered at the bedroom door. The handle turned, rattling loose in its brass enclosure. I didn't reply and it went away.

A scream ran through the house, followed by a toddler's cry. I listened to the wailing voices, not able to stop putting their features to the unholy

IN THE END

cries, the sound still getting through my fists despite being pushed hard to my ears.

I heard fighting, sure I could smell that stench. I turned to Naomi, but despite the space between her breaths, it wasn't coming from her direction.

Gun shots came next, one after the other, the burning smell adding to the mix. Then nothing. No sign of who'd won.

I stood, unable to keep back the tears. I watched outside as a crowd built, funnelling through into the house. I heard my name. I was sure and stopped my heavy breath, wiping the tears from my cheeks. A name, my name. They needed me.

I turned to Naomi and held my palms flat on her chest, then moved to her hand and for the first time felt her grip.

It was too tight, tighter than when she was alive. My fingers ground together and I pulled back.

She wasn't Naomi anymore. Her eyes were open, white, sinking deep into her skull as I watched. It was time.

I reached into my pockets, expecting to find a weapon but I hadn't put one there. I hadn't prepared. My chest grew tight and I realised as the weight lifted from my shoulders I would be no good on my own.

My name was called again, but much more distant this time. These were my people. They were my friends. They were what I had left in this world. I couldn't see them dead at my hands.

"Sorry, Naomi," I said, as she rose, letting the covers fall.

I turned to the wardrobe and shoved it, tried to push it aside. It was much heavier this time.

I turned back to Naomi. No, not anymore; turned back to the creature in her body, shoved her cold flesh down to the bed and heaved the wardrobe to the side.

With the door open, the stench was almost too much to handle and I slammed it shut at my back. My stomach heaved and would have poured out if there had been anything waiting.

IN THE END

I called out, my words stirring movement below. I leaned down over the banister. Those weren't my friends milling in the hallway.

Running to the other bedroom, I dragged out the drawer of the wooden dresser and smashed it apart with one hit to the floor.

Holding the plank of wood out in front, I raced down the stairs and called for Andrew. His reply came, but from far away. So distant.

They'd left, gone. What little choice had I given them?

The first creature didn't know what hit it, the wood crushing through the plate of bone between his eyes, falling back, tumbling the others down the stairs behind him.

I leapt over the diagonal banister, landing on a body. It didn't react as I crushed the bone in its chest, no air left to escape. Behind me I saw a queue forming at the door; a long, orderly line, each ready to take the place of the next I took down.

I rushed to the kitchen, passing the

locked-up back door. I could hear their calls, but they weren't in the garden; only those creatures scratched at the window.

    I turned, backing my way in, hitting out left and right, blood spraying across the walls as my feet battled with the contents of the cupboards strewn over the kitchen floor.

    Even though I'd changed my mind, I'd got what I wanted. I was doing it my way. I would die through my own choices.

78

I swung the board left, then right, jabbing its length forward, smashing the rotting face over and again. Decaying flesh came away with each swipe, but it wouldn't go down; it just kept coming back for more, its hand clawing the air just out of reach.

Somehow, I was keeping it from the kitchen, the cork in the bottle, knowing if they broke through I'd be surrounded and the weapon I'd improvised would be no use.

I could feel my energy relenting. Knew it wouldn't be much longer before I couldn't even lift the board, my mind on the growing deadly queue in the hallway behind.

The voices were back, quiet, but with an intensity of a shout and I could swear they were coming from the cupboard.

A light sprung on in my head; they were behind the closed door. Why hadn't I checked before?

I had one chance and hoped I could make it. When I stopped fighting they would pour in and overwhelm me.

As I took the steps to find out, I hoped my ears hadn't been playing a joke.

Angling my body around to the right, battering hard with a renewed energy and giving all I could with one last jab, I leapt side on to the door, pulling it wide to see the shallow larder, its narrow shelves empty of food and my friends.

I'd done it now; I'd made my choice and the cupboard was where I would have to wait it out.

Feeling a scrape against my jumper, I turned, jabbing the wood into the neck of a woman, her eyes white and wide, her hair missing, torn clean off to leave the red of her skull exposed.

Another was at her side, but I turned before I could take him in. Looking to the fridge and with one push at its back, it rocked, almost dropping to the floor, nearly forcing back the horde but not quite.

IN THE END

I turned, the rest a blur. The floor was gone, the light too and I was falling, but hands stopped my bounce against the steps. The door slammed shut and the fridge scraped along the floor as it slapped hard against the door.

I looked to a candle against a far wall as it flickered in a draft. Hands put me right, turned me through ninety degrees, settling me on my butt.

I was in a basement. Andrew's face peered at me as it moved in and out of shadow with each flicker.

"This is awkward," I said, but he didn't reply, just pulled me into his open arms and squeezed.

"Look what Lane found," he finally said, so quietly I could hardly hear as he released me, spreading his hands out to show me the rest of the tiny room.

The room was about the size of the bedroom upstairs where I spent most of my time in the house, but without the bed and the dated flowered wallpaper, unless it was authentic decaying brick print.

The floor was soft, a mix of rubble

and mud I didn't want to spend much time looking at.

Along the walls were shelves filled with jam jars, but I couldn't make out anything edible inside. The smell was an improvement from above, but only just; the musk and musty odour made me glad when my breath finally slowed.

The three children huddled around the far edge, holding each other's hands for warmth. It was cold down here, almost as cold as outside.

I wanted to talk, but Andrew insisted we kept silent.

To the side of him was Lane, crouched down in what seemed a strange pose. His hand floated in the air, I thought, until light flashed across a pair of eyes. It was Shadow, Lane's hand stroking his back.

I wanted to say sorry as I stood and looked around the room, wanted to apologise for what I'd said, even though it had only been inside my head. I wanted to say sorry for not letting them in.

I wanted to cry out this was all my

fault. If they hadn't had to break the door down, they could have kept the horde from overrunning.

I had no more tears left to cry, had nothing inside me left to give.

So, I waited as patiently as I could. Waited while listening to everyone's stomach groan and complain for food. Listening to the movement on the boards above, the slow methodical placement of one foot after another.

The creak and crack of activity above slowed, but only after some time had past. No one could say how long, but it was less than a day and more than a few hours.

We'd burnt through two candles and had just lit the last when the sound upstairs rattled my nerves.

It was them. It was Logan and Cassie, I was sure. It was their heavy steps, faster than the others had been. It was their vehicle we'd heard rumbling outside, their vehicle which left and came back and now idled on the road.

Andrew didn't agree but wouldn't voice a reason why it was better to stay here than to venture back up, to peer out through the door and contact whoever it was. But he'd been outside; he'd gone with Lane to fetch back the kid.

I'd seen nothing and I would not make another decision which could end someone's life.

Shadow knew it, too, and ran to the stairs before Lane could leap after him; before he could stop him letting loose a bark.

Andrew and Lane subdued him, their hands tight around his mouth.

Now it was too late and we heard their voices, heard Logan and Cassie outside; heard their upset.

The engine revved and they wouldn't be able to hear our shouts, wouldn't be able to hear Shadow's bark echo in the air.

Andrew was first to rise, the first to run up the creaking wooden steps. The first to push up the board covering the hatch and the first to jab the door, to feel it move only an inch as the fridge I'd toppled stayed where it had been pushed

IN THE END

by the creatures clambering after me.

Lane was the second to try it, and the third as they put all their weight behind.

I was the first to find my tears again. The children followed shortly after.

79

LOGAN

"Jack mentioned his house. Maybe they'll be there? Or the supermarket? Whatever's left," I said to Cassie, trying to catch old conversations as they rolled around my head.

When she replied, her voice was distant, her gaze fixed on the road behind.

"They'll be running for their lives," she said, the words tailing off before rising to a shout. "Stop."

I pushed my foot to the brake, looked left, looked right and checked ahead, trying to see what had caused the panic. I couldn't see anything in the fading light and turned in my seat, twisting as she leant against the back door, her hand pushing it wide.

"Cassie," I shouted, as she jumped into the night. Still, I searched the view until I caught movement, something low

IN THE END

to the road in the failing light.

Was it a dog bounding up from behind? "Shadow," I shouted, pulling myself from the seat and following Cassie out.

Forgetting McCole, forgetting the lurking danger, I ran towards Cassie, watching as Shadow slowed. Watching as he came to a stop and turned his head back, his bark rolling over the stone walls and back again.

As Cassie neared, pushing her hand out to pat his head, he turned away and ran in the opposite direction. I'd watched enough episodes of Lassie in my youth not to question what he needed us to do.

With a quick glance in my direction, Cassie continued her chase as I raced back to the Land Rover.

"You know him?" McCole said, as I launched down heavy in the seat.

"Yes, I do," I replied with a grin, turning the Defender in three points.

The headlights lit the pair almost back at the cottage. Soon overtaking, I jumped to the road, pausing only to grab the tyre iron from the front seat as

Shadow raced past and back through the open door.

I didn't need him to lead the way. I could already hear their distant voices calling, growing louder as I passed the bodies we'd stepped over twice before.

Arriving in the kitchen, I followed Shadow's pointed nose towards the fingers hooked around the cupboard door in the corner, his bark rattling the windows as the fridge lay toppled across their escape.

With two heaves, Cassie and I, grinning from ear to ear, dislodged the fridge and slid it across the floor.

Not waiting for a helping hand, the door pushed open and there was Lane and Andrew, with Zoe behind.

Cassie squeezed past them all with her arms open to pull Ellie out from the back.

I paused for a moment, letting my grin lower until Jack led Tish up the steps and into the twilight. To Shadow's barks we laughed and hugged, Andrew trying to calm our voices, reminding us of the reality.

IN THE END

With the tyre iron in my hand, I led them out.

It was the distant calls in the night which hurried everyone into the Land Rover, hurried our introductions to McCole.

Still, I took the time to make sure we'd counted each head twice over.

"Where now?" Andrew asked from the front seat.

I couldn't help but smile, glancing over the questioning faces in the back as I told them we had a plan and were taking a trip to a hospital only a short while away.

Cassie spent the whole time with her arms wrapped around her sister, while Ellie squirmed away from the kisses.

"In the morning," McCole said, causing me to pause.

"In the morning," I added. "He's right. We don't need to be in the open tonight."

I drove us the short distance to the hamlet, not answering any of their questions, but peering as best I could along the road and letting the headlights light up each of the doors until I found the perfect place.

I chose the house next to the one in which we'd spent so much time, a house which hadn't been raided by the looters and stood protected with double-glazed windows.

Tipping a wave across the road to the figure back-lit by faint light coming from a bedroom window, I was pleased to see the old guy was still okay and hoped for his wife, too.

I reversed the car down the side of the house, knocking down the short wooden fence so I could get close.

With guns in hand, Lane, Andrew and I left the car, leaving strict instructions of what to do if we got into trouble.

We cleared the outside of the house in the last of the light. A small window by the back door smashed with three hits from a stone and we were in, leaving the doors intact.

I took the first floor and cleared each room. My heart raced as I saw a

IN THE END

disembodied head waiting on a dressing table, but instead of launching an attack, I let my breath calm and opened the curtains. It was just a plastic wig stand.

With no fuss or fury from downstairs, everyone piled in and we herded them in to the front room as Andrew secured the back door and window, while I fingertip-searched the rucksacks for torches, candles and matches.

Before we lit the place up, we closed all the curtains whilst watching as the flowered wallpaper took shape. We found no hidden basement, just a loft hatch, but no ladder to get us up high if we needed.

By the time we'd finished the search, we knew the house inside out. We knew every route. Knew everything of use in each of its four bedrooms and had decanted the water from each of the taps until it ran brown with the sludge from the bottom of the tank. We knew every morsel of food and had it packed in bags; split by each door and ready if we had to take flight, all before feasting on cold beans, tinned tomatoes and the last of the Christmas chocolates. Orange creams never tasted so good.

Tiredness caught up as stomachs filled. We had no idea of the time, with no clocks hanging on the walls or standing, chiming in the hall.

I told everyone as we ate to be ready to leave at first light. Setting a candle to time each watch, we agreed the rota as we all dissipated around the house.

No one had asked about the plan, I was glad. I had no energy to explain, but I would need to have an adult conversation with Jack in the morning. I would need to decide if I should trust everyone with what we'd unintentionally kept as a secret. Did they need to know about the hope which lay on his head? I was too tired to answer the question.

The kids were given the biggest bedroom. Zoe and Cassie were to share the next, leaving the box room at the front for McCole and a lookout with their dual objective.

The dining room was where the

IN THE END

other watch would stay awake, looking across the vast garden ready to rouse the house. The large, double front room upstairs was where I would take my turn to rest before the candle burned to its base.

I checked in on Cassie, knocking at the door, but Zoe lay there, out of this world, her eyelids flittering in the candlelight, a space beside her.

I found her in the kid's room, laying fully clothed on top of the covers, her arm around her sister, next to Tish and Jack, huddled together.

I couldn't help but stare at the boy. Couldn't help but wonder how someone so little could hold the key to our future.

My gaze drifted to Cassie and her face as it flickered by the candle in my hand. I'd wanted to say goodnight, to talk about the day, about what tomorrow might bring. I wanted to talk about the rest of our lives. I wanted to know if she was excited about the future too.

Closing the door, I drifted to the front room, heard movement downstairs and, covering the candle, I peered outside.

The street was quiet, unmoving and I tried to force myself to relax, tried to unlearn the fear from the last few days. Tonight was where it started to go right. Tonight was where it would go our way. Tonight was the end of the beginning.

I could hear Cassie's laughter in my head and I chuckled to myself as I undressed, pulling on new underwear from the drawer. They were a little tight, but I was learning to get by.

Folding my clothes and keeping them at hand, I slipped into a dream after barely sliding under the covers, until I bolted upright as a frozen hand touched my shoulder.

80

 Her low voice soothed my heavy breath, her other hand so much warmer against my chest as she pushed me down, drawing the covers up and sliding to my side.
 Her cold finger warmed against my lips, her mouth silent as I listened to her breath, mine held so I wouldn't disturb the dream.
 Her scent rolled over me as she drew close, adding to the most lucid experience I'd had in all my years.
 Her palm ran along my chest, bumping over muscles, my ribs pain free as I tensed until her hand settled on my shoulder and there it stayed as our breath slowed and my body relaxed.

 It was light when I woke and I turned to see the bed empty next to me. It was a dream and I deflated as the realisation came.
 The house was silent and no one

had woken me for my watch. I rushed from the bed, smelling a mix of foreign odours, but the hint of smoke in the air made me pull on my clothes and step to the window to see the lone Cord ambling in the road.

My chest tightened as foreign sounds started from downstairs; the noise of activity, of action.

I checked the bedrooms and found them all empty. My heart raced as I searched the landing for anything heavy, but found only the mistake I'd made in leaving everything of use downstairs. I would have to attack unarmed.

Creeping back to the bedroom, I pulled on my clothes and quickly found a bottle of perfume, its tapered cap the best I could do as I took the first step down, willing myself to peer around the corner with sweat building on my forehead.

81

Halfway down the stairs my fist went out, the tapered bottle nestled below my knuckles as a face came around the corner.

Pulling back the lunge, the perfume bottle slipped from my hand as I saw Lane's wide smile staring back. My hands went out, flailing in the air for the glass, taking hold just before it could smash hard against his face.

With an unnecessary juggle between my hands, I had it gripped tight, watching as his wide smile narrowed and his head turned to the side as he locked on to the tapered glass.

"Good morning," he said in reply to my shrug before disappearing towards the kitchen.

I rose back to the top step, leaving the bottle to rest on a bookcase in the landing before hurrying down the stairs with the smell of charred meat filling my lungs.

"Barbecue," I said under my breath

as I peered out of the window to the thin wisp of white smoke.

Following the smell through the kitchen and into the dining room, I found the long table set for eight places with everyone but Zoe sat down as she moved around the table, forking out food to each setting.

All eyes turned to me as I entered; even Shadow took his stare from the plate of food as it moved around the room. At his feet, a bowl already stood empty.

Cassie sat between Andrew and Ellie, smiling in my direction, only turning away as Zoe filled her plate.

"We found a full freezer. It thawed, but the stuff at the bottom was still cold," Andrew said, a half smile filling his face.

"Who's watching?" I replied, my mouth not curling up as it filled with saliva. "There's one out there," I said, looking between the faces.

"Just one?" Andrew replied.

I nodded.

"The doors are locked and everyone

IN THE END

is here," he added, looking around the table. "It'll be fine while we eat," and attacked his food with his knife and fork, sounds of pleasure issuing from his mouth.

I knew he was probably right and I also knew too well the pull of the food on the table.

"Why didn't anyone wake me for my turn?" I asked, still standing in the doorway.

"You needed the sleep," Lane replied, to nods around the table as he cut the food on McCole's plate.

I watched a grin appear on Cassie's face and she looked me straight in the eye, biting her bottom lip as she dipped her head; it hadn't been a dream.

Shadow joined me at my side as I took the seat at the head of the table and ate like it was only the second proper meal I'd had in days.

Despite being able to finish my plate, I let Shadow take the last of the prime meat and watched him gulp it down, barely chewing as I ran my palm down his black coat.

Last night was where it all changed, but the first real change came only moments later.

A fist, not heavy but firm, banged on the front door.

Lane, Andrew, McCole and I shared a look, pausing before we jumped to our feet, knocking the table as we rose.

The three of us who were able had the same thought, grabbing table knives in our fists as we ran to the front door.

"No, no, no," came the voice from the other side as I struggled with the door, finding it double locked; we didn't find a key last night.

I shrugged my jacket on and gingerly opened the back door, a gust of wind rushing across my face.

With Andrew at my back we crept around the corner, my hand fumbling in the pocket for the handgun, only then remembering I was the rifleman now.

Nearing the corner and brushing down the side of the Land Rover, I could hear a low moan in the street and saw Cords ambling in the distance. The procession shared the same pace,

IN THE END

slowing rolling down the street. I turned back and glanced at Andrew, silently confirming with a shake of my head they hadn't been there a moment ago.

At the front was the old man I recognised from across the road, banging at our door and repeating the same word.

"What's wrong?" I asked, letting my fist down, despite the shotgun cracked open in the crook of his arm.

As he saw me, then Andrew at my back, his eyes opened wide, his free arm reaching out.

"What's wrong?" I repeated.

"The smell, the smell," he said.

I stopped moving but didn't need long to figure out he was talking about the food smell still only just dissipating.

"It's drawing them in."

I turned again, looking behind me. Although the creatures still ambled slowly, they were getting close and another pack was coming from the other end of the row of houses.

"Shit," I said, turning to Andrew. "We've got to go and quick."

Andrew disappeared down the side of the house and I turned back to the old man.

"Listen," I said, trying to calm his continued repetition. "We need to go now," but when he didn't react, I built my voice up.

"We've found a safe place, a hospital a few miles away. The military are there, they'll help. You can come with us if you want?"

We didn't really have the room but would have to make do. I couldn't leave these people here when we could give them hope.

He stopped talking; stopped repeating his words and eventually nodded with great enthusiasm.

"Go back to your wife, get ready and we'll come and get you," I said, and watched as he turned, hobbling across the road as the horde drew in from either side.

By the time I was back in the house, thanks to our planning last night, everyone was queuing up at the back door with the supplies in hand, Lane

IN THE END

helping McCole to line up whilst handing me the rifle.

"The old couple from over the road are coming with us," I said, and despite everyone knowing there was so little room, no-one voiced any other opinion.

Before I gave the signal, I ran upstairs, looked out of the front window and lingered on the group merging in the middle. I tried to count, grouping each in ten, but stopped as I got to fifty. At least they were only the slow creatures; a dream to deal with compared to what might have been.

I kicked myself as I checked the back room. Staring out beyond the garden fence I watched as a creature stooped low to the grass and, as if seeing me, it rose high and gave a cry like a wolf howling to the moon.

82

Still, they waited in the line, each turning as I came down the stairs and watched my expression. There was no chance they could have missed the terrifying call, despite the rumble from the crowd outside and the evil smell penetrating through the walls.

I beamed back. If ever there was a time for a positive attitude, it was now. A few faces responded, Lane and Andrew's lifting, Cassie beaming as she looked back. McCole was unmoved as he leaned heavy on Lane's shoulder, his face downcast and growing paler with every moment.

I gave the order and stood to the side of the back door, waving Andrew out with his handgun peering ahead. Zoe and each of the kids followed; I read from their expressions their intrigue to see where we were off to next.

Lane came after with a rucksack on his back. McCole followed, his good hand on Lane's shoulder. He couldn't

IN THE END

lift his leg enough and tripped on the step, separating from Lane and falling headfirst out the door.

Rushing to his aid, we had him the right way up, watching as he nodded he was still okay and exclaimed that the bruise on his head was nothing compared to the throbbing pain beneath the bandage he'd used to slow the fall.

Cassie offered a shot of morphine but pulled back from reaching around to her pack as he shook his head for a second time.

Lane took the lead again, going much slower this time and taking care of each crack in the concrete while checking up at Andrew, who hurried them forward and beckoned them towards the open back door, whilst each moment he swapped his glance to the road.

It wasn't long before everyone had squeezed in. Cassie took the last space next to McCole, resting his swelling hand on her lap. Our eyes met through the glass as I shut the back door, taking great care not to make a sound.

"It'll be okay," I mouthed and she nodded, beaming back.

Andrew took the passenger seat; he'd share the front with the old guy's wife while the husband would have to take his chances in the back.

I jumped in the driver's seat, crunching broken glass under my feet, trying to ignore the slow procession only a few strides away.

They hadn't turned yet. I looked through the door window and remembered the missing glass. I was out again, crashing my foot against a fence panel, each snap causing more attention than I needed.

The shape wasn't right, but it would have to do. They were turning our way now, changing course with their mouths snapping open and closed.

Back in the seat with the rough fence panel at my side, I pulled the door closed, no longer any need for the silence. I didn't have time to settle in, leaning heavy against the panel blocking the space of the window.

I took a breath and the engine

started first time. In the back, the low murmurs stopped and I watched in the mirror as all faces peered forward until the adults distracted the children's glances.

Revving the engine, I let the clutch out. None of the creatures moved to the side. A triangular path didn't open, but the Land Rover had no trouble dropping each in the way below the line of the bonnet.

With the suspension barely rocking as the wheels crushed bone, I saw our chance. The crowd was surging towards us, leaving a space where the old guy and his wife peered wide-eyed through a crack in the door.

"We're not going to have time. Drag them in, you'll have to do all the work for them," I shouted over my shoulder.

Excitement grew in the rear and children hunched as they stood and were pushed further in so Lane could get to the back door.

Andrew readied his hand on the handle and I pushed the accelerator as far as it would go. Flesh slapped against the front, fingernails scraped along the paintwork.

I leaned as heavy as I could against the fence panel, giving more pressure as I felt the grab of hands scratching as fingers tried to get a hold. Still those in the way disappeared underneath in droves.

The cottage door was opening as we grew near, but a Cord clung to the bonnet, refusing to be dragged to its second death. Instead, entangled in the grill, its fingers, hand and arms slapped against the bonnet as it flailed its arms for our flesh.

I started the count from ten.

At five, we'd cleared the main group and I shifted the wheel left and right, the passengers gasping with each turn like they were on a rollercoaster. Still, the trapped Cord wouldn't dislodge, clinging on for what it called a life.

On three, I smashed through the old guy's fence, hitting a post square on the centre grill, but not before it dropped the body and dragged it underneath to give back my full vision.

IN THE END

On one, I slammed the brakes, stopping with the couple standing in the middle of the Land Rover's length.

The back door flew open, Cassie and Lane out. Andrew jumped from the passenger seat. He turned around, raising the gun, his expression bunching as he fired a salvo.

He didn't stay fixed for long and like a member of an elite Israeli snatch squad, he had the woman off the floor. Her calls couldn't hide her surprise as she slid across the passenger seat while he paused a second time, firing two shots in our wake, then crushed up against her to share the seat.

I revved the engine for fear of stalling and without looking, drove off as hard as I could when the rear door slammed closed.

Clear of the front garden, I looked in the passenger wing mirror and watched as the Cords slowly turned to follow. I watched as they overcame the bodies Andrew had dropped.

Checking in front, I saw the empty road and peered left out of Andrew's window. It was clear.

I looked back through the rear-view mirror and let out a breath as I saw the squashed faces; Lane, the old guy and Cassie in the back.

I relaxed against the fence panel, settled into my seat with my breath slowing until Cassie's scream ripped through the air, slamming on the brakes as a gunshot flashed from the back and sent my ears ringing.

83

Andrew and I burst out through our doors. The fence panel flew out to the road as I jumped. Freezing in my stride; I stared back at the creature I'd seen from the house. Its matted dark hair swung wild with its long stride towards us.

A gunshot exploded from the other side of the Rover. I turned, grabbed the rifle from down the side of the seat and dropped to my knee. Despite being scared to take the time, I looked through the sight and lined up the shaking iron.

As I pulled the trigger, I hit the target again and again.

Andrew's shots filled the spaces between mine. Too soon the creature dropped to its haunches, leaping to the air and out of view.

I shouldered the rifle; the abomination was gone. I rose, running to the back of the Land Rover, my gaze cast along the line of Cords who I knew would catch up too soon.

By the rear doors, I followed the trail of thick blood splattered in wide marks across the tarmac. A shot went off from around the side before I could look up; before I could round the corner.

All I could see was the plume spraying through the air and the body rolling to Andrew's side, the back of its head an open mess, the white of sharp bone poking through flesh.

Blood covered Andrew's arm. He'd been hit, bitten, his face contorted in pain. Had it not been for the chaos at my side and the screams of panic in the back of the Land Rover, I would have rushed to his aid.

Ripping the door open, Ellie's face ran with tears as she was pushed towards me. I searched in the darkness, desperate to find what had happened. I caught her before she fell to the tarmac, her face, clothes, everywhere I looked were sprayed with blood. A handgun skittered after her, stopping just before it dropped.

I took a left-handed hold of her and pushed my right into the darkness of the passenger compartment. Grabbing what I felt first, my hand came back with the scruff of the old guy's collar.

I had him out to the road with no complaint, pausing only as I saw the jagged gunshot wound in the front of his face.

A shot went off but not from inside. It was Andrew and I turned. The Cords were going down with every new round, but still there were around twenty left, making their steady progress towards us.

My hand went in a second time and found the arm of McCole's camouflage fatigues. Pulling as hard as I could, I soon realised most of his head had been left behind.

I dragged his body to the floor, blood trailing after, the veins sticking out from what I could see of his skin.

I only had time to guess that McCole must have turned as I drove. Someone had taken action, but the bullet had unintended consequences, taking the old neighbour too.

Screams continued to issue from

inside and so did the rounds from Andrew, until I heard the soft click of the empty chamber, the subtle noise mixed with the screaming chaos.

My reach into the darkness found another, but what I had was so light I felt panic race up my spine when I thought I'd found just a part of someone.

My face lit up as I found it was Tish, her weight suddenly heavy as Jack clung on. I pulled them both out and Ellie took control of the pair, helping them steady to the road and herding them around the side, whilst being careful to move their view from the pair of gruesome bloodied bodies at my feet.

With my fourth reach I had to turn back, letting go of the cloth I'd taken in my hand, the moans of the walking dead creatures so close.

A hand grabbed at my coat but I could do nothing but walk away; had to raise the pistol and let fury burst from its muzzle.

With each round I took a step forward, issuing a terrifying, angry

IN THE END

scream without my command; despite the water in my eyes rounding out my vision, each shot hit square in their heads.

As the gun clicked, telling me it was all over, I put the last three down, emptying the bullets from the rifle.

I went to turn back, but had to take a breath, forcing myself to twist. As I did, I saw the old woman bent down by Andrew, her hand ripping his shirt from his arm. The gun lay down at her side.

To the right, Ellie had the two kids facing in towards her, her arms wrapped tight around their backs. No one else had emerged from the Land Rover and still there was Zoe and Lane, but I could barely bring myself to think of Cassie unaccounted for.

My knees and feet slipped on the vehicle's slick floor, my eyes still not adjusted to the dark, but my gaze soon locked with Lane's, following his hands held tight around Zoe's throat.

Her eyes were blinking faster than I thought possible. Moments later they stopped altogether and she slumped forward. I switched back to Lane, following his gaze again as it took me across the compartment.

Relief filled me with joy as I swivelled around, but it wasn't long before the world fell out from under me. Cassie stared back with a forced smile on her lips, her hand clamped tight on her arm and blood seeping between her pale fingers.

84

Somehow, I switched off the sorrow and cleared the emotion from my view. With a wipe of my hand against stubbled skin, I numbed the fear and pushed back the pain.

My hand found the scruff of Cassie's jacket and I pulled her hard through the slick of blood. Pulling her up into my arms, I shuffled through the back door. With a kiss to her forehead, I lay her on a patch of bloodless tarmac.

Lane was out with his pack open in his hands, the first aid kit already split in two and its contents spreading across the road.

Cassie didn't moan or wince at the pain as Lane cleaned out the wound, but I had to look away.

Standing, I scooped dressings from the floor and, ripping open the pack of QuikClot, I stumbled over to Andrew. The old woman's tourniquet had slowed his bleed, but his arm was going pale and I pushed the dressing into her outstretched hand.

With my palm over my mouth, I took in a full view, drew a deep breath and watched for movement; the road littered with death and destruction, both with bodies which had died for the second time and those for whom it would be their one and only.

The thought struck a reminder in my head, but my step back to the Land Rover paused as I caught a strange noise. My ears were attuned to the terrifying scream those horrific creatures gave off, but this was so different.

Shaking off the contemplation, I delved in the rucksack and pulled two magazines from the ammo bag before retrieving the hand gun from the road next to the rifle. I pushed a magazine home and climbed into the back of the Land Rover.

The smell was already surfacing.

I pulled Zoe's arm and she followed like a doll. Gritting my teeth with her in my arms, I could already feel the ice-cold body reacting as the last of her energy sent her muscles twitching.

IN THE END

I took her past the children, smiling through my clench and kicked the door of the old man's cottage wide before laying her to the sofa, holding my left hand firm on her chest, with the other pushing the barrel against her forehead.

"Goodbye," I said, and with a deep breath I pulled the trigger.

Back out in the open, the air was thick with decay and the stench of blood blowing in my face with every gust of wind.

I'd been right; this was a new beginning. Just not for all of us.

"Back in the truck," I said to Ellie, my words free of emotion. "Back in the truck," I repeated to Lane, ignoring Cassie's outreached hand.

Instead, I strode towards the house where we'd stayed the night, walking at a stiff pace towards the whimper, all the while knowing what I would find.

The sound grew louder and told me I was right; the black body in the garden curled in a ball soon confirming.

Shadow's head raised as high as he could manage, his gaze locking to mine as I approached. He lay on his side and breath caught in my throat as my gaze fell on a great rend of flesh matting down the fur of his chest.

Whimpering as I picked him up, tears ran down my face as his long tongue slapped at my cheek. He'd gone ahead, slipped out of the sight; rushed off to attack the creature in a pre-emptive strike to save the misery of its attack.

The walk seemed so much longer on the return journey as I hoped I wouldn't have to say goodbye to another friend by my hand today.

Arriving back, the Land Rover was loaded; just the bloody remains, liquid slick, the discarded dressing packs and antiseptic bottles left to litter the road.

I placed Shadow just behind the rear door and Cassie's voice came back quiet.

"I'm okay," she said, and I turned to Andrew, his cheeks bunched.

I noted his silence. I couldn't reply. I couldn't voice my anger and give words to the despair when a small hand came

IN THE END

up from out of sight.

"It'll be okay," the small boy said, and I turned in his direction. Taking his hand, he squeezed.

"She told me last night. I can help," Jack said and I saw his bright face, his sister's too, as she sat between his legs. Ellie's hand came out and I took it in my left.

"She'll be okay," she said. "She's the strongest person I've ever known," she added, and I gave a nod, turning to Lane and the gun in his fist.

"Watch Shadow too," I said, trying my best to keep my voice even before slamming the doors as I let go. I couldn't twist away too soon, couldn't turn from their faces any quicker. Ellie was right, but I knew even if Jack held the key to the cure, it wouldn't be in time to save Cassie, no matter her strength.

We had the chance to save other people's lives, but I couldn't stop the tears rolling down my cheeks. I wasn't blubbing. I wasn't losing control, but I couldn't help letting the emotion pour out.

I took longer than I should to collect up the discarded weapons and pile them back on the passenger seat.

The journey was the most solitude I'd had in ages and I pushed bullets into magazines and chambers while I let the Land Rover amble along, knowing the lead had names on them I never wanted to write.

Although I kept my eyes wide open and searched the horizon for hazards while taking a wide path around where danger could be hiding, I'd barely noticed as we finally made it along the stretch of road and I saw the Land Rover we'd used to make our first trip.

It was now pushed to the side and added to the roadblock.

I slowed, ready for the sentries to raise over the hedge-lines.

I was ready for them to take over, to lift this weight from my shoulders and pull away the responsibility.

When the movement didn't come, I cocked a handgun and opened the door. Standing on the sill, I fired twice at

IN THE END

the figure as it rose, their face already blooded, its skull on show.

I gunned the engine, swerving around the angled cars and for the first time noticing the plumes of smoke rising in the distance.

85

McCole had been right; they'd needed taller fences. Stronger ones too; then maybe there wouldn't be great gaps where they'd toppled and the supporting weights wouldn't be strewn to the side. If they had, then maybe the outbuildings wouldn't be on fire, their windows melted, roofs caved in to leave just the rising black smoke behind.

Shells of Land Rovers littered the car park at the front of the low hospital; trucks, too. Bodies of soldiers, their weapons at their sides and bloodied messed up faces lay all around. The more numerous corpses were of the creatures; the normal people who'd been infected, driven of their will. Their bodies paved the tarmac, the grass, everywhere I looked; even wedging wide the main doors dripping with blood, stained with hand prints streaking down the wood.

Bullets strafed brick, the windows riddled; smashed, the glass gone.

Cassie knew something was up,

IN THE END

despite facing out the back doors. She saw before asking, before climbing to her knees, helped up by Lane to peer over the seats.

Rising, she stifled an intake of breath, her good hand to her mouth before she could ask the question to which I had no answer.

We could all guess what had gone before; they'd been overrun, but somehow I could still feel the hope. It was a big building, plenty of places to hide. Only the fast creatures, the unnamed, the hunters, would seek their prey; the others, the Cords, were opportunists and would walk away.

I drove slowly, letting the wheels turn, snaking around the death and decay. I saw no movement other than the smoke. I saw no imminent threat, but I didn't kid myself it couldn't change in an instant.

We travelled halfway around the compound before the fence and the main building were at their closest and the route became impassable, blocked with a sea of bodies for which it was too difficult to tell which side they'd belonged to.

I pictured the last stand in my head. A line of troops with their guns up and expressions set, waiting for the creatures to gather in the bottleneck, waiting for the prime range; only then letting rip, mowing down time and again. But something had caught them by surprise, something in the air bearing down.

I saw the machine gun post beyond the bodies, the heavy weapon mounted in the hastily-constructed fortification of sand bags. The gunner was gone, the assailant too, leaving just the weapon and the road scattered with a sea of shell casings.

To the side was a fire exit, the doors open from the inside with another stack of bodies which were easier to identify. Their white, bloodied coats and camouflage clothes told me of their allegiance. The blood slicked a line down the centre of the corridor behind, its surface ruined by heavy footsteps told me the story; they'd evacuated,

IN THE END

running into the bottleneck and the hail of crossfire before falling to the ground. The soldiers would have been left with no choice; they'd had to make sure they were not coming back.

"I'm going in," I said, pulling off the seat belt and turning away from the thick air drifting through the missing window.

"Why?" Lane replied, climbing into the front seat. "Let's drive, find where the quarantine zone ends and get the hell out of here."

I shook my head.

"Where is that? What direction? Where do we get the fuel? How many of the petrol pumps still work?"

"Logan's right," Cassie said.

I could tell she was doing her best to keep her voice level.

"The place is so big. Someone who can help might be alive."

Lane looked at Cassie, then turned to the children huddled in the back.

"It's a mistake. We're safer on the road," he said, taking one of the handguns from the passenger seat.

I leaned in, pulling him close, pushing my mouth to his ear and whispering the firm words.

"They'll be dead before you get out of the county," I said, as quiet as I could.

He put his hand on mine, gripping my head and squeezed gently.

"I'm sorry," he said, tightening his grip. "But they're dead already."

I let go, pulling out of his grasp.

"Find another," I said. "Go."

He sat looking down at the floor.

"Look, over there," I said, pointing to another khaki-green Land Rover parked at the side of the building. "And there," I said, my voice building. "Take one of those and run."

He didn't move, just looked at me and I turned away. Still, I saw as he turned to Cassie and I knew she would look back with a face full of sympathy.

Lane looked down to where Andrew lay silent, the old woman at his side, Cassie reaching over to put a hand on Andrew's chest.

He looked over at the children, then

IN THE END

to Shadow, his eyes reflecting the light as his head raised.

Then he turned, pulling open the door and left, letting it shut quietly on the hinges before I could open my lips and blurt out our secret about Jack.

I didn't know if it would make him stay. I didn't know if he'd try and take the boy with him. I stayed quiet.

"I thought he was better than this," I said, to no one in particular.

Cassie's hand reached out, resting on my shoulder. She was warm, for now. We needed her strength, needed what she had left.

I handed her the last handgun, pulled open the door and stepped out, not watching Lane as I strode into the corridor whilst keeping to the side, even though the blood had dried hard.

I heard noises echoing. There was life in the building still, but I didn't know if it was their second time around.

86

The sting of antiseptic was all but gone from the air, replaced with the breath of decay and burning plastic clawing at my throat. The hum of fluorescent tubes had gone, too, leaving just my long shadow stepping before me as I approached the first door.

Like the others I'd seen on my first visit, it was tall and white with a porthole at head-height, but rather than seeing to the other side, all I could make out were dark shadows passing behind the white paper blocking my view.

I knew from my last visit what would have become of the people who'd been on the other side.

The cold stung my hand as I twisted the metal handle, slow and calm. After the smallest of pushes, I let go, relieved as it held firm.

Trainers squeaking on the tiled floor, my shadow grew taller as I headed further down the corridor. Glancing down, I watched as the trail of

IN THE END

blood thinned, but the gruesome slick remained my companion with each step.

I searched for any sign of life, death, too, but the doctor's office was the first place I wanted to find; the only place I guessed would be a hideout.

If someone had survived, had held out for the miracle boy, I wanted it to be the place where I would find them.

Along each side of the corridor I counted five doors, before a sharp turn to the right.

A noise came from outside. Was it a call from the people I'd left behind? Or one of those creatures we had no effective defence against?

Whatever had made the noise I knew it wouldn't be smart to stay apart from my friends for long without Lane there for protection.

The next few doors were closed and with no portholes I pushed my ear to the cold wood and listened. I heard vibration through the building; heard movement reverberating along the wall, on the floor above perhaps, but nothing I could pinpoint to the other side.

I turned the handle, regretting I'd left the handgun behind as I did, but time was of the essence as I thought of Andrew's speedy decline, knowing Cassie, too, would look worse with each moment.

The door opened to darkness and when nothing lashed out or pounced towards me screaming, I stepped to the side and let it open its full arc.

The meagre light reaching this far down the corridor was enough to make out the store of medical equipment. Unfolding a wheelchair, I pulled it out of the room and let the door swing closed, cursing as it slapped hard against its frame.

I ran back, pushing the chair at my front.

Cassie hadn't changed; Andrew was no worse, but no better. Shadow's wound wasn't bleeding out like the others.

I drew an optimist breath; maybe dogs weren't affected by the disease. They'd be the new rulers of the world when humans were extinct.

I shook off the thought. The weight

IN THE END

of the rifle felt good in my hands as I grabbed it from the passenger seat.

Along with pulling the torch from the pack, I shouldered the rucksack and made sure Cassie held the handgun out as she slid out to the road.

Andrew woke as I lifted, but slumped to the side as I let him down into the chair. He woke again as I placed Shadow on his lap, his hand reaching to take a long stroke of his back.

Movement caught my eye as scanned our surroundings, but I turned away from the figure, instead looking to the space where the second Land Rover had sat.

I swapped a glance with Cassie. She shrugged, her face full of empathy. I'd wanted to understand; instead, I did what I did best and pushed the pain down, burying it inside.

I turned back to where I'd seen the movement, to two soldiers walking in a line, their backs hunched over, their camouflage soaked dark in different patterns.

I'd made the right decision and

pushed the chair through into the corridor, the wheels squeaking against the floor. I paused just beyond the entrance but pushed on as I abandoned clearing the bodies and pulling closed the doors.

Without voice or command, we fell into a natural formation.

Cassie followed at the back, glancing everywhere we'd walked while I went ahead.

Ellie pushed the chair whilst the old lady shepherded the kids.

As I watched her form them in a group, her face almost as clear as mine, she showed no sign she'd witnessed the death of her husband; the death of her old life.

The floor was alive with tall shadows, except when caught by the swing of the thin torch, as was the wall at our front as we walked its length, listening at each door for a pause and trying each handle before moving on.

I was looking for a sign; some way of knowing if there was anyone left living. It wasn't easy to spot until I

IN THE END

turned the corner.

    I peered around, slow at first, watching the trail of blood end at a door. The words 'Safe Harbour' ran in bold marker on the long wooden panel but smeared over with blood, as if someone had tried to wipe the letters away.

    Rushing forward, barely looking down the length of the corridor, I tried the handle and it gave. My heart raced with delight at my choice to stay; I'd kept faith in others when I'd relied on myself for what seemed like an eternity, even though it had only been a matter of days.

    I let the others know to wait as Andrew's front wheels rounded the corner before opening the door wide.

    The first sign was the darkness, the second the emptiness of the room. The packing crates were still there. The desks in the centre too. Papers were still strewn across its surface, but now scattered to the floor as well.

    I forged ahead, letting the door swing back and I saw the third sign as I rounded the desks.

The body lay, its lab coat once white, face-down on the floor. A gun rested beside where most of the head had fallen.

Blood and grey hair stuck high to the wall.

87

The doctor was gone and with her went all hope, my plan evaporating like the foul smoke.

Lane had been right and the low hurried calls from the corridor told me it would not be a simple case of rewinding our path.

I knew before I stepped from the office the two soldiers would be making their slow way towards us, but I hadn't accounted for the crowd at their back, seven or more figures just behind. The details were lost in their silhouettes.

Cassie levelled her gun, aiming high as I arrived by her side.

I put my hand to her forearm and whispered, "You'll draw more in."

She let me lead her back around the corner where she stayed to the rear, keeping her place in our order as I returned to lead.

I pulled the doctor's office door closed, not voicing what I'd found; not letting them in on my race to figure out what we would do next.

Instead, I took steps, following the torch beam to the slow plod of feet and the squeak of wheels.

Scanning left to right, the corridor was a mess with debris. Large sandbags lay halfway along the centre, piled high either side of the corridor in a haphazard dark mass. Blood pooled at the base, the walls scratched, strafed with bullets. I tried not to imagine the horrific battle which must have taken place.

Along the walls I recognised pairs of doors. The doctor had led us through one of these, but I had no impulse to take the same journey again, knowing what would have happened once we'd left.

Each of my footsteps resounded around the corridor, echoed at my back with the five other pairs and squeak of the wheels. At least the sound following grew no louder.

Tracing the walls up and down, I saw no more writing, no more graffiti guiding our way, just the occasional splatter of blood and pot marks of lead

IN THE END

embedded in the wall.

Walking at a pace no faster but no slower than the Cords, I ran through the layout of the hospital in my head. If I remembered rightly, around the next corner would be the room where Cassie and I had first been taken; where we'd been subjected to the thorough exam to make sure we were not bringing anything in, even though it's what they'd wanted.

They would want Cassie now. She'd been recently infected. Andrew, too; both their bleeding stopped soon after they'd been bitten.

McCole's face flashed into my head. How long had it been before his bandages? It couldn't have been much over five minutes, but still he'd died. Still he'd turned.

I lifted my head from its downward drift, raising high and took a thick, copper-tasting breath.

It was no way to think; this was not the place to reflect.

A light flashed ahead and my reaction was quick; I killed the torch without pause. With the darkness, the close footsteps stopped, the wheels ceasing their irritating noise.

The white light was gone, blinking out so soon, making me think my brain was overworking. I would have carried on thinking the same if it hadn't been for the footsteps, loud and energetic with purpose.

But there was something else. The steps were uneven, like someone walking with a limp. I kept the torch unlit, even though this was what I'd wanted, what I'd searched for.

Someone had come through the double doors, through the entrance we'd been brought through and now they were making their purposeful way down the corridor towards us.

With footsteps slow, I hoped to make no noise, hoped to give no reason for the others to do anything but stand and wait for my command. So far it had worked, the echo of the uneven steps at my front helping to mask my own progress.

One handed, I pushed the rifle out,

IN THE END

digging it into my hip for a second time whilst remembering McCole's advice.

The sound of the steps became so much clearer in an instant. I stopped, tried to slow my breath, realising they'd turned the corner and were right in front of me.

Still I waited, wanted them close; couldn't let them run away in panic if they could help us. I didn't want to scare them off if they were a survivor and we could be the ones to help them. Or maybe looters were already on to this place. I didn't want to give them the chance to escape, either.

As the thoughts rolled around my head, the footsteps stopped and a new noise took up. It was the sound of effort, of strain and I clicked on the torch.

There, in the bright circle, a man stood hunched over; he was halfway through a turn and in his thin, sleeveless arms he held a large sandbag with the contents dripping down.

The man was gaunt, hair stuck to his scalp, his skin so thin in the bright light I could see dark veins running up and down. His eyes were white and his face covered in dark dried blood.

It hadn't been a man for some time and those weren't sandbags in the pile.

The soldier's body fell to the floor and the creature's mouth dropped open. I knew the noise it would issue before the scream began.

88

I was firing, shooting from the hip before the roar of the scream hit my ears.

I stepped back, keeping my speed down, despite knowing the bullets were missing each time. Light flashed from behind me and I turned, regret gripping tight across my chest.

Ellie pushed Andrew through the ward's door, the kids running after to the place I hadn't wanted to go back to, but now I knew it was our only sanctuary.

I didn't turn to face the creature; knew it would be a waste of time, a waste of the energy I craved for which I needed to give a head start on a creature focused on hunting me down.

Perhaps its stomach was full of its feast, but I didn't wait to question how I'd made it to the door before I was dead; before it dragged me off by its jaws.

It had followed, I was sure. The run of its legs, the slap of its feet against the floor told me all I needed to know.

Still, I grabbed Cassie's looped arm, my hand catching as she fired past my ear. I dragged her with me through the doors, pushing her in front whilst catching her eye, but not able to make sense if she'd hit the target.

The room was bright, even though the windows were masked with great sheets of white plastic I could only guess were reinforcing the glass. The plastic inner seal had been pulled down and lay in tatters, its shredded, blood-streaked remains discarded to the side.

There were no guards. No patients. No nurses or attendants left; just a handful of bodies, each with a catastrophic head wound. A wound we knew was the only way of stopping the dead from living a second time; if you could call being under the control of the Zombie Cordyceps Mould living.

The ten beds were still there, rearranged, disordered, pushed to the side, their blankets and sheets each covered in a different bloody motif. Bandages, thin metal chairs and other

IN THE END

debris, the monitors, their screens blank, cables snaking from their mouth lay scattered across the floor.

Shadow whined with pain as he jumped down from Andrew's lap and as he bared his teeth, a sudden fear gripped across my chest. The pressure welled up and almost turned to tears as his head moved and, limping, he turned his attention to the double doors.

"The beds," I shouted, and the able-bodied took action. All but Tish knew what to do, driven by the same instinct to jam whatever they could against the door we had no way of locking; the door which had no jamb to push against and hold it closed.

With the beds pushed up and rolled against the door, they were too heavy to lift or to pile on top of each other; it was a sorry obstacle one of the Cords could summit with such little effort.

The weapons I'd seen the guards carrying were gone and our rushed inventory confirmed we were low on ammunition, with one magazine left for the half-empty handgun and what remained in the rifle's magazine, maybe ten rounds, all we could rely on.

The doors cracked hard against the beds with a great bang and each of us shook as the rattle repeated. With my arms open wide, I turned and ushered everyone back to the far end of the room.

They ran, wheeling Andrew along. Cassie stayed by my side and looped her arms around mine, gripping tight as we turned and took the slow walk to the end of the ward.

"Shadow," I snapped when I saw he'd stayed behind. He started his backward step, limping.

Bang went the door, soon joined by the dull thud. I pictured the slow soldiers catching up, joining the push against the doors. The beds moved as the gap between the doors widened.

As soon as I could see teeth snapping in the gap, I looked again, scouring the room to the rasp of Shadow's bark.

I looked to the ceiling but found it solid, the stainless-steel vents fixed with

IN THE END

screws I had no hope of turning. There were no other doors, no cupboard to hide in our desperation.

My attention again turned to the windows and I stepped away. I could hear the snapping of teeth and I saw a head, soon several, fighting to get through the gap.

I pulled up a chair and threw it at the window, gasps running through the watching crowd as it bounced back, slapping down to the hard floor. Even Shadow had silenced as I pulled up the rifle hanging across my back and fired.

I hit the big target, but watched as a neat hole punched through the centre without splitting or cracking the glass, leaving a space to see shadows across the other side.

Still, I had to hope we were better outside than cramped in here. I launched the chair again and my knees gave way as it bounced off, watching as the barricade of beds swept either side.

I had to get up. I had to raise myself high. The body was willing but I couldn't get my mind to take control, despite seeing the hungry creatures pour through the double doors.

After all that had gone before, could I lay down and not fight to the end? Could I really give up now, not taking my place at our last stand?

89

What choice did I have when I saw Cassie reaching out? How could I draw back from her bandaged hand held open to pull me from where I'd sunk? How could I let her see me like this in our last moments together?

I stood and fixed my gaze on hers whilst ignoring the pain in my knees as they bent, sucking up the sting of each breath as my body remembered the trauma I'd endured in the last few days.

Together, we turned to face the advance as Shadow's bark grew more intense. We drew up our weapons, with no need to be selective. We both fired, loosing off round after round into the crowd.

Lead opened jagged holes, ripping flesh from bone, but few bodies fell to the floor or slowed their momentum.

The click of my empty chamber came too soon. I turned to Cassie to see her rapid fire, but instead she stared back, her gun empty, too.

Still, bullets shocked the air, rounds flying in from somewhere we couldn't see. I scanned the room and saw a window in the centre row where the glass had blown out, its fragments spread across the floor. A flurry of lead streamed from outside and the smoking black-end of a long barrel rattled against the windowsill as it weaved left and right, mowing the dead down, splitting torsos in two.

"Get down," I shouted, turning as I motioned for everyone to hit the floor. My back was to the advance, even though the creatures were almost on us.

"Get down," I repeated, running over to Andrew, the old lady already on the floor as I pulled him from the chair, launching myself to cover his body and burying my face against his cooling skin.

The chatter of the machine gun stopped, but shouts were all around, single shots volleying from somewhere unseen.

The rattle was back and I felt a weight fall on my arm. I spasmed out, rising, prepared to smash the life, or death, with my fists; ready to protect to the end.

No response came back as I shoved it away, the creature just flesh, my fist coming back clotted with blood.

A haze of thick, chemical stink misted the room as the gunfire fell silent. The fog settled enough for me to see two soldiers, one a good foot taller than the other, striding through the double doors. Their faces were stern, looking either way for movement, their handguns aimed in our direction.

I put my hands in the air, ready to switch to the next nightmare.

Still alive as they slowed their advance, they settled their guns pointing to the floor.

My gaze shot to the window and someone climbing through. Neither soldier reacted as Lane jumped to the tiles, dragging the heavy machine gun by a handle with a ribbon of long bullets wrapped around its centre.

"You were right," he said, his face with a thin smile as he picked his way through the mess of bodies littering the length of the ward, tip-toeing around the leeching blood.

I stood to full height, took notice as each one of us rose.

Ellie ushered the children up, taking care to see their wide eyes open. She turned them each away, struggling to find a direction clear of the chaos.

Cassie pulled up and looked to me, checking over my body for any damage whilst I did the same for her. Only the old lady and Andrew didn't rise and together we helped him to the chair, pausing as we saw the bullet hole in the leather seat and a matching crater in the wall behind.

"You found them," I said, turning away, stepping around the children.

The old lady was still on the floor, her body cooling as I touched.

"No, they found me," Lane reply.

We hugged.

"You were right. I told them about you guys."

"I didn't even know her name," I said, looking to the old woman. Cassie took my arm and helped me to my feet.

IN THE END

"Doctor Lytham's dead," I said as I rose.

"No, she's not," said the taller soldier in a deep voice, his gun by his side. "Who's injured?"

With no time to take in the news, I turned to Cassie, not able to look anywhere but her hand. I saw the soldiers stiffen, their pistols jerking just a little but still pointed to the floor; they raised once more as we turned to Andrew.

"But they're okay. We got the bleeding under control quickly," I said.

Both looked at each other and gave a nod as they turned to clear a path, pushing bodies to the side with their heavy boots.

I stroked Shadow and picked him up around his legs, my ribs complaining like they hadn't done in hours.

The taller soldier stayed up front, guiding the way with the wide beam of a torch.

Lane walked by my side as the other soldier held back while we headed through the corridor. I was thankful for Shadow's bulk blocking my view as we passed the piled bodies, with no other choice than to walk through the tacky blood.

A shot went off as we found a double set of doors, the solider at the rear jogging to catch up now he'd made sure the old lady wouldn't rise.

Beyond the doors were climbing concrete steps; the smear of dark liquid on the first few told of the battles won and lost in this place.

Leaving the machine gun behind, Lane and the shorter soldier helped Andrew out of his chair, their footsteps echoing with each heavy breath until we were through the doors at the top and out into light.

We passed another two guards crouched down behind barricades, rifles pointing in our direction. At least I could be sure the bags they used for cover contained sand this time.

The first floor was different, despite having the same layout as below; the stench of decay less pronounced, covered perhaps by the caustic antiseptic hanging in my mouth.

IN THE END

The corridor wasn't littered with battlefield scars and light poured down through skylights after every few steps. It felt like we were in a different place, like a weight lifted, despite the heaviness of the dog.

Led into an anti-room, much like the one downstairs, I watched each of the two separate doorways. Without the need to wait, the left opened and through came Doctor Lytham.

"Who?" I asked, turning back to Cassie, but the words tailed off.

"You look like you've seen a ghost," the doctor said, but she didn't keep her gaze on me long enough for a reply.

Instead, her lids widened as they fell on Jack then squinted small as she scanned the room, settling on Andrew sitting on the floor, his back leaning heavy against the wall.

The second of the two doors opened and out stepped a man with messy, ginger hair. With a nod from the doctor, he rounded up the children, but before he could be led through the door, Jack turned, wide-eyed, for my approval.

"Go," I said, tapping his shoulder as they passed.

The doctor nodded. "He'll be fine," she said.

I nodded a slow reply.

"They'll be safe with us," she added.

"We'll make sure," I replied, and moved to follow.

The soldier stepped in my path.

"You have been injured," Doctor Lytham said, and turned with me towards Cassie and Andrew.

As the door swung closed at my back, I was sure I heard a key turn and a lock snap into place.

The doctor took a step. Lane backed away and she examined Cassie's grey, dirty bandage and swept her long blonde hair to the side as she pushed her hand to Cassie's forehead, then gripped her wrist between her thumb and forefinger, staring out to the wall as if it wasn't there.

Letting go, the doctor seemed satisfied and ushered her to stand beside me. With Cassie out of the way, she knelt down to Andrew, but didn't touch him or take his pulse. She did nothing but look over his paling skin and the dark red stains soaking through the bandage at his arm.

Another man in a lab coat came through the right-hand door, his coat splashed dark with blood.

The doctor pointed Cassie out and he opened the right-hand door, holding it open. Cassie turned, staring back at me the same way Jack had, willing me to answer her unvoiced question. Is it going to be okay?

I nodded without pause. I wanted to go with her, but Andrew's need was more pressing.

Lane followed Cassie through the door, but when I didn't go with them, Doctor Lytham dismissed her colleague with a nod and he let the door close as he followed behind.

"He needs stitches," I said, looking down at the dog.

Doctor Lytham turned sharply in my direction, glancing towards Shadow, but soon her gaze fell on Andrew again.

I saw the look in her eyes, saw her

give an unvoiced order; watched as the taller of the soldiers took a step towards me as the doctor tried not to catch my eye, walking through the left door and holding it open.

I took a step, turning back to ask a question, but my voice dried up as I looked at Andrew.

His eyes were wide open and, instead of the soldier lifting him under the armpits, he held a gun at his temple.

My view became blocked by the other soldier, his arms grabbing around me in a bear hug. I bucked as the bang echoed.

Shadow struggled, squeezed tight against my chest, my arms pinned at my side.

90

I'd been out cold for a while, but for how long I could only guess. The drugs they'd stabbed in my neck felt like they still swirled around my head. They'd been enough to calm my grief, to close my eyes, to get me behind the unbreakable glass door.

With my vision only just becoming clear, I stared out past the glass, watching technicians in white coats hurry around the laboratory as it stretched out, their excitement so clear in their energetic expressions while they busied between the benches. In their hands, many held long pipettes, loading colourful liquids from vial to vial.

I'd woken laying down on a bed to the hum of a generator somewhere close by. Shadow sat at my feet, the hair around his middle shaven, while a line of stitches highlighted the wound. I pushed my hand to his head, making sure they hadn't just given me his body back.

Pulling at the long metal door

handle, none of the heads on the other side looked up as my fist hammered hard when I found it locked.

I stopped only as Shadow woke, lifting his head as if complaining about the noise. The room had nothing I could force against the window. Shiny, thick bolts held the metal bed frame to the floor. The blanket was no use, nor was the bucket sitting in the corner.

I sat close to Shadow and let the pressure in my veins drop, hoping my vision would settle as I stroked across his back. I kept my gaze from the short hair and watched as he nuzzled his head tight against his back legs.

Watching out through the glass, I set about planning my next move. They would have to give me food; when the door opened I would strike forward. I would take the opportunity to launch my revenge for Andrew's death.

Lytham would be the first. I'd look her in the eye and wait for her to tell me he hadn't had a chance, so why give him one? I would tell her she had no chance either, count to three, then blow her out

IN THE END

of existence.

Somehow, I would find Cassie and Lane, would find the kids and we'd go. We'd take our chances on the outside. We'd live whatever time we had left hidden away. Hidden from the creatures. Hidden from the looters. Hidden from the army and those who said they were here on the side of humanity.

With bile rising in my stomach, I stood, hoping to make more of the movement in the far corner of the lab; to see who was heading my way behind the tall desks stacked high with clear pipes connecting great bell jars.

The procession was short; just three. A soldier led the way, his handgun holstered, the strap of a rifle over his shoulder. In the middle was Cassie and my breath fell away as I saw her gaunt features and the striking white of her new bandage.

Behind her was a woman in a white coat, her face pale against her long brunette hair, a khaki shirt under her coat; her walk seemed stilted as if she carried an injury.

Before they arrived, a soldier stepped from the side, his gaze fixed on mine and the black of a pistol held in his hand. He slipped the lock to the side and aimed the gun between my eyes.

I stopped staring as Cassie swept into the room, the cage, the cell, whatever you care to call it. I stopped watching as she opened her arms, tears rolling down her face and she pulled me in close.

The soldiers and the tech had gone by the time we came up for air and my questions fired.

"Are you okay?" I asked and she nodded a reply. "What did they do to you?"

"Tests. Took blood, changed the bandage," she said, her voice low.

"What did they say?" I asked, as I held her good hand in both of mine.

"Not much," she replied, forcing a smile.

"Your sister? Jack and Tish?"

"Tests, too. They have a room set up with toys. They're looking after them," she said, wiping her eyes on the bandage.

"Lane," I said, as she leaned forward to pat Shadow.

"I don't know. I think they have him in another room. What about you? Are you okay?"

Sighing, I let a big smile go.

"I'm fine, don't worry about me. I was just figuring out how I'd rescue you," I replied and she laughed, pulling me close. I wished she hadn't; her skin felt so cold.

Sitting back, she settled in at my side and I swept the blanket over her, but she pulled it up so it covered us both. With my arm around her shoulders, she tucked in and I stared out to the lab, listening to her slowing breath as I tried to calm my own.

Waking with a start, Shadow's head went up too, but Cassie was much slower to react and was only just opening her eyes as I saw three figures walking towards us.

Doctor Lytham, the soldier who had

killed Andrew and the other woman in a white coat from before stood on the other side of the door, holding a piece of paper against the glass.

I looked from comparing the resemblance the two women shared, one old, one not so. I stared at the sign which just read 'Drink,' with an arrow pointed to the floor.

The two of us followed down the glass to the Pyrex conical flask sat on the wooden floor, filled halfway with a dark liquid.

I looked at Cassie and back to the figures. The sign had turned and it read, 'It might save your life,' but I saw from their faces *it might equally kill.*

Cassie lifted from my side, the younger doctor's expression setting in an awkward smile as Cassie struggled with her balance.

I caught her arm before she could fall and helped her back to the bed. Shadow barked as I touched the flask and saw the thick liquid was purple close up as it sloshed against the glass.

"It's okay, boy," I said, and Shadow

IN THE END

tucked his head back in, closing his eyes.

The liquid smelt foul, the rotten stink forcing me to recoil as I sat back to Cassie's side.

"You don't have to," I said, and she struggled to raise her eyebrows.

"What choice do I have?"

I wanted to say something to brighten her spirits. I wanted to tell her of my great idea about how we would get out of this place and live happily ever after, but I had no words. I couldn't save the day. We were passengers on a train; our only choice was to jump to our deaths or stay and hope it didn't smash apart when we came to the end of the line.

I shrugged, regretting the weakness of my reply, but she struggled with a smile and pushed the flask out.

"Drink some."

I shook my head.

"I don't need it. I haven't been bitten."

"You might need it sometime. Maybe it will help," she said, and turned slowly to the door as my head followed.

The doctor and the woman in the lab coat shrugged their shoulders.

I slowly pushed the flask and her hand away.

"You need it. Drink it up. I won't need it. When you're better, this will all be over."

Cassie raised her right brow and my heart melted.

"No, only if you drink it with me."

"Don't be silly. Time is of the essence. Drink it, then we can get on with our lives. When you get better we'll be out of here. They'll want to save you, want to take you with them. Us, I mean. You'll be the one who recovered. Right?" I said, and turned to the glass.

They were a little slow to reply, but eventually the younger woman nodded.

"Now drink up."

"No," Cassie replied, and pushed the glass out to her side as if she would let it smash to the tiles.

"No," I shouted, and took it from her hand. I tried not to sniff the liquid and took a gulp, pushing it down my

IN THE END

throat as I handed it back.

She hurried the rest down in one go.

I took the flask and lifted to my feet, my weight seeming to grow with every step as I bent and placed the glass by the door.

Cassie had already lain down on the bed, my legs too heavy to leap the gap, to cup her head in my hands. It was all I could do to get my leg up before I could do nothing but close my eyes, hoping the guilt I felt wasn't my last thought in this fucked-up world.

91

My head throbbed to the beating of the wind. Air pounded around me, pushing heavy into my eardrums.

Shifting my body as I lay, I tried to release the numb of my shoulder and to move the dead weight trapping me against the bed.

My eyes flew open, shrinking back against the fresh light and I realised it was Cassie's hair in my face as I reached for her shoulder.

Surprised and relieved, I found her warmth, but the joy was short-lived when she wouldn't respond to the shake of her arm.

I slid my shoulder from under her, my legs giving way as I put weight to the floor. Scrabbling up along the slippery tiles in my socks, my vision cleared and her body defined. It was her face buried in my shoulder, the bandage on her hand soaked through and mottled black and yellow. A sickly stench of decay wafted up as I shooed away the

IN THE END

flies.

I hoped this was just her body's response as it fought the disease with the aid of whatever the doctor had given us, and not a sign she was too far gone to pull through and the cocktail we'd both been given hadn't pushed down the nails in her coffin.

Shadow's head lifted in the corner of my vision and he jumped to the floor, his knees buckling as his claws skated on the tiles.

Leaning close, I touched Cassie's shoulder before carefully turning her on her back.

As she settled, I looked to the ceiling; the pound of air was so close now, like something was landing just above our heads.

A helicopter. My eyes twitched, blinking wide. Why had it taken me so long to figure this out?

Shadow's bark rattled the glass and my hands went to my ears for shelter from the pain. I shook Cassie's shoulder again. Who could sleep through this deafening racket? Who could lay there in bed as the world churned around us?

I snapped for Shadow to be quiet, but he continued to bark before moving forward and out of my view.

Kneeling, I stared at her face. Her cheeks were rosy red, so bright against the blonde hair laying across her face. She was hot, vivid red. I knew it couldn't be a positive sign.

"Cassie," I cried. "Cassie," I said, right up in her face. At least now Shadow's bark was getting quieter.

I pushed my lips against hers, but she didn't reply. She flexed none of her muscles and my heart felt like it stopped dead.

I turned, standing, wobbling on my feet and stared at Shadow through the glass and the door hanging ajar side.

This was it. The time I'd been talking about for so long. The moment I'd dreamt about since this sorry mess began.

The helicopter was here to pull out the survivors, to take away the saviours now a cure had been found; we'd been left behind when they couldn't wake us.

IN THE END

I had to show we were okay. I had to show them we were awake. We had to get to the helicopter.

I slapped down to the bed, pushed on my trainers, trying to muster speed. I turned and pulled up Cassie's warm body, praying my knees would let me lift.

She didn't move, didn't react as with great care I hefted her over my shoulder, pinning my arms around her legs; hoping this was the time where everything would go right.

Shadow led the way as I picked my route through the smashed glass. The instruments dropped to the tiles. The remains shattered all around.

They'd destroyed the place to stop it from getting in the wrong hands, I told myself over and again.

Keeping my eyes wide for any movement, I stepped into the corridor, the boom of wind louder than ever before. I could feel the roof complaining at the weight sitting above.

In the corridor there was no sign of a struggle. No new battle scars running along the walls. No bodies once or twice dead and so I followed Shadow along its full length to the other end of the building, our path unerring as he found the climbing set of stairs.

Stopping only a moment to resettle her weight, I pushed through the door to a gale pouring down the stairwell.

With tears in my eyes I climbed, following Shadow, bursting out to squint at the brightness.

A camouflage helicopter sat on the roof the other side of the building, its rotors spinning hard and a line of white coats and soldiers climbing in.

"Ellie, Jack, Tish," I said, as I saw into the packed cabin. "Look, Cassie," I said, even though she wouldn't respond.

I ran, slowing only to navigate around the puddles of ice and knee-high ventilation towers dotted around.

I heard a call and realised there was someone at the back of the group; someone separate from the line running towards the open door. His hands were waving, frantic in the air, his shouts barely cutting through the downdraft.

IN THE END

"Wait, wait," I heard him say, the words only forming as I pushed to concentrate.

With my heart beating out of my chest, I watched as Lane reached the helicopter, but was pushed back by several hands as they tried to slide the door closed.

Lane wasn't giving up, slamming his foot to bar the flow of the door.

An order shouted out and I knew the ending before the gun raised from the packed helicopter. I knew the bullet would fire out before the bang I heard over the rotors. I knew Lane would fall to the ground before the spray of red flew from the back of his head.

I settled my pace; stopped my run, let my feet stick to the tar roof. I let Cassie slowly down to prop her against a ventilation tower.

I pushed my hand in the air, smiling and looking to the kids I could just make out. I waved as the door closed and the engine's whine grew to a high pitch.

I waved a slow-motion circle in the air as it struggled at first to lift, watching as it turned through ninety degrees, growing smaller with every passing moment.

Shadow rubbed against my leg and tugged at my jeans as if he wanted me to pull him up.

I looked down and saw Cassie squinting back. My flat expression lit up as my heart pounded. Like a giraffe on ice, I supported her as she climbed to her feet and took her in my arms, squeezing harder than I should.

My gaze fell on Shadow, following his stare to the village.

Slowly, movement came into focus, settling from one dot-sized face in the distance to another, again and again.

Turning with Cassie in a circle, I watched their slow, steady movement in our direction.

Nothing could dampen my spirits. Nothing could push my elation away.

Together we would live to fight another day and I didn't care how much of a struggle it would be; the children were safe.

I had Cassie in my arms and maybe,

IN THE END

just maybe, we'd helped to find a cure. We'd get out. Things would turn out okay.

We would just have to survive until tomorrow, or maybe another.

We heard a voice high with energy coming from somewhere close.

I turned, still holding Cassie in my arms and she pulled away, opening our embrace, her gaze following mine as I kept her arm around my shoulder.

She saw the advance, but only exclaimed as we both caught sight of a white van in the car park. Bold letters stencilled on the side, cables running from the back to a camera on the shoulder of a man looking into the viewfinder, its weight pointed to a woman in a red pant suit; a microphone held in her hand as she talked at the camera, oblivious to her impending death.

"I wonder what their story is?" I said as I pulled Cassie in close.

Check out the next in the series!

Before The End

Digging up this once-in-a-lifetime story could have lethal consequences...

Visit gjstevens.com for news about new releases and sign up to the mailing list to receive a free ebook and more!

G J STEVENS